LOVE'S TREMBLING TORMENT

He removed her bonnet, tossed it on the table, and began slipping the pins from her hair. "I love you, Garnet."

"No," she cried, shaken. "No, Brant, no!"

"Yes, and what's more, I think you love me, too."

"I'm married... We both know our being together like this is wrong."

"It's not wrong," he said quietly, approaching her again, blocking her defiant retreat. "You're a widow, Garnet, not a wife. Your husband is dead... He was my prisoner. He was shot trying to escape."

She seemed suddenly struck mute and deaf. Her face, gone white and still, appalled him, as if he had driven a knife into her heart. She stood confronting him like an avowed enemy, imbued with bitter hatred and determined revenge. "Murderer!" she said between clenched teeth. "Killer!"

She attacked him physically, clawing, kicking, biting, crying, screaming in wrathful rage. "Damn Reb! I hate you, and I'll hate you till I die!"

Echoes & Embers

Patricia Gallagher

AVON
PUBLISHERS OF BARD, CAMELOT, DISCUS AND FLARE BOOKS

ECHOES & EMBERS is an original publication of
Avon Books. This work has never before appeared in book
form.

AVON BOOKS
A division of
The Hearst Corporation
959 Eighth Avenue
New York, New York 10019

First Avon Printing, February, 1983

AVON TRADEMARK REG. U. S. PAT. OFF. AND IN
OTHER COUNTRIES, MARCA REGISTRADA, HECHO EN
U. S. A.

Printed in the U. S. A.

WFH   10   9   8   7   6   5   4   3   2   1

To Kellie Marie Gallagher,
the joy of my life

Echoes & Embers

PART ONE

Chapter 1

GARNET LANE was adamant. She would travel in mourning. And, though privately her family considered Garnet a widow, Aunt Jennifer protested that Garnet was sailing under false colors. Aunt Jennifer thought the poor girl looked ghastly in black, which transformed her pallor to sallowness, and little better in the severe ash-gray and dark-blue ensembles she had selected for the long journey.

"A pink silk rose under the brim of that gray straw poke bonnet would be adorable," Jenny suggested, "or a curl of scarlet ostrich plume tucked in the crown? And a frilly white blouse or lace jabot would do wonders for the navy *faille* suit." She tapped her own rouge pot. "So would a touch of boxed bloom on your fair cheeks."

"Mother wouldn't approve of paint," Garnet objected, as they packed their trunks. "I still wish I'd bought that black *peau de soie* gown and Empress

3

Eugénie tricorn hat with the long black *ninon* veil—
an elegant costume, didn't you think?"

"Only actresses dramatize death, darling. Widowhood, other than legal, is a kind of masquerade."

"And discouraging to males, Auntie? I'm not traveling for pleasure, as you very well know. And certainly not for romance!"

"Of course not, dear. But you must keep things in proper perspective."

"I intend to. Indeed, I may remain in seclusion for most of the journey."

"Ridiculous, Garnet! There'll probably be a good deal of socializing on the steamboat. I want to meet people."

"By all means do," Garnet encouraged.

"Without you?"

Garnet smiled coyly. "Who's chaperoning whom?"

Jenny winked and patted her shoulder affectionately. "You almost sound like your old self, kitten. I think one reason we get along so well is that you don't see me as a strange old spinster."

"Now, Auntie, stop teasing! You're very attractive, and I know you're single by choice. Mother says you had lots of eager suitors, but no one pleased you enough for marriage."

"That's not quite true. They all pleased me, and I couldn't marry them all, or choose between them. *That's* why your old Aunt Jennifer is still a maiden."

"Forty-six isn't old," Garnet told her, "and that's the most unmaidenly wardrobe I ever saw."

"A little bribery from your parents," said Jenny, eyes sparkling as she smoothed one of her fancy gowns. "I didn't want to go south looking defeated. After all, the North did win the war!"

Jennifer's thick chestnut hair was netted into a heavy mesh snood, the latest coiffure accessory for traveling. Her hazel eyes sparkled like sherry in sunlight, and the vivid glow of her smooth skin was a bit too radiant to be entirely natural. Unlike her sister Eleanor, a slender, blond older model of her daughter Garnet, Jenny was robust and buxom. Even Garnet's father, the most reserved of males, admitted that his sister-in-law cut a fine figure.

Garnet chuckled. "You're a designing woman, Auntie. But where do you expect to wear all that finery?"

"Any place I can!" Jenny grinned. "I just hope the West isn't as primitive as people say."

"Texas, Auntie."

"It's west of the Mississippi, isn't it? Well, for me, that's the end of civilization—and as far into the wilderness as I've ever ventured. If only your parents had listened to me and sent us to one of the Continental spas... Vichy, or Saint Moritz."

"Dr. Forbes wouldn't recommend any spa after the waters of Saratoga Springs failed to help me."

"The charlatan!" Jenny was suspicious of doctors who sought to put great distance between themselves and unsatisfactory patients. "Hot, dry climate! That could fit any number of places, including Hades. That confounded doctor! Sending you away like Hippocrates when he couldn't cure Plato. I could have stuck a pin in a map blindfolded and come up with a better prospect than Texas."

"Better prospect for what, Auntie?"

"Darling, must you be so literal? You know the real deciding factor was Uncle Seth, who just happens to be conveniently located in Texas. Lucky for us he's not in Death Valley!"

Garnet winced, and her aunt turned away, contrite.

Over a year had passed since Appomattox, and, as the women prepared to leave Connecticut, the county was preparing a memorial to its Civil War dead. Garnet's family thought that Dennis Lane's name should be inscribed on the granite base, but his wife wouldn't hear of it.

The offical report had stated only that Private

Dennis Robert Lane had disappeared during reconnaissance duty. The commanding officer had not known the patrol's exact location at the time it disappeared, and the men were presumed to have been captured somewhere in Tennessee, near the Georgia border. But Dennis's name had not appeared on the prisoner-of-war rosters of either state, and a year's searching of both Confederate and Union records revealed nothing of Dennis at all.

Garnet's father, Henry Ashley, had employed an attorney in Washington to check the Department of Graves Registration, but there was no confirmation of the young soldier's burial anywhere. Private Dennis Robert Lane continued to be listed as "missing in action." Numerous other men had disappeared into that military limbo, vanishing like phantoms, but Garnet refused to believe that her husband was gone. Denny was so young, so much in love, so eager for life. He would return. She had only to be patient, confident, and faithful.

She had his picture and a few cherished letters to comfort her. And if she grew thin and pale in her vigil, if she jeopardized her health and her family's sanity, it did not occur to Garnet Lane that she had become a tragic figure, Camille in Connecticut. She was still over two years shy of twenty, much too young for tragedy—as Denny was too young.

Dr. Forbes blamed her all-too-frequent fevers and colds on the long bitter winter, New England's worst in forty years. He seriously doubted that his patient would survive long. Her violet eyes were often feverishly intense and darkly circled in the wan face. Her spun-gold hair, long and loose and wispy on her shoulders, increased her wraithlike appearance. Baffled by the case, the desperate man told Garnet's family that a change of climate was her best hope, and perhaps her only one.

"Hot, dry air?" Mr. Ashley asked, fearing the disease for which that was the standard treatment.

Forbes nodded, knowing his thoughts, and tried to reassure the distraught mother. "I'm sure Garnet will recover completely in the West. I believe you have a relative in Texas, madam." He picked up his hat and bag. "Good day."

Eleanor looked at her sister, both of them thinking of their mother's brother. They had not seen Uncle Seth for over twenty years, had not even heard from him since the Civil War.

An urgent letter was sent to Seth Travers at his last known address, while Jennifer argued in vain against the doctor's advice. After a month, Seth wrote from Texas. The invitation was warm and eager, the traveling instructions concise.

"Take train to St. Louis. Riverboat to New Orleans. Gulf steamer to Corpus Christi. Stagecoach to San Antonio. Register at Menger Hotel, where I will call for the ladies. Looking fondly forward to the visit. *Seth.*"

Good grief! Jenny had thought, reading the letter. If Garnet could survive that itinerary, she would survive anything.

And she continued to think so.

Chapter 2

EN ROUTE to St. Louis by train, Garnet read or talked with her aunt. They spent a night in a hotel near the depot and then boarded a shabby steamboat to New Orleans. The few impoverished Southerners aboard the *Crescent Queen* glared openly at the more prosperous Northerners.

"They act as if they own this river, and we're trespassing," Garnet remarked in their cabin. "The Rebels hate us even more now than they did during the war. They probably blame us for their misfortunes."

Jenny took a kindlier view. "I suppose we'd feel the same way if we were in their position."

But Garnet, thinking of her husband, was merciless. "Well, *they* started the war, and I don't pity them!"

A glimpse of the saloon and rear deck would have convinced any straitlaced moralist aboard the *Crescent Queen* that the boat was a floating Babylon.

An entrepreneur toting a partitioned wicker cage of bristling bantam gamecocks came aboard from an Illinois port and, with the captain's permission, set up a portable arena on the rear deck and solicited bets from the men. Soon the roosters were slashing at each other viciously with razor-sharp blades attached to their spurs, flicking blood all over the cheering audience. Glasses tinkled, dice rattled, and cards were riffled in the saloon, where professional gamblers fleeced unsuspecting players. Gaudy prostitutes took what was left of their money. At night, music and laughter drifted across the decks, rising above the churning paddlewheels, the puffing boilers, the tooting whistles. All of it was standard riverboat entertainment, even after the Civil War.

Jenny listened to the merriment with twinkling eyes, but her niece felt no interest. She went to bed early. "Lord, how'll we sleep with all that racket!" was her only comment on the festivities.

Unable to afford the expensive diversions, Brant Steele lounged in the main saloon, simply watching. Faces, routines were familiar to him. Lacey Lee and Lollipop were on stage. Miss Lee was a striking brunette with large, expressive gray-green eyes, creamy complexion, and a unique act. Her partner, a cleverly trained monkey in fancy rompers, imitated her singing and dancing until, at his mistress's signal, he leaped into her arms and released a strap of her scanty costume. That was the finale.

"Naughty boy!" she scolded, slapping his hands lightly, then bowing to thunderous male applause.

Brant thought Miss Lee possessed more audacity than art, but he admired her ingenuity. Women had made fortunes in the profession with far less talent and fewer endowments. He and the lady had exchanged sensual looks a few times, but after several nights on the river, he had not yet made an advance. Perhaps he would approach her later that evening.

She was mighty appealing, and he had not lain with such a lovely woman in a long time.

Though hardly innocent, neither did she seem promiscuous. Brant was wary of whores, such as the pair working the boat. Both had probably been camp followers during the war and could give a fellow more than he bargained for.

After Lacey Lee's spectacular performance, the two blackface minstrels were anticlimactic. Brant had heard their sorry jokes before. He removed himself from the saloon, thinking that a walk on deck might improve his sleep, which had been restless lately. And he could smoke his cheroot shorter without betraying his poverty.

He had not walked far before he saw the slight figure, clad all in gray, standing at the port rail. Her preoccupation precluded any awareness of his approach. She appeared to be contemplating the dark water despairingly. She might have been weeping, but he couldn't tell.

It was the *Crescent Queen*'s third night out of St. Louis, and Garnet Lane's first night out of her cabin. Ship's gossip had already established her identity.

He drew a final puff on his vanishing cigar, savoring the aroma before tossing the stub overboard and whispering, "Anything wrong, ma'am?"

She jumped. "Sir, you startled me!"

"My humble apologies, ma'am. I thought I might help."

"Help?"

"You seem distressed."

Garnet shook her head. "It was warm in the stateroom, and I came out for air. I don't believe we've met, Mister—?"

"Steele," he replied. "Brant Steele. And nobody stands on ceremony aboard ship."

"Oh?" Garnet demanded. "I thought it was customary to exchange cards with passengers one wished to meet."

Brant first perceived the object in her hands as a thin prayer book, then recognized it as a small folding leather photograph frame. "That was true once," he acknowledged, "but the war changed some social customs. This is not an ocean liner, after all."

"Not everywhere, Mr. Steele. Some proprieties still exist in my part of America." She paused slightly. "Furthermore, this isn't even a ship! It's a riverboat, and a sorry one, at that."

"It is. But the *Crescent Queen* had her reign, all right. A glorious one." Brant remembered glimpsing her tall twin smokestacks from the upper gallery of Great Oaks Plantation and hearing her regal, deep-throated whistle as she passed the landing.

"You don't sound like a Southerner, Mr. Steele. Your accent is Western, isn't it?"

"I'm part Texan," he explained. "My father was educated in New Orleans, where he met my mother. And though Pa balked like a mustang at first, he finally agreed to live on her family's sugar plantation, where I was born. He used to tell me about Texas, though, and took me there to visit my grandparents a few times. They're all dead now," he added, lost in his thoughts. "I inherited the plantation, which is now in ruins and going to be auctioned off. I can't muster the means to save it."

Garnet asked, "Did you try to keep the plantation?" Curiosity was getting the best of her.

"Oh, yes. I foolishly hoped to get the money by gambling. But I'm no match for the professionals on the riverboats. I can't cheat well enough, you see. Playing cards with gentlemen friends for leisure is quite different from challenging sharks for money."

Intrigued by his smooth baritone voice, Garnet cast him a covert glance. His profile was somber, brooding, and as clear-cut as the image on a medallion. Exceptionally handsome, if one liked dark types. She preferred fair men. Denny's eyes were light blue, his hair the color of sun-ripened wheat. His pale, downy beard had not even required daily shaving. Mr. Steele's hair was too thick and black, his eyes too dark and devilish—rather like a pirate's leering at a maiden. If he had a beard or mustache, he would appear starkly villainous, she thought. For those and other vague reasons, he made Garnet nervous.

She asked cautiously, "Were you in the Confederate Army?"

He nodded grimly, but volunteered no further information, and she didn't press him. The two remained silent for a while, gazing at the muddy yellow river, which took on a deceptive golden glint in the moonlight. Stars gleamed in the velvet sky, and Garnet wished she were anywhere on earth except on this chugging craft which was bearing her relentlessly into Rebel territory.

"I'm on my way to Texas," she broke the silence, "traveling with my aunt, Miss Jennifer Temple. She took supper in the dining saloon this evening and remained to watch the show."

"Yes, I saw her and was told who she was. Lovely lady. May I ask where in Texas you're headed?"

Garnet shrugged, uncertain. "Oh, a town called Longhorn Junction. Near San Antonio, I believe. My great-uncle, Seth Travers, operates a general store there. We're going to live with him for a while."

"I've been to San Antonio," he said. "Do you know much about Texas?"

"No. Uncle Seth isn't much of a correspondent, and we really weren't interested in knowing much about a place we never expected to visit."

"Well, it should prove interesting to you."

"I doubt that."

"Then why are you going?"

After some hesitancy, Garnet admitted, "Our family physician recommended the climate. For health."

Steele did not have to wonder which one of them was under a doctor's care. Garnet looked ethereal in the moonlight, her skin so pale, soft, and as dewy-white as a gardenia. Her hair looked more silver than gold, and her features were as exquisite as the face on his mother's favorite cameo. Although much too slender and delicate, she was breathtakingly beautiful. But where was the man whose wedding band she wore?

"Will Mr. Lane join you in Texas?"

After a silence, she answered quietly, "I don't know. He was reported missing early in '65, and I've heard nothing since."

Brant pondered a moment, then decided to say what was on his mind. "I'm sorry, ma'am, but don't you think he would have returned by now..." He hesitated before adding, "If possible?"

"If he were still alive, you mean?" she said harshly.

Before he could think of a kinder approach, Jennifer appeared on deck, fanning herself. She eyed the tall, dark stranger standing with her niece. "It's such a heavenly night, except for the mosquitoes. Big as vampire bats, some of them, and as bloodthirsty." She smiled and nodded to Brant. "Mr. Steele, isn't it?"

"Yes, ma'am."

"I'm Mrs. Lane's aunt, Miss Jennifer Temple."

"My pleasure, Miss Temple."

Garnet explained, "Mr. Steele has Texan ancestry on his father's side, Auntie. His mother's people were Louisiana planters." Afraid that Jenny would become too friendly, Garnet rushed on, "It's been a pleasure meeting you, Mr. Steele. But I'm tired and would like to retire. Please excuse us."

He bowed. "Good night, ladies. I wish you a pleasant evening."

"Hah!" cried Jenny, suddenly feeling the sherry she had drunk. "I just hope this relic doesn't sink. Why, there are some bullet holes in our cabin!"

"The *Queen* was in military service," Brant said.

"Really?"

"Come along, Auntie," Garnet urged, leading away

the tipsy lady, charming in her lavender *moiré* ball gown. "Things will look brighter in the morning."

Jenny shook her head. "I doubt it, dear. I have a feeling that I shall be indisposed tomorrow."

Chapter 3

AT BREAKFAST the next morning Jenny ignored all food in favor of black coffee, grimacing with each sip, for the galley cook had laced it heavily with bitter chicory.

"Captain Beam says we'll put into Memphis today, dear, and the passengers may go ashore if we like," she said.

"I'd rather not, Auntie," her niece said firmly.

Garnet didn't want to meet Brant Steele again. Obviously he considered her a widow and had little patience with her belief. He even acted like a hunter—alert, wary, stalking. She resolved to avoid him.

Her aunt, however, had her own plans. "I wasn't suggesting that we go alone, sweetie. The women say Memphis is the toughest port on the Mississippi, and no decent woman would dare appear on the streets unescorted. It used to be a den of river pirates and rum smugglers, and it's even worse since the war. But I'm sure if we wanted an escort, that nice Mr. Steele would be happy—"

"Nice? Why, Brant Steele was the enemy! And still is, as far as I'm concerned."

"Darling, we Yankees are considered the enemy here! It behooves us to try and make friends with the Southerners. Mr. Steele seemed like a nice gentleman last night."

"Your vision was blurred last night, Auntie."

"Nonsense! I had only one small glass of wine. Well, maybe two. Or three."

Garnet suppressed a smile. Aunt Jennifer was enjoying her sabbatical. The farther they got from Connecticut, the more it seemed that she, Garnet, was the chaperone and Jenny a young lady tasting freedom.

"It might be wiser to stick with ginger ale and sarsaparilla," she said, smiling at her aunt.

The Memphis docks bore the scars of many Union gunboats. The bales of cotton stacked there no longer represented Tennessee's principal source of revenue. The bankers, brokers, traders, and speculators were gone, and planters and plantations were ruined, along with their culture.

Negroes wandered the streets in the rags of freedom, aimless and bewildered, begging handouts from whites no better off than they, or sat idly on the wharves and levees. Youngsters of both races danced for the pennies tossed to them by the *Crescent Queen*'s passengers. Shanty-boats were tied up to the willow-tangled island in the harbor, and the air reeked of frying catfish, boiling cabbage, rotting garbage, sewage, and river mud. Memphis's chief assets and concerns appeared to be saloons, gambling halls, and brothels.

On the promenade deck, Jenny was gazing at the scene when she became aware of Brant Steele. "Are you going ashore, sir?"

He shook his head. "I've seen Memphis before. Most of Tennessee, in fact." He gazed beyond the hub of the waterfront, beyond the Choctaw bluffs of the city proper, seeing in memory Shiloh, Murfreesboro, Chattanooga, Chickamauga.

"During the war?"

He nodded, his face grave. "There was a lot of action in this state. Like the rest of the South, it's a carpetbaggers' mecca now."

Jenny was glad that Garnet was not there. "War talk upsets my niece, Mr. Steele."

"I'll try to remember that, ma'am, if I have the pleasure of meeting her again. She keeps to herself pretty much."

"Too much," Jenny declared. "I worry that she'll become a recluse, and at her age!"

"Is she ill?"

"She isn't well, but I don't believe the trouble is entirely physical. Not knowing whether her husband is dead or alive is a terrible ordeal even for a mature woman, and Garnet is hardly more than a girl." She sighed. "War is very hard on the families of fighting men. I'm sure your relatives could vouch for that."

"My father and brother were killed in battle," he said quietly. "Malaria killed my mother last year. I have no one else, really, just a few cousins scattered here and there."

"That's too bad." Jenny pitied anyone who didn't have a loyal, loving family.

Just then Lacey Lee appeared on deck, the monkey clinging to her neck. Jenny nodded politely and Brant tipped his yellowed Panama hat. He asked if she intended to try her luck in Memphis.

"No, I think New Orleans would be better." She petted her partner, allowing Lollipop to kiss her cheek and nibble at her ear. "Don't you think so, sir?"

Jenny began speculating furiously about the woman's past. She appeared to be alone in the world, and had the added burden of a difficult profession.

How had she chosen her act, and how had she trained the animal to cooperate? Jenny knew that the act would be forbidden in most legitimate theaters, considered obscene and permitted only in carnivals or in Barnum's Museum, where anything was allowed.

"Frankly, ma'am," Brant was advising Miss Lee, "your best prospects are probably out West. From Texas to California, you'd create a sensation in any mining town!"

Lacey Lee was listening to him intently.

"Really?" she murmured, half to herself. "Then I'll think about that if I don't go over big in New Orleans."

Brant grinned, appraising her. "You'd be a star in some place like Denver or San Francisco. Why not go out West?"

Miss Lee smiled, inspired by his apparent confidence. "Do you happen to be heading in any of those directions, Mr. Steele?"

"I may, eventually."

Garnet never again ventured out of the cabin. She dined from trays, picking delicately at her food, taking Dr. Forbes's medications. The Delta landscape enchanted her and at the same time made her mournful. Long draperies of moss shrouded the trees, as if the land were in mourning. Mosquitoes swarmed in the cane brakes. At twilight, wild creatures called plaintively in the dark woods and marshes, but there were no lights or sounds from the abandoned plantations.

"Is it always so quiet on the Delta?" she asked the steward who came in to fill the water decanter.

"It is now, ma'am. Some folks claim to see ghosts on the levees and hear voices wailing."

Garnet shivered, close to believing it. She was almost tempted to accompany Jenny to supper that evening. But she resisted and read a novel instead.

Later, as she was drifting into sleep, whispers outside the cabin woke her. She raised the window shade cautiously and peeked out. Apparitions? No, Mr. Steele and Miss Lee were strolling on the deck, arm in arm. Suddenly they paused, murmuring, then embraced and kissed. They were long, deep, passionate kisses.

Embarrassed, Garnet lowered the shade and sat back, twisting her wedding ring. Denny had never behaved so boldly, either before or after the ceremony. Never once had they been totally naked together, even in the dark. Virgins on their nuptial night, adolescents of sixteen and eighteen, childhood sweethearts who had rushed to the altar before his conscription into the army, neither had been able to instruct the other. Their brief honeymoon was a fiasco of juvenile ignorance and frustration. Garnet still cringed at the memory.

After a week of embarrassed couplings, he marched off to war in his new blue uniform. A short Christmas furlough reunited but scarcely reacquainted them before their second and final parting.

Nevertheless, Garnet cherished his love and her vows, and she refused to believe that she wasn't married. She carried his picture, touching it whenever doubts assailed her. Before embarking on the journey, she had made an oilskin pouch to protect the tintype, and she always either pinned it under her bodice or hung the drawstring pouch around her neck.

That night, tossing restlessly in her berth, Garnet wondered whether Denny was still faithful to her. Had he ever bedded some loose female out of loneliness or plain animal need? Some men regarded war as license, and she wondered if Denny was any different.

Assuring herself that Denny was as true blue as his uniform, she finally slept.

Chapter 4

A HUGE EXPLOSION jolted Garnet from her berth onto the floor, numbing her. She could hear people screaming, crying, pleading for help. The shade had rolled up and she could see flames through the glass. They *were* flames. It wasn't a dream. The boat was on fire.

Jenny burst into the cabin. "Garnet, where are you?"

"On the floor, Auntie! What happened?" Garnet stood up carefully.

"A boiler exploded. We have to abandon ship!"

"Oh, Auntie, how awful! Help me dress!"

"There's no time for dressing." Jenny grabbed the life preservers off the wall and thrust one at her niece. "Hang onto yours, Garnet! There aren't enough for everyone, and passengers are fighting over them. Hurry!" she cried. The *Crescent Queen* was already rocking and tilting.

The stern was fully ablaze, shooting fragments of
blazing timber into the sky. They fell, sparking and
hissing, into the dark river. People had been killed
in the explosion. Some were wounded, or were being
trampled by panicked passengers. The panic was
fierce as people rampaged over the decks, away from
the inferno.

Jenny clutched Garnet's hand. "Hurry, for God's
sake! The boat is sinking!"

"Wait!" Garnet cried, searching for the oilskin
pouch and draping it around her neck.

When Jenny opened the portal, the fire was raging
in the passageway, feeding quickly on the dry, rotted
wood. Pumps sprewed water over the foredecks and
midship exits, but it wasn't enough. People leaped
over the gingerbread railings without life preservers. Horns and whistles blasted, as the captain bellowed orders to abandon ship.

Slamming the cabin door shut on the flaming corridor, Jenny pulled Garnet toward the window.
Breaking the glass with a chair, she cried, "This
way!" Slipping the large cork rings over both of them,
she shoved her frightened, stunned niece over the
rail.

They hit the water simultaneously. Aided by fire-
light, Jenny was able to catch the rope of Garnet's
preserver and tie it to her own. "Paddle your hands
and kick your feet," she instructed, "or else we'll get
caught in the suction as the boat capsizes."

Garnet's obedience was automatic, and Jenny
guided them away from the powerful current of the
main channel. The eerie glow of the blazing vessel
revealed survivors treading water while clinging to
pieces of furniture, planks, and carpetbags. Men in
underwear, or stark naked, tried to swim to a nearby
sandbar. Women and children wailed on makeshift
rafts.

Suddenly, seemingly out of nowhere, a floating
door approached Jenny and Garnet. A chattering

monkey sat in the center, and two people clung to the sides, heads bobbing above the water.

"Hey there!" Brant yelled. "You folks all right?"

"So far," Jenny replied.

"Any injuries?"

"I don't think so!"

"Well, the river is fairly shallow here—we could walk ashore except for the mud. Grab hold of this door, and between us we can maneuver it toward the bank."

"Yes, sir!" Jenny cried gratefully. "Anything you say!"

Soon they were in reach of the sturdy willows edging the river, and they wedged the raft between the trunks. Silt sucked at their feet as they struggled to safety, grasping the flexible branches.

"Give me your preservers," Steele panted, and Jenny and Garnet tore them away and handed them to him.

Brant swam back into the river, hoping to save other lives. Instead, he had to fight for his own. Desperate men attacked him, wresting the corks from him, forcing him to swim back to the bank on his own.

The ladies watched in awe, and Lollipop, hanging from a limb, looked as distraught and anxious as his sobbing mistress.

Lacey Lee's tears surprised Garnet almost as much as her own reaction surprised her. Her heart began to flutter as she joined the chorus cheering Brant on.

After what seemed like an eternity of touch and go, Brant reached the willows and pulled himself onto the bank. Exhausted more from the wrestling than the swimming, he staggered a few feet, then buckled to the ground.

Miss Lee knelt beside him, rubbing his bare chest. "Brant? Darling, speak to me!"

"Those dirty bastards," he gasped. "I could have saved a mother and child. They were clutching a

beam, but were swept away before I could reach them.
If I'd had a gun, I'd have shot those bastards!"

"It wasn't your fault," Jenny soothed, stroking the
wet hair from his forehead. "We saw what happened.
So many people died tonight."

Brant sat up, coughing water. "That tub was a
death trap," he declared, gazing gravely at the sinking remains. "She carried only one lifeboat, and that
was blown to bits. There weren't half enough preservers. There ought to be a law against that kind
of negligence. They'll be fishing out bodies all the
way to the Gulf of Mexico. Why, two-thirds of the
passengers must have died."

The women nodded solemnly, knowing the miracle of their own rescue. Their soaking hair streamed
over their shoulders, and only Jenny was decently
clothed. Garnet was acutely aware of her sheer linen
nightgown. She wished she could hold back the dawn,
but it was already breaking over the treetops, and
soon she would be as blatantly exposed as that trol-
lop, Lacey Lee. Jenny would have to share her petticoats. Garnet became aware of her grip on the
oilskin pouch. Her wedding ring still bound her finger, but all the rest of their possessions, their money
and jewelry, were gone.

"Thank you for rescuing us, Mr. Steele," Jenny
said, nudging her niece. "We will always be grateful,
won't we, dear?"

Garnet nodded. He was brash and he was a Rebel,
but he had saved her life.

"What now?" asked Jenny, following an exchange
of female garments, which took place behind a clump
of bushes. She wore her ruined taffeta evening gown,
corset, and drawers, and Garnet and Miss Lee wore
Jenny's bedraggled petticoats, secured by strings over
their breasts and barely covering their knees.

"Fortunately, we're not too far from New Orleans," said Brant. "Another fifteen miles or so. Great

Oaks is fairly near, however, and we can take temporary refuge there."

"Great Oaks?" Jenny repeated.

"My family's plantation—or what's left of it. It'll do for emergency shelter. I can get us there. I'm familiar with this region because I used to hunt here."

"For runaway slaves?" Garnet snapped, and was sorry.

"For game," he replied blandly. "Deer and ducks, mostly. But there are also some large black bears around here."

"Bears?" cried Garnet.

Jenny suggested they wait on the riverbank for another boat. Surely searchers would come out to look for the *Crescent Queen*'s survivors.

"Eventually, perhaps, but there's no guarantee, Miss Temple. And the weather is getting bad. This is hurricane season. Great Oaks has survived more than a few and will harbor us, if we can reach it in time." A weighty pause emphasized the danger Brant felt they were in. "I'm convinced that Captain Beam ordered full steam, taxing the weak boilers, in the hope of reaching a safe port before the storm struck. We must get to Great Oaks. There's no other shelter for miles."

"But, as you know, my niece is rather frail, Mr. Steele. She can't hike very far."

"I'll carry her, if necessary."

Garnet set her small oval chin firmly. Jenny's allusions to her health embarrassed her. "I'm perfectly capable of walking," she announced emphatically, crossing her hands over her chest, feeling her nipples taut against the thin fabric and fearing that even more of her anatomy was visible under the thin petticoat. What a wretched experience! Two Yankee females marooned with a former Rebel soldier, an apparent harlot, and a loquacious and inquisitive monkey.

"Move, ladies! I'm sorry I don't have a machete to

whack away the underbrush." Brant grinned. Picking up sticks, he handed them to his charges.

"Stay together, ladies, and every so often, beat the ground around you in a circle—that will chase off most snakes."

Garnet cringed. "How deep into this jungle must we go?"

"Until we reach River Road, which leads to most of the plantations, including Great Oaks," replied Brant. "Watch those brambles ahead—the thorns are sharp as needles."

Jenny and Miss Lee cleared the obstacles safely, but Garnet snagged her petticoat. Furious, she jerked it free before Brant could reach over to help her. *What* was he staring at now? Certainly his hussy had more to reveal, and far less compunction about doing so.

"Your... string up there is loose," he mumbled.

"Thank you," she murmured, fumbling in a hasty effort to fasten it. An annoying tangle resulted, but she scorned assistance, brushing his hands away. "I can do it!"

"Then hurry up," Lacey Lee called. "You're holding up the caravan. Why are you so bad-tempered, anyway? Survivors should cooperate."

"My feet hurt, my arms and legs are scratched, I'm snagging my hair and clothes on the bushes, and the mosquitoes are eating me alive! Should I enjoy this abominable expedition?"

"I've offered to carry you, Mrs. Lane."

"And I've declined your offer, Mr. Steele."

"Garnet, dear," her aunt pacified, "Brant is doing his best for all of us. Please forgive her temper, sir. She really isn't well."

"Oh, Aunt Jennifer, hush about that!" Garnet cried, slashing furiously at a plant in her path. "Lead on, General—or whatever your former rank was—Rebel!"

His laughter infuriated her. "Nothing so exalted, ma'am. I was a mere major."

"In the cavalry?"

"Affirmative."

They proceeded in silence, the monkey swinging from tree to vine, as happy as if he were in his native habitat. They came upon some marshland and a bayou whose course bewildered Jenny. It appeared to flow in the wrong direction.

"Don't the streams of the west bank of the Mississippi run into the river, Mr. Steele?"

"Not all of them, ma'am. Some seem to defy gravity—it's one of the peculiarities of this region."

"Not the only one," Garnet muttered, starting across a bog, only to be swiftly jerked backwards.

"How dare you!" she fumed, for his hand had caught her just below her breasts.

"My apologies, madam! But that log is an alligator."

Garnet screamed, Jenny jumped, and Lacey gasped as the reptile waddled toward the bayou and disappeared into the brackish water.

"Be on guard," Brant warned. "His mate may be nearby. And that slithering tangle over there is a nest of poisonous cottonmouth moccasins. Wild hogs breed in these marshes too, and the boars' tusks can rip a man to shreds in minutes. There's also quicksand here."

Faint, Garnet suddenly collapsed. She regained consciousness in Brant's muscular arms, her head resting on his broad, hard, bare chest, his dark hair prickling her tender cheeks. Her feminine instinct was to relax and enjoy the masculine protection. Reluctantly, she bade him release her, but he was firm.

"You're not strong enough yet, and I don't want you swooning again."

Lacey's glance riled Garnet nearly as much as her own reaction to Brant riled her. Why should she, Garnet, feel favored because she was the one in his arms? Appalled by the sensations pervading her, she again demanded to be freed. But she was astonished by his abrupt compliance.

"Foolish girl," Jenny chided *sotto voce*. "He's not to be bullied. You'll be the loser in any battle with Brant Steele."

Chapter 5

BEFORE they had gone much farther, they came upon a huge rattlesnake coiled in their path, tail buttons shaking warningly, fangs bared in its striking head.

The women watched in awe as Brant killed the snake with several swift and accurate blows of his sturdy oak limb.

"Bravo!" Miss Lee cried, and Jenny echoed her. Even Garnet felt a grudging respect for Brant's prowess. She tried not to stare at his broad shoulders and chest. Her husband had not been built that way. But, of course, neither he nor she had attained full maturity before their marriage. When they met again, they would be adults, not adolescents. Oddly, the prospect was disturbing. What if they had changed emotionally?

"People and situations change," her older and wiser

aunt had often told her. "Nothing in this world stays the same always and forever."

Her silence was born of bewildering personal thoughts and unutterable weariness. The unfamiliar sensations aroused by Brant Steele engendered more trepidation than Garnet cared to admit, even to herself.

Observing her puzzled frown, Brant inquired solicitously, "More problems, Mrs. Lane?"

"Our circumstances are obvious, Mr. Steele."

"May I remind you, madam, that we are lucky to be alive?"

There were dark, roiling clouds in the south, and gusting breezes rustled the jungle. The monkey's excited behavior indicated more than just the jittery nature of his species.

"Lollipop senses a storm," his mistress explained, soothing him with gentle words. "Animals have a natural instinct about the elements."

Garnet asked, "Did Lollipop save himself from the burning boat?"

"No, animals are more frightened of fire than of any other danger. But he had the sense to cling to Mr. Steele when we abandoned ship. And when Brant salvaged that door—"

"We know the rest," Garnet interrupted, certain then that Miss Lee and Brant had been together when the explosion occurred.

"My feet hurt terribly," Jenny declared, hoping to avert an argument. "Any suggestions, Mr. Steele?"

"One. We can rest long enough to improvise some shoes for everyone."

"A cobbler, too?" Garnet scoffed, upset by her suspicions and conclusions. "Do you plan to skin an alligator for our bootery? Why didn't you put on your own shoes along with your pants!"

"Why didn't you grab your slippers instead of that oilskin pouch?" he countered suavely. "Is it so vitally important? I hope it contains money and jewelry, for you'll need currency." A grim twist of his mouth accompanied the sarcasm. "This isn't exactly a land of plenty, since it was stripped by the 'blue plague.' Few of us have anything of value left, and Confederate currency is worthless."

Jenny intervened before Garnet could say anything. "We intend to telegraph home as soon as possible, sir. Our family will help us."

"If you can contact them, ma'am. Communications haven't been fully restored yet, even in Southern cities, much less out here. The Yankees had a penchant for destroying rail and wire facilities once they had used them. If the hurricane moves up the Mississippi, New Orleans may be isolated for days or even weeks."

As he spoke, Brant ripped away fibrous leaves and sturdy vines and said, "Wrap your feet in layers of leaves and tie the leaves with vines. It'll be better than nothing."

Garnet was not as adept as the others, and Brant fashioned the shields for her, promptly and neatly. Ashamed of her dependency, she averted her eyes as he helped her to her feet. Why couldn't she be as competent as the others?

Brant brushed away several leaves from the pale cascade of her hair, remembering its silvery sheen in the moonlight and longing to feel its silken texture. The faint flush of her pallid skin suggested a slight fever, and not even the voluminous petticoat could disguise her slenderness. Beside the voluptuous Lacey, Garnet Lane was actually skinny, yet eminently more beautiful. Her haunted purple eyes intrigued and mystified him. A hardy and defiant spirit lived in that frail body, surfacing every time their temperaments clashed, and Brant knew she would trudge along now until she dropped of exhaustion, rather than admit to weakness.

At one point the long-unused hunter's trail narrowed, diminished, and finally disappeared altogether. Dense vegetation shut out all daylight. They followed Brant single file, moving very slowly, scourged by lashing branches and cruel brambles. Once Brant had to beat away a blocked passage, creating a tunnel through which they crawled. Lace and ruffles were tattered, and Garnet feared they would all be stripped naked.

"I thought you *knew* this country," she gasped, hanging onto his leather belt.

"I did once, but I haven't hunted here in over five years. Jungles grow fast. But take heart, there's a clearing ahead. Only a few more yards."

"Voilà!" cried Jenny, glimpsing a patch of murky sky.

Able to straighten out at last, Garnet declared, "What a wretched land!"

"Not all of it," Brant defended. "Parts of this state are enchanting. Longfellow thought so when he wrote *Evangeline*. And you'll see its beauty for yourself, when we reach Great Oaks."

"If we ever do."

"Garnet," her aunt placated, "Mr. Steele did what he felt was best. Bad weather is definitely coming, and fretting is useless. Let us proceed in peace, please."

Approaching a wide, tree-lined lane, Brant explained, "This is River Road. It serves most of the plantations and farms in this parish, which is what we call a county in Louisiana. We don't have far to go now."

"Thank heaven," Jenny murmured. "The Lord was with us all the way."

"He wasn't when the steamboat blew up," Lacey said wryly.

Garnet recalled the drinking, gambling, cockfighting, and other vices aboard the *Crescent Queen*. "Perhaps God had reason."

The earthy entertainer laughed. "In that

case, there wouldn't be a riverboat afloat anywhere."

"No matter," Jenny temporized quickly. "He
provided a Moses to lead us out of the wilderness."

Amused by the bickering and wisely refusing to
participate, Brant walked straight ahead without
speaking, the monkey perched on his shoulder. Hours
had passed since they had begun the hazardous trek,
and exhaustion and hunger had set in long before.
We look like rejects from a carnival, Garnet thought
morosely. What kind of refuge awaited them? The
atmosphere was heavy and the very land seemed
hushed and expectant.

Long avenues of moss-draped live oaks marked
the entrance to almost every plantation along the
River Road, most estates in ruins by then. A full
quarter mile of those monarchal trees, planted by
Brant's paternal ancestors over a century before,
formed an enchanting colonnade to Great Oaks.
Their spreading limbs extended like gargantuan
arms, shading and protecting visitors, and the in-
itial glimpse of the pillared white manor at the end
of the lane had once been a breathtaking sight.

Now the master of Great Oaks paused in somber
reflection, flinching visibly. Public notices were
nailed to oak trees. The property had been vandalized and many of the outbuildings, including the
slave cabins, had been burned, but the main house
had been spared by one of General Benjamin Butler's
officers who had taken a fancy to it. Brant expected
that man to be among the bidders at the imminent
auction.

Miss Lee was affected by the wanton destruction.
"Oh," she cried as they neared the broken steps of
the first-floor gallery, "why did they have to harm
this lovely place! What did the house and gardens
ever do to them?"

"The owners kept slaves," Garnet said, although she, too, was shocked.

"Union soldiers did this before they were ordered to stop," Brant said bitterly. "Decades of work were destroyed in a few hours, and there's no sane defense for this. Even the President deplores the cruelty."

Brant opened the massive carved-cypress portal. The graceful fanlight above was shattered. Bayonets had slashed the furniture, draperies, paintings. Animal urine and feces stained the carpets. All food and livestock had been confiscated before the torching of the barns, stables, and storehouses. Brant knew all of that from the letters written by his mother not long before her death, and the diary she had secreted in the attic.

"Welcome to Great Oaks!" he drawled ironically, bowing his guests into the defaced foyer. "You may choose your own bedchambers. I regret that my hospitality is necessarily limited. I trust you'll understand."

Garnet entered the once-elegant drawing room, now in shambles. Ancestral portraits had provided target practice for malicious knife-throwers, and one in an ornate gilt frame seemed to have been a particular favorite. Garnet gazed at the canvas remains of the lovely, dark-haired lady seated on a tufted ivory satin settee, two small boys at her exquisitely gowned knees, until she sensed Brant Steele observing her. Turning, she found him leaning against the arched entrance, arms folded across his chest.

"Your mother?" she asked softly.

"And her two sons," he nodded. "That portrait was my father's pride and joy. Thank God he never saw it like that."

In a rush, she felt pangs of sorrow for Brant Steele. "Why do you keep the portrait now? Surely it must be painful to look at this way?"

"Pain is not always eliminated through its sources," he replied cryptically. "You should know that, Mrs. Lane. Do you not carry the source of your pain with you? Isn't your husband's picture in that oilskin pouch you cherish?"

As she nodded, Brant wished he might have a look at the man who inspired such devotion. The glorified biblical spouse, cleaving unto her helpmeet until death, and even beyond, by sealing herself in a tomb made of memories!

His curiosity finally provoked the request and, though Garnet hesitated, reluctant to share even Dennis's picture with a Rebel, she slowly opened the drawstring and extended the tintype toward him.

Private Dennis Lane appeared to Brant to be a callow, scared boy with illusions of heroism and fear of dying. Brant had seen thousands like him, on both sides of the lines—raw meat thrown desperately and too late to the battling lions. Lane's insignia identified a Connecticut company familiar to Brant, which may have explained the odd sense of recognition. During the final phases of the war, Brant's regiment had captured a detachment of bluecoats near the Georgia border, just as General Sherman was preparing to assault Atlanta. Frightened kids that squad had been, inexperienced, poorly trained, incompetent soldiers blundering through their first important mission involving military secrets. After a swift and easy surrender, the captives had panicked at the possibility of imprisonment in the notorious Andersonville prison, and they had tried to escape. Rifle bullets stopped them.

Good Lord, Brant thought as the realization began taking hold. That was where he'd seen the young man in uniform. Private Dennis Lane had been one of the men in that ill-fated reconnaissance patrol! And the officer who had interrogated Lane had been...Brant Steele, of the Confederate Army.

Yes, the baby-faced young man had indeed been captured, but Lane was not missing in action. He was dead.

And what threw Brant into a storm of confusion was the recollection that, while one of the other men had shot Lane, it was Brant who had issued the command. He had passed the death sentence on Garnet Lane's husband.

His thoughts closed in on him. He could tell her the truth, he realized. He could free Garnet from the limbo of wondering whether Dennis was alive. He could do that—but could he ever make her understand? What, really, would this genteel young woman know about the exigencies of war? Would she see that Dennis, in Brant's place, would have done what Brant had done? Could Brant *make* her see that? *Never,* he scoffed at himself. *Never. She'll never see it the way you want her to.*

Abruptly he handed the tintype back to Garnet, keeping his gaze riveted on the picture.

"A fine-looking fellow," he muttered hoarsely, unable to meet her eyes.

"Thank you," she murmured.

"I wonder where your aunt and Miss Lee are?" he said, desperate to change the subject.

"Exploring upstairs, I suppose. When do you think the storm will strike?"

"Tonight or tomorrow, unless it stalls over the Gulf of Mexico or changes course. But Great Oaks was built to withstand violent assaults from the sea. The house may tremble, but it'll protect us."

"I hope so," Garnet smiled. "After what we've endured to get here."

"Yes," he agreed. "I'm more concerned now about food. I planted a garden and stashed some staples a couple of months ago, before I got the impractical idea that I could win the astronomical tax assessment by playing cards. Not many scavengers on River Road anymore, so Great Oaks may not have been raided recently. I'll soon find out." He turned to leave, then paused. "Can you cook?"

"Not very well. I never had much practice. But Aunt Jennifer is terrific."

"Good for her. Magic may be required to produce a palatable meal around here now. Why don't you go up and choose a bedroom for the next few nights?"

Chapter 6

BESIDES feminine caprice, Brant knew of nothing more temperamental than a tropical storm. French-speaking Negroes called them "grand tempests." Unlike the average Louisiana planter, however, Brant's family had owned few slaves of mixed blood. His mother's people had brought their Kentucky house servants with them and purchased field hands from Mississippi and Alabama. They had to be taught the culture and processing of sugarcane into sugar and molasses, and special hands were trained for that duty. The cotton workers knew their business thoroughly too, and between them, the excellent overseer and diligent master and mistress, Great Oaks had prospered as one of the largest and most efficiently run plantations in Louisiana.

But all that was gone, of course. The quality of the volunteer cane was too poor for commercial value, and the idle sugar-mill machinery was rusting in

the swampy dampness. Long since picked of their
meager, untended yield, the cotton fields lay fallow.
The wagon trails, eroded by the frequent, drenching
rains in southern Louisiana, were scarcely discern-
ible any longer.

Leaving the ladies, Brant conducted a perfunctory
inspection of his property. Before the war, that had
been a frequent ritual which he, his father, and his
brother had undertaken. Only a small part of the
vast acreage was accessible on foot, and Brant still
smarted over the surrender of his fine mount to the
Union cavalry and the humiliation of returning to
Great Oaks not only in defeat but on foot, bearded
and bedraggled, toting his battered haversack like
a hobo.

The lonely silence of the plantation then was the
stillness of death and ghosts. The great manor was
a besieged palace brooding over a deposed empire.
Weeds invaded the once lush, lavish gardens and
choked the pools. Rampant vines bound the statues
and fountains, and the tenacious oleanders, mag-
nolias, and jasmine spread their cloying fragrance
like incense over the dead.

Passing the untrimmed boxwood labyrinth, Brant
recalled his first romantic rendezvous in the intri-
cate, concealing mazes, where an eager young couple
could be assured reasonable privacy. He and his
brother Corey had put the place to use on numerous
occasions. His father and Corey were decaying in a
Vicksburg trench, and Brant had no intention of
bringing them back to rest in ground that would soon
belong to someone else. His mother and the two sisters who had died in childhood lay in the plantation
cemetery, their elevated vaults slowly sinking into
the spongy earth. He paused by the twisted iron fence
for a few moments.

The neglected vegetable patch, unable to compete
with the lusty natural flora of the fertile soil, had
not prospered. But some hardy carrots, turnips, beets,

and parsnips had grown. And with the gun which was hidden between the attic rafters, he could shoot pigeons, quail, or rabbits for stew. Visualizing the netted hams, sides of bacon, and rows of sausages there had been in the smokehouses, his mouth watered. That life of wealth and luxury, of ease and plenty, was as extinct as the culture that had fostered it. Somewhere, somehow, after the sale of Great Oaks, he would begin a new life and he would never allow himself to mourn the past.

Returning to the manor, Brant found Garnet in an old calico dress, faded and mended, once worn by a house slave. A pair of his mother's slippers, one size too large for her petite feet, replaced the makeshift shoes. Jenny wore a long full-length mammy-style apron over her torn garments. Miss Lee, on the other hand, had latched on to an old scarlet satin ball gown and high-heeled opera pumps, which Garnet thought typical, considering her profession. Brant refrained from saying Lacey's costume had been worn by Corey's fiancée in a masquerade, impersonating the notorious Madame Du Barry.

"How do we look?" Lacey asked pertly, modeling the ridiculous gown.

"Gorgeous," he declared. "You did yourselves proud, ladies. Too bad we're not having a ball this evening."

"I suppose there were many grand balls here?" Lacey began to hum, waltzing about the room, hoping Brant would take the hint, disappointed when he presented the bunch of vegetables to Jennifer with a gallant bow, as though they were a bouquet.

"See what you can do with these, ma'am. Nimrod will try his luck at bagging some meat for our table."

"What about the storm?" Garnet worried.

"The calm indicates a reprieve. It may be hours

before it comes ashore. The coast will bear the brunt, but we'll catch our share."

"I'll do the cooking," Jenny said. "Set the table, Lacey, with whatever you can find in the cupboards. Garnet, why don't you gather some flowers from the garden—add a nice touch to our first meal together?"

"What are we celebrating, Auntie?"

"Why, being alive!"

Garnet left the house shortly after Brant, rifle slung over his shoulder, strode toward the cane fields. Fowl flocked there in the afternoon, seeking seeds left by smaller birds. Garnet was cutting rosebuds and ferns when the shots rang out, startling her. How many men had he killed with that gun? She knew he had used it in the military, for CSA was carved in the stock. No doubt he had carried a pistol and saber too, standard equipment for the swash-buckling cavalryman.

Poor Denny had been in the infantry, a common foot soldier. Dear God, *where* was he now? Wandering in a daze, in a hospital, or lying in an unmarked grave?

She was sitting dolefully on a cracked marble bench, lost in bewildered preoccupation, when Brant came to her, holding out several birds and a bottle of port. "Our supper, milady."

"Where did you get the wine?"

He smiled, pleased. "From a secret cache the Yankees never discovered. And there's more."

"I don't drink alcoholic beverages, Mr. Steele."

"Moral objections? Even Christ approved of fermented grape juice, you know. Didn't He change water into wine at the wedding feast in Cana?"

Immediately he regretted his mistake. He should not have mentioned marriage. "It's getting late," he said, listening as the woods creatures began to cry and croak. "We'd better go inside. The pests are worse at night, so sleep under netting if we can find you some."

Within minutes, he prepared the quail for boiling. Jenny added the cleaned, chopped vegetables with some seasoning from the herb bed near the kitchen door, and soon an appetizing aroma permeated the room.

"Wine?" Lacey exclaimed over the dusty green bottle. "Oh, Brant, you're a genius!"

He grinned. "I didn't make it, ma'am, just managed to preserve it. Light a candle. I think Mrs. Lane is creating a centerpiece."

Later, Jenny carried in the steaming tureen like a chef's *pièce de résistance*. "Shall we be seated? Our host at the head of the table, naturally."

They took their places, and Brant poured the cool wine into the crystal goblets which had been rejected by the plunderers because of chips. "Sure you won't join us in a toast?" he asked Garnet.

She shook her head.

"Well, here's to the survivors of the *Crescent Queen*! May they be blessed with good fortune from now on—calm seas, blue skies, golden sunshine!" With a significant glance at Garnet, he added firmly, "Most of all, may North and South forgive, forget their differences, and reunite the country in brotherly love and Christian spirit."

"How beautiful," Lacey commented, lifting her glass in admiration.

Jenny was equally impressed. "You're a poet, sir."

The compliments embarrassed Brant, who cleared his throat huskily. *"Bon appétit,* everyone!"

"No grace, Auntie?" Garnet had never eaten a meal at home without asking this blessing.

"Oh, certainly, dear!" Jenny obliged with a short grace, of which Garnet, aware of Brant's gaze on her, heard hardly a word.

The door between the adjoining bedrooms selected

by Jenny and Garnet was open. Brant was in the master suite, Miss Lee directly across the hall. A convenient arrangement, Garnet thought, tossing restlessly. Although miserably sore and tired, she could not relax. Accustomed to fresh, soft linens and eiderdown pillows, she found the bare mattress hardly appealing, and the tattered mosquito net was a vast web in which she became entangled several times. If this was the state to which Confederate mansions had been reduced, what would they find on the Texas frontier?

Heavy clouds obscured the moon, and the room was in utter darkness. Strange sounds emanated from the forest and bayou.

Garnet was still awake when a door squeaked open, followed by footsteps on the bare boards of the upper gallery. Someone else could not sleep, either. Tobacco smoke wafting through her windows soon betrayed the other insomniac's identity. She listened quietly as he paced, his face vaguely lit by the glowing cheroot. A ragged robe hung on his tall frame. Occasionally he paused and stared intently into the dense blackness, as if his vision could penetrate it. She was about to speak to him out of her own loneliness when she heard more footsteps and a sensual contralto whispering, "Brooding won't help, darling. Please come back to bed. It's lonely in there without you."

So they had been together again! Was sex a nightly occurrence with them regardless of circumstances? Her face burned.

"I can't rest, Lacey. My mind is as unsettled as the weather."

"Let me soothe you," she coaxed. Garnet heard their footsteps as he obeyed, walking back to the bed with Lacey.

The storm struck at midnight. It was awesome. Rain pounded the slate roof like heavy, violent fists,

and winds ripped out shutter slats. In the flashes of
lightning, Garnet could see great trees bowing humbly to earth. She heard limbs cracking. Thunder
echoed like angry voices. A stricken oak smashed
against the galleries, and Garnet's involuntary
scream brought her aunt, a flickering taper in hand.

"Are you hurt, dear?"

"No, but I thought the walls were crumbling!"

Brant rushed in from the hall, Miss Lee close
behind him. Both had needed time to clothe themselves, he in the baggy robe, she clutching a frayed
silk wrapper to her body, the tops of her bare glob-
ular breasts protruding above the deep V-neckline.

Garnet glared at the lovers. How dared they flaunt
themselves!

"That falling tree barely grazed the house," Brant
assured her. "The large ones are kept trimmed and
were planted far enough away to avoid just that."

Jenny said, "I suppose this means the hurricane
is coming inland?"

"Like a demon! And there's nothing to do except
wait it out. Try to conserve the candles, please. They
burn faster in drafts, you know."

His eyes were on Garnet's indignantly quivering
bosom for several seconds before she realized that
she was wearing a sheer linen nightgown. She crossed
her hands modestly over her breasts, which were
small and perfectly molded.

Damn lecher! Wasn't one woman enough for
him? Did he lust after her, too? Maybe he wanted
several at once—a Roman orgy! Why did he always
leer at her delicate, inadequate form, when he had
a robust Venus de Milo *with arms* eager to embrace
him?

"Snuff the candle, Auntie. You heard what Mr.
Steele said."

Blandly, with the most unmitigated gall, their
host said, "I'm just down the hall, Mrs. Lane. If you
should need me, don't hesitate to come."

"But knock first," Lacey advised with a smile.

"Good night, all!" Garnet murmured, furious. And as the violent hurricane continued to lash the house, she lay awake, thinking about companionship and comfort.

Morning brought no break in the weather, and Garnet was sullenly silent at breakfast. The grits, biscuits, and gravy tasted of stale flour and rancid lard, edible only by pretending they were pancakes and maple syrup, bacon and eggs, muffins and marmalade. She refused a piece of the dried, moldy sausage, which had been hanging in the pantry for months.

"The mold won't hurt you," Brant said. "Just scrape it off. And sop up some gravy with your biscuit. Our men kept themselves alive on far worse in the field, believe me."

"And ours in your prison camps," Garnet countered. "Oh, we read about the horrors of your torture chambers, especially at Andersonville, Georgia!"

"And we about yours at Rock Island, Illinois, and Libby Prison in Richmond," he responded. "The bugles blew a truce, Mrs. Lane—why don't we?"

"He's right, dear," Jenny said firmly.

"Sure," Lacey added, scraping her plate for the last morsel. "Let's be friends, honey."

Garnet lowered her eyes, ashamed of her temper, which flared at the slightest provocation or even none at all. "I'm sorry. The weather is unnerving. Please excuse me. I'm not hungry."

She retreated to the drawing room and sat on the sad remains of a Chippendale sofa. Faint, gloomy daylight penetrated the unshuttered windows. Rain still lashed the panes. Garnet could hear her aunt apologizing for her, blaming it on illness.

Suddenly a match flared, touching the candle wick in a tarnished brass holder on the mantel, grotesquely illuminating the vandalized portrait of mother and children.

"Weren't we supposed to save on candles, sir? You don't follow your own orders very well."

"It's dark in here, and I don't think you like darkness. Indeed, you seem to have a childish fear of it."

"You know why I screamed last night! Only a fool wouldn't be frightened in a hurricane. Dear heaven, how much longer will it continue!"

He shrugged. "No telling. There may be many hurt on the coast. New Orleans is undoubtedly flooded. It's below sea level, which is why the cemeteries there are above ground."

Garnet twisted her wedding band. And how were dead Union soldiers buried in southern Louisiana?

Brant again considered steeling himself and telling her the truth about her husband. Again he changed his mind. What unnerved him most was the horror of realizing that he actually possessed a few of Private Lane's personal effects. They were to have been interred with the body, but orders to move on had been given before the burial detail had arrived. The gold watch, ring, and wallet, tied up in the Yankee kerchief, were still in Brant's haversack. He had forgotten them until he saw the tintype.

When and how to give them to her kept him frozen in silence, lest he appear to be a ghoul, a battle-trophy hunter. Oh, God! Why did his prisoner have to have been Private Dennis Lane?

"If only there were some way to send my parents a message," Garnet worried, "or telegraph my uncle in Texas."

"As soon as possible, I'll beg, borrow, or steal a horse and locate an operating telegraph station," he promised. "Most of the lines around here may be down, however."

"I haven't seen anything in the South worth fighting over," Garnet remarked bitterly, "much less worth the deaths of hundreds of thousands of men."

"The war wasn't fought over material things,"

Brant said. "And you haven't seen much of the South. There's far more to it than you glimpsed from the steamboat."

"And even that was more than I ever wanted to see," she snapped. "I have no desire to go to Texas. I shall insist that Aunt Jennifer and I return to Connecticut as soon as we can."

"I don't blame you, ma'am. In your place, so would I."

"What do you mean?"

"It takes a real woman to survive in that land."

Her violet eyes blazed. "And you don't think I qualify?"

"Maybe, maybe not," he drawled, deliberately goading her. "You'll have to prove that to yourself, ma'am."

Before she could hurl a stinging retort, Miss Lee appeared on the threshold. "Am I interrupting?"

"Yes," Garnet replied, rising and rushing from the room.

"Whew!" said Lacey, pretending to fan herself. "She has a sharp tongue for a fine-bred lady, and more gumption than I imagined."

Brant nodded. "An ice-capped volcano, burning within... and she doesn't even realize it."

"Do you intend to enlighten her? Melt the ice, so to speak?"

"Someday, perhaps." But again he was thinking of the articles in his haversack.

Lacey linked her arm through his. "I know you don't have any money, Brant. None of us has. But if I could get to a military camp or a town near one, and perform, I'm sure I could earn some."

"No doubt of that, honey. Any soldier would give a month's pay to see your act. Where's your clever little partner?"

Lacey's hand flew to her forehead. "Oh, mercy! Lollipop is still upstairs. He's housebroken, but he's been locked in there for hours now. If he soiled anything—"

"Never mind." Brant gestured to the profaned drawing room. "The Yankees did a lot worse to Great Oaks than that tiny creature could ever do."

Chapter 7

TORRENTIAL rains fell for several days after the raging winds swept north. The saturated earth became a bog, and, stripped of foliage, the trees hung limp and dripping.

Confined indoors, everyone's nerves were strained. When their host suggested card games, Garnet snapped, "I don't gamble!"

"I had only amusement in mind," he said. "After all, we have nothing to gamble with."

Lacey giggled. "I could propose some stakes, but I doubt Mrs. Lane would be interested. I can't speak for Miss Temple, but you've already won my affections, sir."

And more than affections, thought Garnet sourly.

The entertainer caught Garnet's look and laughed, unperturbed. "You don't drink spirits, you don't play cards even for fun, you never once caught the riv-

erboat show. What do you do for diversion, honey?
No wonder you're bored!"

Brant interrupted. "That's enough, Miss Lee. Mrs.
Lane has a right to her principles."

The words were scarcely spoken before Garnet,
upset by his quick defense, seated herself at the table
and muttered, "Deal."

"What game are we playing?" asked Jenny.

"Hearts?" Brant suggested blandly.

Garnet blushed under his gaze. "You'll have to
teach me."

"Gladly, my dear."

They played for an hour. Then, while the others
were out of the room, Brant tried to encourage her.
"You did very well."

"Don't patronize me, sir. The monkey could have
done better."

"You weren't concentrating," he said. "Your mind
was elsewhere."

"So was yours."

"Oh? Where was mine?"

"On Lacey, of course. I may be naïve, but I'm not
stupid." She bit her tongue, appalled at herself.

After a silence, he said smoothly, "Why should it
disturb you?"

"You flatter yourself. It doesn't disturb me at all."

She turned to leave, but he swiftly grasped her
arm. "You're determined to be a martyr, aren't you?
From your attitude, one would think the Union had
lost the war."

"Let me go," she muttered.

His fingers squeezed a little harder into the soft
flesh.

"Do you intend to grieve for the rest of your life?
And do you hold all Southerners responsible for your
husband's fate? Answer me, Garnet!" he demanded
harshly.

"Yes, I do!" She struggled to free herself, glaring
at him. "Release me, damn you!"

As he obliged, his expression was triumphant. "I knew it. Embers under the glacier."

"Well, don't count on stoking the embers for your benefit, Rebel! You're the most monstrous man I've ever had the misfortune to know!" With that, she flung herself away and ran from the room.

Her rage only convinced Brant that the attraction was mutual—which made the ultimate revelation harder. How in God's name could he ever tell her the truth?

The sun eventually shone benignly upon nature's own devastation. Innocent white clouds floated in a gloriously blue sky. The floodwaters began to recede, and the ravaged trees to regain their dignity. Damage to Great Oaks was minor—only enough, Brant gloated, to delay the auction. Bidders from New Orleans would be delayed by washed-out bridges, and those from farther up the Mississippi would be unable to locate the destroyed river landing of Great Oaks.

By foot and pirogue, Brant made his way to a neighboring plantation, but they had no horse to lend and did not know of any nearby.

"We'll be marooned here forever!" Garnet cried, avoiding his eyes, as she often did.

"No, not forever, but longer than you expected. I'm sorry, Garnet, but I can't swim that raging river. The entire Delta is flooded, and the upstream tributaries continue to gush more water into it. Levees are broken all the way to Vicksburg, and probably beyond."

"My parents will be frantic."

"The occupation forces will have to get some communications in order. I'll try to go to New Orleans in a week or so."

"A week! I don't think I can bear it."

"You are not in a prison, my dear. Address your grievances to the Almighty. He created the storm."

"Oh!" Garnet said hotly. "You really are the most unfeeling...irreverent...*heathen*." She turned away. "If you don't mind, I would like to read now. I was delighted to see that your library is intact. Why wasn't it destroyed along with the rest?"

"Because most of the thieving raiders were illiterates," he said. "Help yourself, ma'am. There are some rare manuscripts and first editions. They won't fetch a fraction of their worth."

Garnet relented. "My father appreciates fine literature. If it's all right with you, I'd like to bid for him on the entire collection and ship it, payable on delivery?"

"Very well. But you needn't *buy* the books, Garnet. Take them, with my compliments."

"Don't you wish to keep any?"

A grim, dark mask fell over his features. "Possessions are burdens to a displaced person. I'll be traveling light from now on. Free and easy. No obligations."

"Not even memories?"

"Memories can be the strongest bonds of all, if you let them," he said. "And binding one's self to the past..." He paused, shrugged. "Well, you know what I mean, Mrs. Lane."

"Excuse me, sir." She headed for the library. Soon, standing by one of the long shelves, she heard Lacey's bubbling voice in the foyer.

"There you are, darling! Could we walk outside? I want to discuss something with you."

Minutes later Garnet saw them pass the library windows, strolling toward the old red-brick sugar mill. An impulse to follow was quickly suppressed as Jenny entered.

"Good heavens, Garnet! Why don't you go out in the sunshine? At least sit on the veranda. You've been reading at home for over a year!"

"I want to mark the best of these books for Father.

Mr. Steele has offered to give them to me, but I intend to buy them on consignment."

"That's an insult to his generosity, Garnet."

"Why should I accept gifts from him? Besides, he needs money for a stake somewhere away from here. I wonder where he expects to go."

"Does it matter to you where he goes?"

Lacey's laughter drifted in, soft, merry, flirtatious.

"Not really," Garnet said, "although wherever it is, she'll probably be with him."

"Can't blame her for that, dear. He's really quite a man. If I were younger..." Jenny sighed.

"You can't mean that! He's a Rebel, a damned, murdering Rebel!"

Jenny tapped the thick book her niece was holding. "You've read *Uncle Tom's Cabin* a dozen times or more. I wouldn't have expected to find a signed copy in a Southerner's library. Maybe his family wasn't as prejudiced as some of them."

Garnet abruptly replaced the book. "We should be writing letters home, Auntie."

"On what? There's no stationery. And how would we send mail—in a bottle cast into the Mississippi? Things float downstream, you know, not up."

"Do you suppose they're aware of the explosion of the *Crescent Queen*?"

"The newspapers would surely have reported it by this time."

"Maybe they think we're dead."

Jenny nodded, and Garnet said softly, "Sometimes I wish I *were* dead."

"No, you don't, Garnet. You fought as hard to survive as the rest of us. You want to live more than you realize. You're stronger than Dr. Forbes or any of us thought. I think we can return home as soon as transportation is available."

Although this had been Garnet's desire, Brant's

taunting had gotten to her. He didn't believe she was woman enough for the West? Well, she'd show him!

She squared her shoulders and thrust out her chin. "Uncle Seth is expecting us," she pronounced firmly.

Jenny's eyes widened. "You confound me sometimes," she said, shaking her head ruefully.

"I confound myself, Auntie," Garnet replied, with the first smile she had shown in days.

"We'll go, then," said her aunt. "But not until Mr. Steele can help us."

"*If* he can find the time," Garnet scoffed, the sunny mood gone. "Miss Lee keeps him rather busy."

After a moment, Jennifer ventured, "Why should you mind?"

"They're lovers, Auntie."

"Of course! She's an attractive female, and he's a virile male. You criticize and insult him, while she adores him. But I don't think it's a serious involvement, for him. You're so immature, Garnet. Can't you see he's really in love with you?"

"That's preposterous! We hardly know each other."

"Nevertheless—"

"Hush!" Garnet interrupted. "I don't want to hear any more about it."

"Oh, yes, you do! Everything about Brant Steele interests you, my dear niece, and provokes you. You're seething with jealousy right now, because he's with her."

Garnet covered her ears, crying as she fled the scene. "I won't listen to nonsense! I won't listen!"

For the remainder of the day she sulked in her bedroom, unable to concentrate on the inscribed Jane Austen novel.

Later, from the windows, she watched Brant and Lacey picking vegetables from the muddy garden. Then they went hunting together in the woods, Lacey wearing an old pair of his army breeches, a torn shirt, and his cavalry hat. This time Brant bagged a deer, which they carted home on a pole. Jenny roasted a haunch with herbs and crab apples. It was delicious. Garnet had never tasted venison before. Her father was not a hunter, even of small game. Where had Jenny learned to prepare game? She would do all right in the wilderness, Garnet decided.

When River Road became passable, two soldiers arrived on army mounts. They had been sent by the colonel who was interested in buying Great Oaks. Garnet was overjoyed at the sight of those blue uniforms. Greeting them, she introduced herself and her aunt and explained their predicament.

Brant leaned against a flaking white column, a cynical half-smile on his lips. Their soldiers' courtesy to these Yankee ladies was in marked contrast to the treatment of Southern females.

The sergeant wrote down the information Miss Temple wished dispatched to Connecticut.

"We heard what happened to the *Crescent Queen*," he said. "You folks are among a very few survivors."

"Thanks to Mr. Steele," Jenny told him.

"Yeah. Well, it's lucky for you Colonel Grimes sent us out here, ain't it? You know, he plans to buy this place next week."

"They're not postponing the auction?" Brant asked, straightening.

"Why should they?"

"More bidders could get here."

The sergeant grinned. "More competition for Colonel Grimes, then. The colonel ain't nobody's fool. He'll get this plantation for a pittance—though why he wants it is beyond me. Me, I just want to get the hell out of here and back up North. I miss the Green Mountains of Vermont. This state ain't nothin' but a swamp ridden with pests."

"Many of them in uniform," Brant muttered.

The soldiers' attention was arrested by the appearance of Miss Lee in the scarlet satin gown, the monkey in her arms. They saw her as a higher-class harlot who catered only to officers, while enlisted men settled for the common whore.

Brant interrupted their leering enjoyment. "This is Miss Lacey Lee—a unique *stage* entertainer."

"That's some dress," the corporal drawled.

"It's left over from a costume ball," Jenny explained. "Try to remember, gentlemen, that we were shipwrecked on the *Crescent Queen*. None of us is wearing our Sunday best."

"We understand, ma'am."

"How soon can you send the telegram for us?" Garnet asked impatiently.

"We'll try as soon as we return to headquarters. But I tell you frankly, Mrs. Lane, we got a heap of military communications on the agenda. They got priority. But we'll do our best for you."

As they tipped their hats to depart, Lacey Lee asked, "Are there any local theaters featuring variety acts?"

"Near camp?"

"Anywhere in the vicinity, Sergeant."

"Well, there's some burlesque houses in New Orleans. Also saloons with dancing girls. You looking for work?"

"Yes, sir. I need the money."

"One evening's performance at the officers' mess could mean a sheaf of greenbacks." He jotted down some names on a scrap of paper. "Or you might try these places."

"How kind of you, sir! Could you also suggest some means of transportation?" she wheedled, batting her long eyelashes and forcing her dimples.

"I'll speak with Colonel Grimes," he promised. "I'm sure he can do something."

"I'd appreciate that, Sergeant."

Brant scowled, watching the troopers mount their sleek horses. He had recognized them as two of the many confiscated from Great Oaks. "May I see that list, Lacey?"

"Of course." She handed it to him. "Are any of the places known to you?"

Garnet smirked. "No doubt they all are."

His refusal to be goaded infuriated her. "The Theatre Royale might be your best bet, honey. I know the manager, and I'll go with you to see him."

"Oh, thank you, Brant!"

"And are we to stay here alone?" Garnet demanded.

"You'll be safe enough, my dear. You're Yankees, remember? But I'll leave a loaded gun for you. Just don't shoot yourself." He paused. "I think I'll try to hook some fresh fish for supper."

"Let me help," Lacey begged, "after I change."

"Of course." He glanced hopefully at Garnet. "Would you care to try your luck?"

Before she could reply, Lacey scoffed. "Oh, Brant! One of those big catfish would yank her right into the bayou! But fix a pole for Lollipop, will you? Monkey see, monkey do, you know. I'll be with you in a flash, honey!"

Chapter 8

COLONEL GRIMES sent transportation the next day. After obtaining Miss Lee's signature acknowledging responsibility for the government property, the driver departed on the saddled horse that had trotted behind the buggy. Brant took over the buggy reins and drove toward River Road, Lacey and Lollipop beside him.

"I hope we never see them again, Auntie."

"Poppycock, Garnet! We need Mr. Steele far more than he needs us."

Garnet shrugged, blotting her moist face. "This dreadful heat! How the field hands must have suffered in the summer! I wonder how many slaves the Steeles had and how they treated them."

"No matter now, dear. Brant told me many of the plantation owners are now working their own land, hoping to hang onto their property. But he has resigned himself to the loss of Great Oaks."

63

"Shall we go inside, where it's cooler?"

"You are rather pale, child. Better take a nap."

"I'm not a *child,* Aunt Jennifer! I'm a fully grown woman. And I want to finish in the library before the auctioneer takes charge. He may realize the value of some editions and include them in the sale. There are some priceless diaries and papers."

After supper, Garnet insisted on sleeping in her aunt's room and keeping the tallow candle burning for comfort, although it smoked and smelled abominable. She longed for the bayberry-scented tapers of home. There was not enough moonlight even to cast shadows in the limbo darkness, and she silently cursed Brant for deserting them. She decided that he couldn't care much for her, Garnet, and she assured herself once again that she had only contempt for him. She listened fearfully to the weird cacophony of swamp creatures and, while Jenny slept, she removed the tintype from the oilskin pouch, gazed at it in the dim, smoky light, then fell asleep hugging it to her bosom. The feeling of this reverence was somewhat lacking, but she attributed the lack of fervor to the late hour and strange environment.

Toward dawn, Garnet rose and wandered through the house with the guttering candle. Somehow she wound up in the master suite, and her eyes were drawn to Brant's haversack and the stenciled black markings, *Maj. B. C. Steele, C.S.A.* A strong temptation to open it took hold of her, despite her respect for other people's privacy. Only her aunt's sudden appearance in the doorway prevented the invasion.

"Garnet, what on earth are you doing here?"

"I—I woke up early."

"That's no reason to be here." Jenny grasped her arm firmly, guiding her toward the hall. "No point going back to bed at this hour. We may as well make breakfast."

"That awful corn mush again?"

"Hominy grits, dear, and it's better than hunger.

I'll soak some dried black-eyed peas for supper. Too bad the storm spoiled the peaches. Perhaps Brant will bring back something good to eat from New Orleans. I have an idea Miss Lee will charm some rations out of the mess sergeant, even if she has to—"

"Sleep with him?" Garnet finished, surprised at her own indelicacy. "That would hardly be a novelty for her!"

"Women have done worse for food, Garnet."

They descended the stairway together, Garnet's mind still on the haversack. It was an hypnotic thing, beckoning her without her knowing why it did.

Brant returned from New Orleans with several sacks of delicious food, which he spread on the table with a flourish.

"Compliments of the officers' mess, ladies!"

Garnet gazed hungrily at the bounty. "How did you acquire all this?"

"I didn't. We are indebted to Miss Lee for the ambrosia of the Yankee gods—who now rule Louisiana as if they really had descended from Olympus. After observing her act at the Theatre Royale, a brigadier general took a fancy to the fascinating lady. When his bouquet of flowers arrived backstage, she hinted that she would prefer food. We shall feast for days."

"Is she with him now?" Garnet asked tersely, watching his face for signs of jealousy.

"No, he managed to find a nice apartment for her in the Vieux Carré. I'm afraid you underestimate our benefactress, Mrs. Lane. She has some very clever and cunning ways with men."

"Especially with men," Garnet quipped.

"Was the city badly damaged, Brant?" Jenny asked.

"Less severely than I'd expected, and military details are at work restoring operations," he answered. "The message was telegraphed to Garnet's father.

The reply will be received at headquarters. There should be a response by tomorrow or the next day."

Jenny said, "I suppose the auctioneer will be here by then, too?"

"It seems that Colonel Grimes had enough influence to prevent a public auction of Great Oaks. I sold it to him outright—at his price, of course. I have a week to vacate."

"I'm sorry," Jenny sympathized.

A resigned shrug. "Beggars have no choice."

"And the books?" Garnet asked softly.

"We'll ship them to Connecticut, as we agreed. Grimes is sending some crates for my personal belongings, but I only need one."

"Father will insist on compensating you," Garnet told him, "when he hears the whole story."

"Then don't tell the whole story," he suggested. "Now I must get back to the city and deliver the deed to Great Oaks."

Donning his campaign-battered hat, now stripped of official insignia, he snapped the brim with a kind of reluctant anger. But there was no feeling of defeat in his manner, and Garnet was acutely aware of the tall shadow he cast as he strode to the buggy.

The news he brought the following afternoon caused mixed emotions. Via telegraph, her father had established credit for them with a banker and booked passage on the next ship bound for Corpus Christi, Texas.

"We'll have to buy some clothes before we leave for Texas," Jenny said, reading the message again.

"Aren't you ladies returning to Connecticut?" asked Brant.

Jenny sighed. "No, for some inexplicable reason my niece now regards Texas as a challenge to her womanhood."

"Indeed?" Brant grinned at Garnet's embarrassed frown. "Surely not because of anything I said?"

"Certainly not! You have no influence whatever,

sir! I—I just decided to visit Uncle Seth, that's all.
When I tire of Texas, I'll leave."

"May we ride to town with you tomorrow?" asked
Jenny.

"Of course. I'll take you to the bank and shops. If
it's too late to drive back here, you can stay in a
hotel. The Saint Charles is still in good shape."

"Where will you stay?" Jenny asked, as Garnet
pretended disinterest in his plans.

"Oh, I'll find a place."

"I think we should leave quite early in the morning, Auntie." She nibbled on a fresh, ripe strawberry.
"And let's try to return before dark, Mr. Steele. It
would be a shame to waste any of this wonderful
food."

"A sin," Jenny agreed. "What wonderful jams and
desserts these berries would make! They don't raise
better ones in the Hudson River valley."

"Enjoy yourselves," Brant invited. "You're not
likely to find such a cornucopia in Texas."

A large sum of money had been placed at their
disposal in the bank selected by Henry Ashley, and
they proceeded to buy the necessary things for a
water and land journey to Texas. Although somewhat leery about sailing the vast Gulf of Mexico so
soon after the Mississippi River tragedy, Garnet
adopted a philosophical attitude. It would be a new
adventure, and she had not realized before what a
venturesome spirit she possessed. She steadfastly refused to credit Brant Steele's comments with having
inspired her.

Brant visited Lacey in her charming flat in the
French Quarter. She had four rooms on the second
floor of a long row of brightly painted stucco houses,
all joined by wrought-iron-trimmed balconies. The
residents below her were busy repairing the hurricane damage. Brant always marveled at the city's
rapid recovery from disaster. Its proud citizens were

determined to survive war, plague, the elements, and any other possible devastation. They worked together with a sense of humor, insisting things could be worse.

"You like it here, Lacey?"

"It's interesting, and I'm earning good money. But what will you do after leaving Great Oaks?"

"I don't know yet. No more gambling, though, that's for sure. I may just head west and see what develops."

She was not beguiled. "Are you going in Mrs. Lane's direction, perhaps?"

Brant shrugged. "Well, there's Texas blood in my veins, you know."

"You never told me that before, dear. You're so tight-lipped about yourself. But then, I'm not exactly talkative about myself, either. Shall we both talk a little?"

"Later, honey. Right now, I have other ideas."

Lacey smiled. "Are all Southern men so lusty, or only the part-Texan ones?"

He laughed. "You'd have to conduct your own survey on that, ma'am. What time is your first performance?"

"Same as yesterday and the day before. Seven o'clock. We have plenty of time to play, lover. Will I have the pleasure of your company again tonight?"

"No, my Yankee guests wish to make use of the transportation and fine chow provided by Colonel Grimes. Too damn many Bluecoats on these streets for my liking now. New Orleans will never be the same for me again."

"Did you have a beautiful little quadroon here, like other planters before the war?"

"What a question!" he exclaimed, but she noted that he didn't answer it.

His mouth silenced further conversation. But Lacey sensed patronage in his lovemaking, as if his mind were elsewhere, and for the brief and blissful interlude she possessed only his body.

Wedged between Brant and Jenny in the single-seated buggy, Garnet was acutely conscious of his hips against hers. She was also aware of a heavy perfume on his clothes, suggesting where he had been.

Garnet had chosen another conservative wardrobe, including the dark-blue traveling ensemble she was wearing. Her aunt looked cool and summery in a frock of apple-green *voile* and a matching bonnet adorned with silk flowers.

"I trust you weren't bored waiting for us, sir?" Garnet inquired smoothly.

"Not at all," he drawled. "It was a pleasure."

Garnet clenched her teeth and kept silent until they reached Great Oaks at twilight. Suffering Brant's assistance as she stepped out of the buggy, she rushed into the house and upstairs. She did not appear again until Jenny's summons to a late supper, and then she ate in silence.

When the meal was over, he asked, "May I speak with you for a few minutes before you retire, Mrs. Lane?"

"I suppose," she said.

"Go ahead," Jenny gestured. "I'll clean up here."

He escorted her to the library, a lighted candle in his hand.

He hesitated, setting the candle on a table. "Your boat sails in three days, Garnet."

"I know."

Brant flexed and unflexed his hands. How could he let her leave without telling her the truth about her husband? Yet he could not find the words, or the courage. Damn it!

Unexpectedly, he announced, "I'm sailing with you."

She gaped at him. "What do you mean, *with me?*"

"On the same ship."

"Why?"

"To try to locate my father's relatives." He quickly summoned the words.

"If you have some chivalrous notion about accompanying Aunt Jenny and me, please forget it. We don't need your protection."

Spinning on his heel, he retreated. "Don't worry about my troubling you on the voyage, madam. I won't."

For Garnet, it was another restless night, which left her weary in the morning. She was barely civil to Brant, and he made an elaborate pretense of ignoring her, seemingly absorbed in the final tour of the plantation.

"It must be awful for him," Jenny remarked, as they crated books in the library, "having to give up his home."

Garnet nodded, thinking how difficult it would be if the situation were hers. "Aunt Jenny—he's going to Texas. I can't imagine why."

"Can't you? You can't be as obtuse as you pretend."

Garnet sighed, twisting her hands. "Oh, Auntie, he's sailing on the same ship!"

"I'm not surprised."

"You sound pleased."

"I am pleased," Jenny said. "And if you weren't such an obstinate little goose, you would be, too."

Chapter 9

H AVING spent its fury in the recent tropical storm, the Gulf of Mexico was obligingly calm. Realizing that Corpus Christi meant "body of Christ" in Latin, Garnet wondered why the Mexicans had called it that. She was soon to wonder about many other aspects of Texas.

She had not seen Brant Steele once during the voyage, but they met on the stage to San Antonio. She was surprised to find Lacey Lee on the stage, the monkey riding atop the baggage rack. But she knew she should not be surprised at all.

There wasn't much scenery along the route, mostly coastal plains on which mustangs and longhorn cattle roamed in search of grass. Summer was hard upon the land, and Garnet thought it looked arid and desolate. Brassy sun, glaring sky, and endless horizon were relieved only by the scrubby growth of salt cedar, mesquite, and cactus.

71

Where were the trees, lakes, streams, mountains? And what did she expect to prove to herself or anyone else in this God-forsaken place, which General Philip Sheridan had called "a part of Hell"? That damn fool doctor! Surely he had never been to South Texas. He'd been right about one thing, though, the climate was certainly dry and desert-hot. Her parched throat had craved cool water since they'd left the ship.

When finally they arrived in San Antonio, a sizable town on a winding, tree-shaded river, Garnet was further disappointed to learn that they would not be living there. The nice hotel on the plaza was merely another stopover, where they would wait for Uncle Seth.

Mr. Steele and Miss Lee sought less expensive lodgings down the street, where Lollipop was accepted, and Garnet's gaze trailed the odd trio out of sight, Brant toting their luggage.

"Isn't it ridiculous?" she remarked to her aunt as they entered the spacious, well-appointed Menger Hotel lobby.

"What?"

"The way the once proud Rebel planter caters like a lackey to that wench and her monkey! Next she'll have him grinding an organ on the streets."

"I doubt that, dear. He's still very much his own man, merely helping a damsel in distress."

"That creature in distress? She could charm her way out of a snake pit! Why is she following him, anyway? I thought she was employed at the Theatre Royale."

"Forget them," Jenny advised.

"I intend to. Forever."

"Of course, darling."

The clerk presented an addressed, sealed envelope to Miss Jennifer Temple. She opened it immediately and read the message to her niece.

"'Welcome, Dear Family! Have a good night's rest,

and I'll call for you early in the morning. Your loving and anxious Uncle Seth.'"

"Thank heaven," Garnet sighed. "I couldn't bear another mile on the road today."

Jenny had last seen her mother's brother thirty years before, when he had left Connecticut for the frontier. She had been sixteen then, a romantic girl impressed by handsome older men, and twenty-nine-year-old Uncle Seth had seemed especially attractive, with his roguish black mustache and bold black eyes, bright with the prospect of adventure. The females of the family wept at his farewell party as though it were his funeral. The village youths had envied Seth his travels.

Jenny barely recognized the man who greeted them after breakfast the next morning. His hair was cotton-white, long and shaggy, his weather-beaten face was as wrinkle-tracked as the bottom of a dry creek, and his once stalwart frame was bent, although he was only fifty-nine. Her first suspicion was that he felt himself on the verge of invalidism and wanted a housekeeper, but she was ashamed of the thought. After a round of hugs and kisses, Seth confided that his wife Sarah had died five years before. He hadn't known how to get the news back East with the mails cut off by the war, and he hadn't mentioned it in his invitation, because he feared it might prevent their coming. He had wanted so desperately to have them.

"We thought you lived in San Antonio," Jenny said, as disappointed as Garnet.

"No, I run a general store at a prairie junction about thirty miles west of here, and we'd best get moving before the sun climbs too high," Seth said. "My buckboard's on the plaza. I'll get some help with your baggage."

Beckoning a couple of Mexican lads waiting hopefully in the lobby, Seth spoke to them in Spanish, and they agreed to assist for "dos centavos."

"How much money is that?" Garnet asked, as they were loaded into the small wagon.

"Two cents."

"Labor is cheap here."

"You bet, especially since the war."

"Muchas gracias, señor," the little porters called, clutching the pennies.

Driving off, Seth pointed to a crumbling rock-and-adobe building. "In case you don't recognize it from pictures in your history books, Garnet honey, that's the site of the famous Battle of the Alamo."

"No wonder the defenders died, if *that's* all they had to protect them."

"It was just a mission, child, built by Franciscan monks. San Antone's constructing a real fort now, named for the hero of San Jacinto, General Sam Houston."

Jenny nudged him. "Let's not talk about war, Uncle. It upsets Garnet—and she's here for her health, you know."

"She don't look sick to me," Seth observed. "Just needs some meat on her bones and roses in her cheeks. We'll try to fix that, *pronto.*"

Periodically, as they jounced over the rutted road, Garnet glanced back to see if they had company. But they were alone in the wilderness...except for the horses and cows, jackrabbits and rattlesnakes, buzzards and coyotes. Heat waves shimmered like mirages, and hot winds swirled the dry soil into choking dust. She drew her veil closer about her face.

"Is all the land so drab and flat?" Garnet asked mournfully.

"No, there's plenty of hills and even mountains further west, and the East Texas forests are as green and pretty as any back home. I don't exactly know why I settled in Longhorn Junction, except that it was where I happened to be when I got tired of roaming the territories. I married a sweet little gal and took over her pa's business after he died. Had a good, happy life, too, before we lost our young daughter to typhoid. Then it was just Sarah and me till the Lord called her away, too." He blinked. "Didn't mean to get soppy, ladies."

Longhorn Junction, which they reached in late afternoon, formed a crossroads for cattle trails and pony express routes. Seth Travers occupied quarters connected to his store. He did business with the local farmers and ranchers, and currently with occupation troops from the nearby camp.

"Just can't get used to them uniforms," he muttered, as several troopers galloped by the store. "But at least the Yankees and carpetbaggers ain't confiscating our property as freely as they did in other Confederate states. They want cultivated lands, plantations and fine manors, not undeveloped pastures. Anyway, we're getting a few new settlers—folks not afraid of hard work. Someday this may be a nice town."

But if Seth was content with his life in Texas, Jenny was appalled. It was only bare essentials. She thought he could hardly provide for himself, much less accommodate two females, one in delicate health. Although she did not go so far as to accuse him of exaggerating, her tone implied it. "The letters you wrote some years ago, Uncle? You said you were doing so well—that you were practically a rich man and wanted for nothing."

Seth looked sheepish. "I did all right, Jenny. Made enough to support my family and save a little. We had tough times, sure. Everybody on the frontier does, but I didn't see no point whining to the folks back home. Didn't want to worry them, or receive no charity bundles and advice about giving up, either. I could never move back East. Texas is my home now. I belong here. I expect to be buried here, beside Sarah and our child." A wistful look at Garnet revived painful memories of his precious little Pearl, snatched from life on the brink of lovely womanhood.

"If it's just sunshine and hot, dry air you need, honey, you'll be well and strong in no time," he said gruffly.

Like your daughter and wife? Garnet thought glumly. If this climate was so good, what happened to them? And why did he look a hundred years old?

Seth put their luggage in the small room next to the one he had shared with Sarah. "I hope you'll be comfortable and happy here, ladies. And I want to say again how glad I am to have you. Soon's you rest up, I'll show you around town."

Town? All Garnet could see was a wide space in a dirt road, an old store, a blacksmith shop, a saloon, one church, a dozen frame houses in need of repair, and a small, shabby hotel ... all built around a patch of withered grass and stunted trees.

Jenny sought to alleviate her melancholy with practicality. "I guess we'd better unpack, dear. I hear wheels approaching. Customers, probably."

Garnet glanced curiously through the cracked windowpane, simultaneously feeling anger and joy.

"It's them, Auntie! Mr. Steele, Miss Lee, and Lollipop!"

"Really?" Jenny grinned. "Well, that should liven things up a bit!"

"They're going to the hotel. Uncle Seth is talking to them now."

As she watched, she mused aloud.

"Why did they come here? There was certainly more opportunity for *her* in San Antonio!"

"Perhaps they're just passing through on their way to a more prosperous place."

Seth was smiling when he came back. "Business just picked up. We got two new guests in the hotel, and they aim to stay a spell. I reckon you know 'em, since they rode the same stage from Corpus to San Antone?"

"And the same ship from New Orleans," Jenny nodded. "They're friends of ours, Uncle. I'll tell you about it later. But I wonder how they expect to earn a living in this hamlet."

"Oh, he could work on a ranch," Seth said. "He told me his pa was a Texas cattleman before he married a Louisiana belle. All Mr. Steele needs to know is how to handle a horse and a gun, and every Southerner knows that. She's an entertainer. I bet the cowboys and troopers would ride for miles to see her and that cute little critter."

"No doubt," Garnet agreed grudgingly. "I suppose the hotel owner was happy to rent them a room?"

"Two rooms, honey. They're not married, just traveling together."

Their concern for appearances, evident in their taking separate rooms, surprised Garnet. Why had they done it? It would cost some money, this new modesty of theirs.

Never lazy, Lacey Lee was soon looking for work at the Silver Spur Saloon. She took along a fetching costume of pink satin tights, sequin-spattered pink satin bodice, and a net ruffled skirt, short enough to expose her enticing thighs. Simulating a ballerina's tutu, it had always thrilled male audiences. Lollipop wore matching pink silk rompers and a bellboy cap fastened under his chin.

The proprietor of the Silver Spur Saloon was a stocky, bearded, fat-bellied man reminding Lacey of newspaper caricatures of New York City's notorious Boss Tweed. Sully Voss, chewing a long black stogie, stated flatly that his patrons did not care for animal acts.

"Mine ain't exactly an animal act," Lacey said, smiling to show small even white teeth between the most lusciously red lips Voss had ever seen. "I'd better demonstrate, sir. I've got a costume with me. Where can I change?"

He pointed to a storeroom. "Come out when you're ready."

The saloon's last entertainer had been a plump singer and dancer from Denver, fired from her previous job because of drinking. She had often received more catcalls than applause, and her engagement in Longhorn Junction did not last long. The good acts, like the good-looking women, invariably moved on to larger towns. The Silver Spur was lucky to get the rejects and has-beens—or, as Voss often lamented, the never-had-beens.

Still, Miss Lee would have to exhibit more than beauty to satisfy his customers, most of whom were tough hombres. The men were sometimes so rough that Voss had private guards to keep order in the place. They were obliged to protect his person and property during business hours. It was worth a man's life to insult Sully Voss, to toss a bottle at his prized Venetian mirror, or to whittle on the polished mahogany bar.

As Lacey emerged in her costume, his eyes bulged. She had to suppress a giggle, for he reminded her of the bullfrogs she used to gig in the ponds along the Southern routes her family's medicine wagon had traveled. The few customers lounging around that afternoon stared as if they could not believe their eyes.

"Got any music, sir? Can anybody here play that old piano?"

Perspiration beaded Voss's forehead. "Yeah, but he ain't here. Can't you hum or something?"

"Sure. I sing and dance. I'm an actress, too."

"Regular bundle of talent, ain't you? So give us a demonstration, honey. I can hardly wait."

Before she had sung five notes Sully Voss knew he was going to hire that gorgeous doll and, furthermore, that he would kill any bastard from San Antone who tried to take her away. The patrons gave her a standing ovation, stamping boots and jingling spurs, yelling for more. Lacey heard only the applause, having trained herself to ignore the obscene shouts. She pretended that she was a star on the stage of a legitimate theater, bowing to an appreciative, high-class audience, while she was actually retying the bodice ribbon released by her partner.

"Encore, encore!" cried the voices in her mind, genteel voices, not the bellows that deafened her now. But she declined an encore, having discovered at an early age that samples were the most effective means of selling a product.

Voss had chewed his cigar to shreds. When the word got around—and it wouldn't take long—the cowboys and troopers would be pounding the trails to his watering hole. His coffers would fill with cash every Saturday.

"You're hired, honey," he said, grinning as if he had just signed the late Lola Montez. "Eight this Saturday evening. I'll make some handbills and send riders out to post them. Now, how'd you like to come upstairs to my quarters and toast your future?"

"No, thank you, Mr. Voss. I'm not quite settled yet, and I'd like to work on my act and costumes."

"I understand, ma'am. Go on to the hotel, and if they don't treat you right, let me know. That fella you arrived with ain't got no legal claim on you, has he?"

"No, we're just friends."

As she prepared to leave with Lollipop, a drunk shouted from the bar, "Hey there, sister! That's a mighty famous name you got! Any kin to Gen'l Robert E. Lee?"

"Remotely, suh," Lacey drawled, "though Ah reckon Ah'd be quicker to admit it than the general would," and she left on a roar of laughter.

Outside, Seth Travers was showing his relatives around. Lacey waved and announced, "I got a job!"

"Congratulations!" Jenny called back warmly.

Seth gazed after Lacey speculatively, watching her swish along the board sidewalk. "Ain't she something?"

"Something," Garnet echoed, convinced that men of every age and condition were alike about women like Lacey Lee.

Community milk cows and goats were staked on the square, and chickens scratched in the grass for seeds and insects. Tired and too warm, Garnet was ready to return to the shade of the Mercantile Mart, but she refused to say so in the presence of the entertainer's seemingly boundless energy.

Observing her niece's flushed face, Jenny took Garnet's hand and they crossed the road, their skirts ruffling the dust. She got Garnet to their room.

"Lie down," she ordered. "You look exhausted. I'll bring you some milk. Thank goodness we can get it fresh every day. And meat too, though it's usually tough as an old boot. I'll make a hearty stew for lunch, with some vegetables from the root cellar."

"Could you bake some wheat bread tomorrow, Auntie? I don't care much for those sourdough biscuits and corn pone Uncle Seth favors."

"Yes, dear. Just rest now. Your job is to regain your health and strength, so we can leave Texas."

Garnet sighed wearily, suddenly looking perplexed. "And what then?"

"Make a new life for yourself, Garnet," Jenny said evenly.

"To do that one must first escape the old one, Aunt. I hope there's some mail from home soon. It's been long enough, hasn't it?"

"Yes...but I doubt the letter you're expecting will ever come, child."

"That's cruel," Garnet said, her voice tremulous.

"Oh, no, darling. It's realistic." And she hurried to fetch the milk.

Over supper two weeks later, Jenny asked Seth, "What do the people here do for social life?"

"Well, the ladies have quilting bees, when they

can save up enough scraps for a comforter and don't
need them to patch the family duds. And they have
taffy pulls when they can get molasses. We ain't had
no county fair since the war, and only one church
festival. Used to have harvest barn dances and ranch
barbecues all the time. When folks could afford it,
they went to San Antone. There's a nice ballroom at
the Menger Hotel. And there's a popular spa, boat
rides on the river, and other things. About the only
entertainment around here now is the Silver Spur.
I hear Miss Lee's a howling success."

"Too bad ladies can't go into saloons," Jenny remarked.

"Don't mind her, Uncle," Garnet said. "She was
always shocking Mother with radical ideas about
female emancipation. She went to the Suffragettes'
lectures whenever she could, and even tried to or-
ganize a chapter in Avalon. She wanted to wear
bloomers when they were first introduced. Mother
was always afraid she'd disgrace the family."

"Fiddlesticks!" Jenny scoffed. "I was just tired of
knitting shawls and crocheting antimacassars. And
what's so scandalous about divided skirts? I've seen
some in leather and canvas on Texas women. They're
very practical for riding. As for the Suffragettes, I
admire their goals. I wish them luck. Women should
have more freedom and independence. Certainly
women are entitled to vote."

"They can in the Wyoming Territory," Seth spoke
up.

"Really? How did they accomplish that?"

"Pioneering spirit, I reckon—or maybe the men
were afraid they'd leave unless they humored them
with the vote. It's hard to lure ladies out West, and
even harder to keep them on the frontier without
giving them reasons to stay. There just aren't enough
women out West. No wonder Miss Lee packs the
saloon, and Mr. Steele rides in from the Duke Ranch

whenever he can. But with all the cowpokes there are here, she seems to be a one-hombre woman. That don't make old Sully Voss none too happy. He obviously wants her for himself."

Chapter 10

To GARNET, the mail carriers were the real heroes of the West. Their twice-weekly delivery was the most exciting event in Longhorn Junction.

After weeks of running out onto the porch at the sound of galloping hoofs, she was finally rewarded by two letters from Connecticut. While Jenny shared hers with Seth, Garnet went to the bedroom to open her own. Breaking the wax seal on the ivory vellum envelope, she was thrilled to count nine pages of the familiar monogrammed stationery.

My Dear Daughter,

I take pen in hand this lovely but lonely Sunday afternoon to tell you how much your father and I miss you and Jennifer. We fervently hope that the remainder of your journey was pleasantly uneventful.

You had been gone only a few hours when

doubt and fear began to torment us. Later on,
news of that dreadful disaster on the Mississippi River reached us. What a relief it was to
receive the telegram assuring us of your safety!

We realize that you have suffered a terrible
ordeal, but when you feel up to it, please write
and give us more details.

Jenny has written of the rescue by a fine
young man from Louisiana, whom we would
very much like to thank. Do you know his address? We hope that postal service between the
North and South will improve soon and render
correspondence easier and swifter....

Garnet rushed through the closely written pages,
then read them again slowly to make sure she had
not missed anything. There was no mention of Denny,
not even an inference from which to take heart.

Garnet sat on the narrow little frontier bed that
had belonged to the dead cousin she had never met,
victim in girlhood of this "salubrious" climate, and
surrendered herself to melancholy nostalgia.

The long, chatty letter was the next best thing to
a visit with her family and friends.

Eleanor detailed the weather that Sunday in Avalon, the subject of the sermon at the Congregational
Church, and the parishioners' inquiries about Garnet and Jennifer in Texas.

Eleanor continued:

Your father sends his love, dear. He is very
pleased with the fine books and manuscripts
the Louisiana gentleman sent to him. He is also
quite busy at the mills, now that cotton trade
with the South has resumed.

I trust there is a satisfactory seamstress
there, for I am shipping you and Jennifer some
lovely new materials, along with the latest
fashion magazines and Madame Demorest's

newest pattern designs. Hoops are still in vogue,
but less wide, and not all Paris and New York
ladies are wearing three petticoats any longer.

Bonnets are exceptionally feminine, with
both flowers and veiling, and shoes are daintier
now that the leather-goods manufacturers can
concentrate on something besides boots and
saddles.

Garnet smiled at the space devoted to fashion and
frivolity, thinking wryly that the only female in Longhorn Junction other than Jenny who might be interested was Miss Lee.

The entertainer had already made two trips to San
Antonio to replace the wardrobe lost in the riverboat
explosion. With a loaded pistol handy, she drove herself in a livery equipage, declining the loan of Sully
Voss's fancy rig.

Evidently she was still faithful to Brant, who rode
in from the Duke Ranch every Saturday. His experience with animal husbandry and plantation records had gained him the position of foreman-
bookkeeper at the ranch.

Garnet tried to avoid contact with Brant when he
came to the store for supplies, or merely to pay his
respects. He looked quite fine in his Western regalia,
and could probably ride and shoot with the best of
the cowboys. His skin was even tanner than before,
and there were squint lines when his dark eyes narrowed against the sun.

Garnet clutched the letter to her breast, home-
sickness washing over her. She longed for the blue
waters of Long Island Sound instead of the brownish
sea of parched grass beyond Seth's windows.

Foolish girl, she had taken so many things for
granted! Her mother's lovely face, for instance, with
its fine features and heavy ash-blond chignon tilting
her head backward ever so slightly, giving her graceful throat a regal arch. The portly figure of her father,

his hair, eyes and beard all the color of freshly ground ginger. Would she ever see her parents again, and the gracious white Colonial house and charming garden? She missed even the heirloom furniture, the window seat in the parlor oriel where she had sat reading or watching the snow.

The mignonette-scented sheets rustled like dry leaves in her tremulous hands. Eleanor had discreetly omitted mention of the Civil War Monument, but Garnet knew it would be finished someday soon, the names of the fallen county heroes chiseled in its granite base. There would be dedication ceremonies and annual commemorations and...dear God, was she obstinately, unrealistically, denying Dennis Robert Lane those honors? No! No! She had had no official notice of his death. How awful to bury him when he might not be dead.

She did not hear Jenny enter the room and was startled when she heard, "Well, what a nice long letter! I feel slighted. Mine was shorter. Would you like to read it, dear?"

"Not yet, Auntie. If I put it off a while, it won't seem so long until the next one. But you may read mine."

"No, I feel the same way. Always save something for a rainy day—especially a letter from home—and it's bound to rain here eventually. You're a smart girl, Garnet, and I think you're adjusting."

"Compromising, Aunt Jen. I think that's what life out here must be—one long compromise. And resignation."

The older woman sought to lighten their mood. "Guess who just rode into town?"

"The Rebel, of course. It's Saturday."

"You mustn't hold his Southern origin against him, Garnet. And I'm sure he did only what he thought was right, just as our men followed their consciences."

"That's rationalization, Auntie."

"Will you see him, if he stops by?"

"No. I'm not feeling very well today," Garnet said in a tone that brooked no argument.

"You look better. Your color is better, and you've gained a pound or two."

"All that beef and potatoes! And the milk from Mrs. Mason's jersey cow seems to be pure cream."

"Yes, it makes marvelous butter and cheese. I just churned a fresh batch this morning. We'll spread it on hot bread for lunch, along with some of that delicious algerita jam from Mrs. Slattery. Then you can take your nap."

"Eat and sleep, sleep and eat," Garnet fretted. "If I die of anything, it'll be boredom!"

"And your own fault, too. Mr. Steele could relieve the monotony, if you'd let him take you driving or something."

"Mostly something," Garnet murmured nervously.

"Brant told Seth that the Dukes are throwing a barbecue soon. The whole county is invited."

Garnet frowned. "Which means the Scarlet Lady will be hanging on one of Brant's arms and the monkey on the other."

"Oh, Garnet, you stubborn girl! The slightest show of interest from you could change that."

"But I'm not interested," Garnet shot back.

"So you say, dear, but you are lonely and very unhappy," her aunt returned just as quickly. Jenny sighed. Perhaps she had said too much. She hurried off, hoping her niece hadn't taken offense.

PART TWO

Chapter 11

D R. BERT WARNER had come to Texas straight from the Boston College of Medicine. His first patients had been twenty-four families traveling in the wagon train he'd arrived in. Fevers and fluxes, broken bones, wounds from Indian arrows, and several maternity cases kept him busy. During his long residence in Texas, he had served at several forts and outposts, and at one of the forts he had met and married the adjutant's daughter.

Mildred Cade had been sixteen, a child trying desperately to be a woman, an exquisitely delicate creature. She had had tiny breasts and narrow hips, but, as such females often are, had been exceptionally fertile. Despite his precautions to protect her until she reached maturity, Mildred was soon pregnant. Bert brooded about it, while trying to control the size of the child by restricting Mildred's diet. Contrarily, everything she ate went to the fetus, which grew

abnormally large, distorting her body so hideously
that Bert felt like a ruthless brute who had raped a
helpless little virgin. As her pregnancy advanced,
Mildred's face became pale and gaunt and her large
hazel eyes protruded, projecting fear and bewilderment.

As her labor began, and Bert realized that he
couldn't deliver her normally, he contemplated Cae-
sarean section. But he had never performed or even
observed that operation, and feared he would kill
Mildred with his own scalpel. Instruments were the
alternative, but the fetus was solidly lodged and re-
moval threatened rupture and hemorrhage. The
speculum and forceps were useless. Instead, Bert
worked with her manually, through the day and
night, until her strength, which had been steadily
dissipated over the past nine months, was finally
gone. Mildred died of exhaustion, sheer physical exhaustion, suffocating the infant inside her.

In the carpenter shop of the fort, soldiers constructed a special coffin to accommodate the grotesque bulge of her body, for Bert refused to mutilate
the corpse to remove the baby. She was buried in the
Post Cemetery, and her devastated husband slept on
her grave every night for a week after the funeral.
He castigated himself in grief and despair, merci-
lessly ridiculed his medical competence before others, and resigned his army commission.

He wandered aimlessly for some years before settling in Longhorn Junction. The successful baby de-
liveries he had made since, the maladies he had cured,
the fractures he had mended, the victims of ven-
omous snakes, cattle horns, or horses' hoofs he had
healed, the lives he had saved, never made up for
the one he had lost. Nothing obliterated the memory
or assuaged his feelings of terrible guilt.

Nevertheless, Bert Warner considered himself a
better doctor than the one who had sent that young
Garnet Lane to Texas. She was no consumptive. He

didn't need to examine her lungs to know that. But it was none of his business unless they consulted him.

Dr. Warner wondered what Brant Steele thought of Mrs. Lane, since he'd had ample opportunity to observe her, and he bluntly asked the intelligent new foreman of the Duke Ranch about her when Steele came to town for medical supplies.

"Nice girl," Brant replied.

"That all?"

"She's married, Doc—or thinks she is."

"What do you mean?"

"Come on, Doc. You've surely heard the story from Seth Travers or somebody else by now."

Bert nodded. "Yeah, I have. Her family figures her husband is dead, but the girl won't believe it. Pretty little thing, isn't she? Delicate, though. Reminds me of my lovely Mildred, whose story is a familiar one in these parts, too."

"Things like that get around," Brant said softly. "What do you think is wrong with Mrs. Lane, Doc?"

"She's not my patient. But I daresay her troubles are more emotional than physical. It'll take a damned good man to cure her—and I don't mean a physician. You might be hombre enough...."

"I doubt that," Brant said lightly. "There's a geographical barrier between us, for one thing."

"Yankee-versus-Rebel type of geography? But you're both in Texas now."

"Well, there's more than that involved, Doctor." Brant was stowing supplies in his saddlebags.

Seeing that Brant wanted to change the subject, Bert joked, "Anxious to get over to the Silver Spur? You sure did Sully Voss a favor when you brought that gal and her monkey to this burg." Bert paused, gauging Steele's expression. "I hear Miss Lee wears your brand. If that's true, you better watch out that Voss doesn't rustle her."

"The lady belongs to herself," Brant said without

rancor, slinging the saddlebags over his shoulder. "I've got to get this stuff to the ranch. Mrs. Duke needs her rheumatism medicine, and Mr. Duke needs his gout remedy."

"You tell them I said to come in for a visit soon. Some ranch folks pay more attention to the health of their animals than their own. The Dukes are lucky to have a foreman with some savvy about things besides animals and ranching. Their last one wasn't too bright...drunk half the time, and either falling off his horse or accidentally shooting himself. Once he did both at the same time—which is why you have his job now."

"I'll try to be more careful."

"Please do. Look after the hands, too," the doctor advised. "If you notice anyone carrying his male equipment around in a sling or tobacco sack, send him to me for mercury pills. The clap arrived here with the first armies, and you know Texas has been under *six* flags."

"That's a lot of mercury pills," Brant calculated, touching his hat brim in a military salute. "So long, Bert. See you sometime."

Chapter 12

LACEY LEE was a smash. No one quite like her had ever appeared in the West before, and some of the cactus critics were authorities on frontier entertainment, having seen all El Paso, Santa Fe, Denver, Cheyenne, and even San Francisco had to offer. The sensation of the Silver Spur occasioned more comment than the mysterious fireball that had recently streaked across the night sky, blasting a fifty-foot crater in the chaparral flats when it landed. Lacey Lee drew more feminine protests than the last public hanging in the county had done.

Sully Voss had a gold mine, but his efforts to stake a personal claim to his star lode had failed absolutely. Lacey threatened to leave town whenever he got too close.

Voss, hating the fellow she apparently preferred, brooded over the rejection. He scowled every time Brant Steele rode into Longhorn Junction. In a land of tall, lean, muscular men, Brant's height and physique were still impressive, and he carried himself with a commanding air.

Lacey focused her attention on Brant while singing her most sensual ballads, and between performances she sat at his table, Lollipop perched on the back of her chair. She insisted on pouring his whiskey herself from bottles sealed at the distillery.

"I don't want Mr. Steele paying for whiskey when he's really drinking bark-colored water," she informed Voss. "I know the other girls are required to fleece the customers, but I won't do that to a good friend."

Voss's jealousy erupted. "He's more than a *friend*, ain't he?"

"That's my business!" Lacey snapped belligerently, hands on hips. "You get your money's worth from me, mister!"

"Yeah? What does Steele get—besides the best goddamn booze in the joint?"

Her fast reply was unflinching. "Whatever I want to give him. Does that answer your question?"

"What if I decide he ain't welcome here no more?" Her expression made an answer unnecessary. "Damn it, Lacey! I ain't asking to own you, just to share you."

"Sorry, sir. I'm a one-man woman."

"One at a time?"

Fury smoldered in her eyes. He had gone too far. As she walked away, Lollipop performed one of his many tricks—thumbing his nose.

Voss swore under his breath. Never had his rapist instincts been more keenly aroused, nor his sadistic desire to rawhide someone been greater.

That evening Lacey further incensed him by concentrating exclusively on her lover. "You better circulate," Brant advised. "Voss is getting hot under the collar."

"Not only under the collar."

"Is he crowding you, Lacey?"

"Yes," she admitted, "but I can handle him."

"You sure? I don't want you to get hurt."

"You're sweet, darling. But Voss is the one who'd get hurt if I left this dump, and he knows it. Every Saturday night is a bonanza for him. He could open his own bank." She refilled his glass with the proprietor's private stock. "Enjoy it, dear. Genuine Kentucky bourbon—the Southern gentleman's favorite, I believe. Pure stuff, too."

"Then I'd better sip lightly," Brant laughed. "Don't want to get crocked. Besides, it's more expensive than the regular red-eye, and my wages aren't that high."

"Do you like your job, Brant?"

"Yes, more than I expected. I'd like a spread of my own someday. Maybe there's more rancher than planter in me."

"You don't miss Great Oaks?"

"Of course. I never knew any other home. But that Louisiana planter's life is gone forever, and this Texas one is just beginning."

She thought there was another reason. "I saw your horse at the Mercantile Mart this afternoon. Seth Travers is a nice old fella. How are his Yankee relatives?"

"Don't you ever see them?"

"Only when I need something from the store. Miss Temple is still friendly, of course, but her niece's attitude toward me hasn't changed."

"Nor toward me," Brant admitted. "I guess I'll always be the Confederate enemy to Mrs. Lane."

With an incredulous shake of her head, Lacey said, "Can she honestly believe her husband is still alive?"

"I guess so."

"Do you believe it?"

He glanced away. "Voss is signaling you. Must be time for your next show."

"And my last for the evening, thank God. Will I see you later, Mr. Steele?"

Brant grinned. "I'd like that, Miss Lee, but there's no room at the inn."

The repartee was their private joke: Lollipop had already slipped her key into his shirt pocket.

Brant was standing in the dark, silhouetted against the window overlooking the moonlit square, when Lacey, still in her costume, entered the room. She dropped Lollipop on the bed and ran to embrace him.

"I'm so glad you came!"

"It's impolite to refuse a lady's invitation," he drawled, still playing their little game. "My mother taught me to be a gentleman."

"Who taught you the rest?" she teased.

"You, mostly."

"Hah! You knew it all before you ever met me." She patted his cheek. "Draw the shade, and we'll slip into something more comfortable—bed."

While Brant drew the shades, Lacey struck a match to light the kerosene lamp. The milk-glass globe glowed like an opalescent bubble, enhancing her beauty. Her amorous kisses and caresses made Brant realize how empty his daily life often seemed. He knew his desire was pure lust, but she did not expect him to profess eternal love, only to match her own desire. That was one of the great joys of their relationship, no misgivings to wrestle with afterwards, no wake of remorse.

"Unhook me," she whispered, turning her back, for Lollipop was trained to release only one shoulder strap.

"Who helps you other times?" he asked, obligingly.

"The chambermaid. But she speaks very little English, so I'm learning more Spanish every day."

Working deftly, he unhooked the long row of fasteners from neckline to tailbone.

"I knew a fella in St. Louis once, a real swell. Anticipation was everything to him—and I mean *everything*. He was sort of impotent."

"I'm not," Brant said, slapping her buttocks.

She chuckled. "I know *that*."

The tights were the last barrier. After she was naked, she watched him strip. Lollipop was sitting in the middle of the mattress, in the classic pose— paws covering his eyes.

"Isn't he cute? But the little dickens sometimes gets jealous, as you know, so we'd best put him in the closet, as usual." She did.

Her sensuality never failed, and Brant suspected that he was the envy of every male in town that night—especially Sully Voss.

Later, Lacey murmured, "I long for this, lover. It's the best part of this miserable little junction."

"You have some options, Lacey."

"Working in other dives? That's not my real ambition, Brant. I've got something, and I think it could make me rich and famous."

"You sure have, honey, and it sure could."

"You too, if you're willing."

He gazed at her, admiring the opaline glow of the lamp on her bare breasts. "That sounds like a proposition."

"It is, darling." She paused. "Theatrical managers of good acts make money, Brant—probably far more than you earn from the Dukes. There are showboats on the Mississippi now, you know, and some do very well. I think we could make enough to buy our own paddlewheeler and take it on the Ohio River, all the way to Pittsburgh. From there it's just a short distance to New York and really big money! We could even go abroad one day—to London and Paris!"

"Are you serious?"

"Absolutely! I can do more than sing and dance

with a monkey, Brant. With some training and a few breaks, I could be an actress. Most of the famous ones began as protégées. All my life I've wanted to go on the stage."

"You can accomplish that without me, Lacey."

"But I want you with me, Brant! We get along, don't we? Why not make it a business partnership?"

"You're doing fine on your own, honey. Anyway, your aspirations aren't the same as mine. I'm fairly settled here. You need an ambitious entrepreneur."

She traced her fingers along the dark bristles on his bronzed chest. "You said you'd like your own ranch someday, darling. Well, all it takes is wampum. Why not be my manager?"

"There's another name for a man who lives off a woman," he said grimly, reaching for the labeled bottle on the bedside table.

"That's ridiculous! You'd be peddling my act, not my body."

Her bluntness amused him. "I didn't mean *that*, Lacey. But, look, I'm already drinking another fellow's liquor and smoking his cigars. Don't you think I realize you're pilfering this bonded stuff from Voss?"

"Oh, don't worry. I'm not stealing. He's billing you for it. That greedy bastard wouldn't give his mother a free drink if she was dying of thirst. Why, he even gets kickbacks from the bar girls who sell favors on the side."

"Is he aware of our...Does he know?"

"He knows."

"And does he think I'm paying you?"

"He knows I'm not a whore. I've certainly refused his gold often enough."

"I'm sorry, Lacey. I just wanted to be sure that skunk isn't padding my tab with false charges. I hope I didn't offend you."

She smiled wryly. "I don't offend that easily, Brant. I've been on public exhibition since I was born in my parents' medicine wagon in Missouri. It wouldn't surprise me to learn they had sold tickets to watch the birth. They made money any way they could. I used to help my father hawk potency pills and my mother sell contraceptives and abortion medicine."

"Poor kid."

Lacey shrugged. "Pa died when I was eleven, and right away Ma married a bum ten years younger than she was." There was a pause before she went on. "He raped me before my thirteenth birthday and told her that I had seduced him! Can you imagine? My mother threw me off the wagon that day, to get along as best I could. I begged in the streets until the law put me in an orphanage." She shuddered and closed her eyes. "Oh, Lord, that place! The matron liked to whip naked girls. I ran away when I was fourteen and did housework for room and board, but after I matured fully, no wife would hire me."

Brant held her close, wishing he could comfort the girl she had been. "Why didn't you ever tell me any of this before?"

Lacey sighed. "It's hardly a proud story—and I don't know why I'm telling it now, except that you're different from other men. I don't want to hoodwink you. Surprised? Shocked?"

"No," he said, his hold tightening. "I admire your honesty, my dear, and I certainly don't judge any of your actions."

"There's more," she smiled up at him ruefully. "At seventeen I was mistress to a wealthy Chicago man. I had served in his house as a chambermaid. He was fifty, socially prominent, and his wife had died of a lingering illness. He traveled a lot, to the big Eastern cities. He gave me a pet for company during his absences."

"The capuchin?"

"Right. I named him Lollipop because he loves candy suckers, and I devised a little act to entertain my keeper. Then one day he went off on a long trip to Washington and returned with a new bride. Presto,

Elvira Schwartz was out on the street again!" His quizzical look made her wince. "That's my real name, but I couldn't visualize it on marquees. I'm fond of feminine fluff, which is how 'Lacey' came to mind, and General Lee was a great hero to me. I may have to christen myself again so I can become a serious actress."

Drawing her close against him, Brant said, "You've had it rough, Lacey. I thought I had, during and after the war, but your trials top mine."

Lacey cuddled against him, warm, soft, compliant. Her mouth opened hungrily to his, and her experienced hands worked their special magic. She was never reticent, never reluctant, never a tease. Loving with her was good. So how could he be still thinking of another woman? But he was. Was Lacey aware of it? Somehow, Brant sensed that she was, and that she tried with all her charms to exorcise the pale little trespasser who always came between them.

"You're a lot of woman," he said later.

"You're a lot of man."

"That's a good combination."

"But not good enough to make it permanent, huh?" she lamented. "I don't stand a chance, do I? Mistress, but not missus."

"Lacey, let's not spoil it."

"You'd rather be with her, and that hurts. I guarantee she wouldn't be as much fun—but you'll have to discover that for yourself. With a ring, you may be sure. Her type don't give free samples."

"You talk too much, honey. Did I ever tell you I admire a quiet woman?" He grinned, rising to dress. Lollipop had begun to resent his imprisonment and was chattering and scratching at the closet door. "Should I let him out?" Brant asked, picking up his holster.

"That's up to you, lover."

Brant kissed her, touching one nude breast. Instantly her flesh was yearning again. "Later," he decided. "I'll release the critter later."

"Well, at least put down that gun, cowboy!"

"Cowboy?" He laughed, shucking his clothes again. "Yep, I reckon that's what I am now, all right— cowpuncher. And you know something? I like it, I really do."

Chapter 13

GARNET had never before needed a calendar to learn when summer was over. In New England the seasons were distinct. In Longhorn Junction the seasonal changes were barely visible at all. The square was little different from the first time she had seen it, the grass a bit drier and browner, perhaps, and the mesquite leaves yellowing. But this autumn sun still bore down hard on the land. The prairie winds created swirls of silvery dust.

"Remember Indian summer in Avalon?" Garnet asked her aunt wistfully. "The blazing beauty of the countryside?"

Jenny was darning a pair of Seth's socks. When they had arrived, all his clothes had needed patching. "Quite a contrast, isn't it?"

"I want to go home, Auntie!" It was a passionate cry, and it startled her aunt.

"Darling, you know that's not possible now. It's a

long journey, and winter would arrive before us. But if you keep improving, I'm sure you'll be strong enough to leave next spring. Let's not take any unnecessary risks."

"Sometimes I think you *want* to stay here, Aunt Jen. That you actually *like* Texas," Garnet said sullenly.

Jenny smiled. "Well, don't make it sound like treason, sweetie. There are better places, I'll admit, but there must be worse ones. Don't fight it so hard, Garnet. It's easier if you accept it."

"That's surrender."

"Adjustment," Jenny corrected. "Death is the only surrender, and you're far from defeated. Dr. Warner is highly pleased with your physical improvement, if not your mental attitude."

"What does he know? I was recovering from that cold even before Uncle Seth asked him to look at me."

"Nevertheless, the tonic he concocted has helped you," Jenny insisted, moving the wooden egg from the toe of the sock to the heel. "And he doesn't agree with Dr. Forbes's diagnosis of your condition. Warner claims the West is full of respiratory cases that were never asthma or consumption, so the percentage of supposed cures is phenomenal." After a wary pause she said, "I think much of your trouble has been the plight of a woman without a man."

Garnet's eyes widened.

"Why not, Garnet?" Jennifer rushed on. "You've known love and the physical side of marriage, and you must miss that now. This solitary life isn't normal. You're a warm, vital person, and much too young to seclude yourself. That's why you're morose and petulant at times and finicky at others."

"Really, Auntie! That's disgusting! You talk as if I were a—a heifer in heat!" Garnet protested. Refusing to hear more, she ran into the store, where Seth was looking over the dwindling supplies.

"Aunt Jenny has some of the strangest notions!" Garnet cried.

"Mind the store," Seth said, heading for the living quarters. "Another crisis, Jen? Should I go for the Doc?"

Jenny sighed. "No, Seth. He'd be the first to tell you he can't cure what ails her."

"Got any ideas?"

"One," Jenny nodded. "Invite Brant Steele to supper the next time he's in town."

"I been considering that, Jen. But Steele don't come to town much, you know. Once a week, maybe, to pick up supplies for the Duke Ranch...and visit that saloon gal."

Jenny frowned. "I was hoping Miss Lee would move on."

"Voss is paying her very well, I'm sure."

"That's not the only reason she's staying, Seth, and you know it."

"Reckon so. But getting Brant over here is one thing. Making Garnet take notice of him is another."

"She has noticed him, Seth. She has been aware of him for quite some time. Unfortunately, she feels she shouldn't be. If only she could get that straight! I've been tempted to forge some kind of government paper, but I just couldn't do that."

Seth clawed his whiskers pensively. "The real problem is that she wants to fool herself, Jen, and there's nothing much we can do about that."

"Mr. Steele will stop by Saturday, won't he, to pick up those cheroots he ordered?"

"Yep, but they ain't come in yet. All I got the last shipment was some snuff and chewing stuff, and lucky to get that. Lots of fellas are gonna be disappointed."

"But it'll keep Mr. Steele coming back. Southern gentlemen are connoisseurs of Havana cigars and bourbon whiskey, fine horses and beautiful ladies, though not necessarily in that order."

Seth grinned. "You know you got the makings of a scheming woman, Jen?"

"Don't flatter me, Seth, help me scheme."

"Well, the Dukes throw two annual barbecues, which the whole county attends, and the autumn shindig is coming up in a few weeks," Seth said. "Maybe we can persuade Garnet to go with us?"

"Marvelous idea! And if Brant would invite her himself, we wouldn't look like conspirators. I'll ask the butcher to save me a nice rump roast. If you have any basil, thyme, or bay leaves in stock, don't you dare sell them!"

Garnet was sitting on the porch, watching the vivid glow of sunset. The western horizon appeared to be on fire. Honeysuckle entwined one of the posts, its cloying fragrance oppressive in the evening air, reminding her of Lacey Lee's sensual perfume.

As the last streaks of scarlet, orange, and saffron disappeared from the horizon, the lights went on in the Silver Spur. Then the wall sconces flared in the hotel lobby, the only other building with a sheet-glass window. People had been arriving since noon, for it was Saturday and all trails led to town.

Music and laughter and maybe even a drunken brawl at the saloon or a gun duel on the square would keep the more sober citizens awake much of Saturday night. The two taverns of Avalon would never have permitted such rough behavior, but it was a way of life in Texas. People did not travel as much as a mile unarmed, and Seth said some women could shoot as well as the men. To Garnet, Texas was not only the frontier, it was the end of civilization. She could not understand the pioneers' love for the place.

Brant Steele rode in at sundown, hitching his horse to the post before the Mercantile Mart, removing his hat when he saw Garnet on the veranda.

"Evening, ma'am."

"Good evening, sir."

"My order in yet?"

"You'll have to ask the storekeeper."

The savory aroma of pot roast, one of Jenny's specialties, wafted out from the kitchen. Garnet knew her aunt intended to invite Brant to supper. He would accept, of course. It would be rude to refuse, and Brant considered himself well-bred.

Brant sat on the banister near her, hooking his high-heeled boots under the lower rail, looking as much a Texan as any native. "You're looking well." He smiled at Garnet.

The store lamp shone through the window on Garnet's face, outlining her pale, lovely profile. "Everyone tells me that. It's a community conspiracy." She turned her violet gaze directly on him, openly curious, neither coy nor flirtatious. "Isn't she expecting you?"

"Who?"

"Miss Lee."

"Oh...maybe, but not until later."

"She's a spectacular creature, isn't she? Anyone else is bound to seem dull beside her."

"I wouldn't say that."

No averted eyes, no fluttering lashes, no simpering. If she possessed any feminine wiles, she wasn't practicing them on him. She was as aloof as a snow-capped mountain, and, as always, he was fascinated. Damned if he could get her out of his system!

"You're liable to get trapped into a boring evening of talk and checkers," Garnet warned, arranging the folds in her skirt. "Uncle Seth needs a partner for the game, and Aunt Jenny is fixing to tempt your appetite."

"I'm highly susceptible to temptation."

"All temptation?" she asked, quickly regretting the indiscretion. But he gallantly ignored it.

"Aunt Jenny's a fine cook," she said, glad to change the subject. "I can't boil water."

"Don't you think it's time you learned?"

"Why?"

"Well, you may get married again someday."

Garnet glared at him. "Again? I'm married now."

He shook his head slowly. "Why do you persist, Garnet?"

"Why do *you* persist?" she hissed, as Jenny appeared in the doorway.

"Why, hello, Brant! I thought I heard your voice. You must take potluck with us this evening."

"Oh, I couldn't presume on such short notice, ma'am!"

"Nonsense! It's just pot roast."

"Smells tempting, and I'm hungry as a wolf."

"Don't they call them coyotes here?" Garnet said sarcastically.

He grinned, and Jenny began tentatively, "I suppose they're preparing for the autumn barbecue at the Duke ranch?"

"Yes, ma'am," he nodded. "It'll be quite something, too. Rodeo, turkey-shoot, hoedown in the barn, and a moonlight hayride. I hope you folks are coming?"

"We're looking forward to it, sir."

"Auntie," Garnet began, "you know I—"

"Shall we go in to supper before it gets cold?" Jenny asked, leading the way. "I'm afraid your Havana cheroots haven't arrived yet, Brant, but perhaps Seth saved a stogie or two for you to enjoy later on this evening."

Jenny would not allow Garnet to help with the dishes, insisting that she and Seth could manage.

"But I thought Uncle Seth wanted to play checkers."

"No, no, honey," he said. "Why don't you young folks sit on the swing, or take a stroll on the square?"

Brant reacted quickly. "I'd enjoy that, sir, if the lady is willing."

He extended his hand, and Garnet took it, angering herself.

As they walked, he said quietly, "You're so honest with others, Garnet, be honest with yourself. Why continue this pretense about your husband? You must realize that he can't possibly be alive. The true test of honesty is applying it to yourself."

"I don't need any frontier philosophy, Brant Steele!"

"But you need something to wake you up, Sleeping Beauty."

"Not a Plantation Prince!" she retorted.

"I'm a ranch foreman now," he said, holding her arm more tightly.

"Unhand me, Rebel!"

"Does my touch disturb you?"

"It annoys me."

"It wouldn't, if it didn't disturb you."

"You're arrogant, conceited, and presumptuous." She tried to keep her voice low.

"Guilty on all counts," he grinned, inspired by her indignation. "And you're still disturbed."

"What are you trying to prove, Brant?"

"I've already proved it, Garnet."

The piano was banging in the Silver Spur, and Miss Lee was singing one of her bawdy ballads. "You're missing her first performance, Mr. Steele."

"The evening is young. There'll be more."

"Probably *much* more for the two of you!"

"Jealous, Garnet?" he asked softly, turning to look at her.

"Hardly. I just know you don't spend your Saturday nights in town so you can go to church on Sunday!"

"I would, if you'd accompany me."

"No, thanks," she scoffed. "Folks might think we were courting."

"Perish the thought—if it's so abhorrent to you," Brant drawled with deceptive nonchalance. "But there's no harm in being friends, Garnet, and having a little pleasure together on occasion."

"I'm here to recuperate, not to revel."

"There's nothing really wrong with your health." He glanced up at the great golden moon. "Fine night for a hayride."

"I wouldn't know. I've never been on one," she said wistfully. Her parents had not approved of hayrides.

"You've missed a lot, haven't you, Garnet?"

"I don't think so," she said hotly.

"Matter of opinion, I guess."

"I'm tired. I want to go back now."

"Of course, my dear." But he slowed his steps as they neared the store. At the entrance, he stopped. "May I kiss you good night?"

"You may not, sir!"

"On the cheek," he amended. "Like a brother, or a cousin?"

"I have no brother, Rebel, and I lost all my male cousins in the war!"

Lifting her skirts, she turned away from him and went inside, closing the door. His shadow passed the window as he headed for the saloon.

Garnet braced herself, breathing with difficulty, as if she had run across the square.

Chapter 14

WHILE Garnet bathed in a wooden tub in the kitchen, Jenny pressed her niece's best gown, a pink muslin with flounces, bound in rose velvet. The gown, two voluminous petticoats, a pair of fancy lace-edged drawers, and a crinoline were laid out on the bed, and Garnet eyed her aunt with suspicion.

"Remember the busybodies and matchmakers in Avalon, Auntie? How contemptuous you were of them? Once, when they were pushing you at some bearded old bachelor, you complained, 'This isn't Noah's ark, for heaven's sake, where every animal must have a mate!' So what are you doing now?"

Jenny, alternating the flatirons on the back lid of the cookstove, replied innocently, "Just trying to help your fragile little vessel over some rough seas."

"You and Uncle Seth think you're so clever, don't you? A couple of conniving cupids! Well, it won't work. The only reason I agreed to go is that I knew

113

you wouldn't go without me, and I didn't want to spoil your fun." She scooped up a handful of foam from Jenny's Castile soap and blew on it, scattering wisps.

Her aunt smiled, filling a pitcher and scenting it with a few drops of her precious cologne. "Stand up, and I'll rinse you off."

"You're wasting scarce water, Aunt Jenny."

"So we'll use less for a few days."

When Garnet complained that the rinse was too cold, Jenny insisted that it was good for the circulation. Then she reached for a large huckaback towel and began to dry the fretting girl vigorously.

"You're rubbing me raw, Auntie!"

"Just perking up your color, dear, giving your skin a glow. If only you'd gain some more weight! Your bosom is still too small...perhaps a little cotton supplement?"

Garnet shook her head emphatically. "No false front, Aunt Jen! That's the worst kind of deception."

"Oh, I don't know," Jenny argued. "People wear false hair and false teeth, and your mother wrote in her last letter that women in Paris are beginning to wear false behinds. They're called bustles. Eleanor is sending us a *Godey's* with pictures."

"Lot of good a fashion book does out here," Garnet muttered.

"Don't pout, Garnet. There's nothing pretty about petulance. Dimples are far more charming."

Finally, Jenny brushed Garnet's silver-gold hair until it glistened like silk, and perched a pert rose-velvet bow in the smooth crown.

"Why don't you tie a ribbon on my tail, too?" Garnet had never felt more like a heifer being auctioned off.

"Well, I'd better groom myself now," Jenny smiled. "Do you think my topaz taffeta is too formal?"

"Yes, but you'll wear it anyway. You'd wear it to a roundup, just to show it off."

Nothing could ruffle the elder woman's good humor. "You're right, dear. But Seth is proud to show us off. Go into the store and keep him company. But don't sit down—you'll wrinkle your dress. And don't go outside yet—the wind will muss your hair. It seems to blow constantly out here."

"May I breathe?" asked Garnet in an overly polite voice.

"Deeply," advised her mentor. "It'll swell your chest and fill out your bodice."

The Duke Ranch was measured in miles, not acres. No fences marked the boundaries. Stakes defined the original grants and claims, going off in all directions. The main house was an unusual structure combining Spanish, American, and Texan architecture. Built of native stone and timber and adobe, it sported gables and arches and galleries on three sides. The numerous outbuildings that rambled over the property, bunkhouses, barns, stables, saddlery, storage sheds, corrals, had been built willy-nilly, without any common architectural theme.

Expecting a great hacienda with a lovely courtyard garden to inspire romance, Jenny was disappointed. "How quaint!" she remarked. "Rather unique, actually."

"They build more for utility than for beauty here," Seth explained. "But the big house is right nice inside and always kept spotless by the Mexican servants."

Garnet thought the entire ranch a tacky hodgepodge, the like of which she had never seen before. She could understand why they were called "spreads." Did Brant live in the big house, or have a small one of his own? How could he abide this place after the lovely, gracious Great Oaks? She might have pitied him, but loyalty to Denny precluded compassion for any former Confederate soldier.

The grounds were already crowded with wagons,

buckboards, buggies, saddled horses, and more were arriving. Guests wandered about, calling out greetings.

"Howdy, George, ain't seen you in a coon's age! Me and Amy been aimin' to come over to see you and Effie Lou, but just ain't had no time."

"Jud, this cain't be your li'l Melinda all growed up so pert and purty? Why, the last time I seen her she was in pigtails and pinafores!"

"A new baby, Tess? No, we hadn't heard. Ain't that nice? Makes a even dozen, don't it?"

"Hope the fiddler don't break a arm or leg afore he gits here! Ain't danced in so long my bones is rusty."

"Reckon y'all heard Ben Becker's barn burnt down? Yeah, flat to the ground, with his whole harvest. Stored the stuff green, and it exploded. Ben shoulda knowed better. Guess we'll have to throw a barnraisin' for the Beckers, if we can git holt of some lumber somewheres."

"Can you understand them, Uncle?" Garnet asked between introductions.

"Why, sure, honey! They're talking Texan. We got a language all our own." Seth waved at the busy host and hostess, who had already welcomed them. "Hey, if y'all git a minute to spare for jawin', we got lots of catchin' up to do!"

Mr. Duke, in canvas breeches and scuffed boots, limped slightly with gout, and Mrs. Duke smelled of wintergreen liniment. Her face was darkly tanned and wrinkled, her hands rough and splotched, and several teeth were missing from her broadly smiling mouth. Like the majority of the female guests, she was wearing a simple gingham hubbard, slatted sunbonnet, and brogans. Some wives were obviously pregnant, and feminine style was the least of their concerns.

Embarrassed by her finery, Garnet whispered to

her aunt, "We're overdressed. They must think us awful snobs."

"Just rich Yankees ignorant of local customs," Jenny shrugged, glancing around the gathering. "I wonder where Mr. Steele is. Surely not out on the range!"

"Who cares?" Garnet muttered. "Maybe he's spending the day elsewhere, if Lacey Lee wasn't invited. None of the saloon people seem to be here."

"Did you ever see so much food? Even the air smells delicious!"

Six yearling beeves and six prime pigs were roasting over long pits of burning mesquite coals. The skewered meats, slowly turned by hand cranks, could be smelled for miles. Pinto beans and bacon were boiling in huge blackened iron kettles suspended on tripods. Tables and benches waited under the dusty trees, and Mexican female domestics carried out trays of fried chicken, potato salad, coleslaw, biscuits, butter, jams and jellies, relishes, cakes and cookies.

"They could feed an army."

"Ours should have been so lucky," said Brant Steele from behind them. "Glad you could make it." He extended a friendly hand, grinning widely. "Just in time to tie on the feedbag, too."

"You didn't speak that way in Louisiana," Garnet said.

He shrugged. "When in Rome..."

"Were you ever in Rome?" Jenny asked with genuine interest.

"Yes, ma'am. On my grand tour I traveled for two years. England, Europe, Greece—all over."

"We've also been abroad, but I'm afraid my niece was only five when we went to the World Exhibition in Great Britain, in 1853. Do you remember worrying about London Bridge falling down, dear?"

Garnet blushed, wishing she could lock her loquacious aunt in the Tower of London. "This sun is giving me a headache, Auntie. Shall we move into the shade?"

"You need some chow," Brant said, as the triangular dinner irons were rung, "and the chuck wagon is now officially open. Choose a table, ladies. I'll fix some plates."

Although most of the fare was alien, Garnet found herself eating heartily. Observing the others, she held the spareribs in her fingers and wiped the greasy juices from her chin and hands on a flour-sack dishcloth. Jenny had an improvised napkin tucked into her basque. Seth sat with a group of cronies, wolfing down great chunks of meat and dozens of sourdough biscuits. They were eager for the afternoon's entertainment—playing cards and checkers, pitching horseshoes, target practice, and the amateur rodeo. They wagered bets.

Garnet's hopes of an early departure faded. Seth was in his element, and Jenny was making new friends and looking forward to the evening dance. They would be there until midnight and possibly until dawn. Well, she might have to tolerate dancing with Brant Steele, but there would be no hayriding.

As if sensing her thoughts, he suggested a daylight drive on the prairie. "Unless, of course, you feel it would tax your strength too much, or interfere with your rest," he challenged cleverly.

"I feel fine," Garnet declared. "Will you join us, Aunt Jen?"

"No, thanks, dear. I want to visit with the ladies."

"But we can't go alone, Auntie! What will people think? I'm married, after all."

"Which is precisely why you no longer need a chaperone," Jenny said smoothly. "I'm sure everyone here knows that you are a lady and Mr. Steele is a gentleman."

Brant smiled as Garnet glared. "I'll take good care of her, Miss Temple."

"I'm not worried about that, sir," said Jennifer.

* * *

Bouncing over the rough terrain, Brant advised her, "Better open that parasol, my dear. It won't do you any good closed."

Garnet did, and a sudden swirling gust of wind yanked the ruffled organdy thing out of her hand like a feather. "Oh!" she cried, as it sailed into the air and landed in some thorny brush.

"I'll get it," Brant said, turning the horse.

"Don't bother," she told him, remembering that she and Jenny were the only women who had carried parasols to the barbecue. "It's ruined, anyway, from the cactus and bramble bushes."

"Chaparral," he informed her. "And the natives call those spontaneous whirlwinds 'Texas diabolos,' because they're created by heat, appear swiftly, and are black with dust in dry weather. The Indians had better start dancing for rain."

"Indians—around here?"

"A few, I'm told, but they're fairly harmless. The warring tribes have migrated to the West Texas plains, along with the buffalo. Hundreds of miles away."

Garnet relaxed and began to scan the limitless horizon. Somewhere in infinity the pale blue sky appeared to curve toward the earth. The landscape was one of intense solitude and utter desolation, and she doubted that even the most gifted artist could capture it on canvas just right.

"The animals in this state must outnumber the people by a thousand to one," she said.

"Far more than that, Garnet, since they multiplied quite rapidly during the war."

"Well, I certainly don't like this brush country. It's nothing but a huge briarpatch. Take me back to the ranch, please."

"We're still on the ranch, my dear. I'll show you one of the camps used during roundups."

He drove toward a shack in the distance. "Come spring, there'll be a cattle drive north—the first from the Duke Ranch in over five years."

"Are you going?"

"Yes. Mr. Duke is not in shape for a long, harsh drive, and I'm his foreman. I also want the adventure."

"Uncle Seth did some trail driving in his younger days, and he says it's dangerous. But you like risking your neck, don't you? I bet you volunteered to fight the minute you heard the news about Fort Sumter."

"Didn't your husband?"

"Dennis was too young, then. Later, he had no choice. The North was never as rabid about the war as the South. The Union had conscription. You were all fanatics."

"The Confederacy had conscription, too."

"Really? I thought all Rebs rushed to defend their glorious cause while still in knee pants."

"Propaganda," Brant said, pulling up to the weather-beaten bunkhouse.

"Is *this* what you brought me to see?" Garnet cried scornfully.

"Not entirely." Brant jumped down and lifted her out of the rig. "I wanted to get you alone somewhere, to talk. You've always managed to run away from me before. But don't try it now, Garnet. You'll get lost...and there are rattlesnakes and coyotes all over here."

"Some in human guise," she said indignantly. "You tricked me!"

He carried her into the building, which was furnished with bunks, a hand-hewn oak table, and chairs with cowhide seats. Furious because the over-the-threshold ritual was for brides and grooms, Garnet raged, "Put me down!" She was most disturbed by the drumbeat of his heart near her face.

Brant obliged, setting her gently on unsteady feet.

Garnet stepped back, bumping into a chair. The small shack suggested a cage, and she felt trapped. Her pulse thudded in her ears, and her eyes were wide.

"Don't look that way," he pleaded. "Please, Garnet."

"What way?"

"Like a scared rabbit in a snare. I'm not going to harm you."

"How do I know that?"

"Because I tell you so."

"And you've never lied to a woman?"

"Not a woman who meant anything to me."

She gazed at him silently, motionless, entranced. He touched her gently, stroking her back, and Garnet submitted docilely. Very slowly, he leaned forward and kissed her.

She had never been kissed with such tender ferocity. Trying to recall Denny's kisses, she was surprised to find the memory vague and less sacred than she used to. She moved away from Brant's mouth with some reluctance and hid her face in his hard shoulder, wishing she might stay there forever.

He removed her bonnet, tossed it on the table, and began slipping the pins from her hair. "I love you, Garnet."

"No," she cried, suddenly shaken. "No, Brant, no!"

"Yes. And what's more, I think you love me."

Garnet touched the gold band on her finger, her protection.

"Take the ring off, Garnet."

"No."

"It doesn't belong there anymore. Stop using it as a barrier. Remove it."

"I feel faint, Brant. I want to leave."

He shook his head. "Not yet."

"Don't be a fool, Brant! I'm not Lacey Lee, remember. And besides that, I'm married."

A scowl covered his face. "If that tintype I saw is

a fair likeness, you were married to a boy, Garnet. I've known some women in my time, but I doubt you've ever known a man."

"And you want to introduce me to one?"

"I told you, I love you."

"And I told you, it's impossible!"

"Listen to me, Garnet! I'm not some adolescent milksop. You liked what I was doing a while ago. You had forgotten your past enough to respond to me as a mature woman. Go ahead, deny it—and add that lie to your other self-deceptions."

"You're one tenth chivalry and nine tenths conceit, Brant Steele! The South was championed by men like you. That's why it's dead now!"

His mouth twisted. "Ah, the truth at last! That's the real trouble between us, isn't it? You've got to try and understand, Garnet." He stopped a moment to collect his thoughts. This had to be explained just right. She had to see things his way, even if only for a minute, or she would cling to her prejudices forever. He drew a deep breath, then looked at her with a gaze so intense she could not look away.

He began, "When Louisiana seceded from the Union and joined the Confederacy, my family had no choice. It was our home, our land, and we fought for it. You think it was an easy decision? You think we gloried in the horror? We didn't, but we had to declare our allegiance, just as General Lee did, when he left the United States Army to defend his native Virginia. And we suffered and lost a hell of a lot more than the Yankees did. Than your family did."

"Pain well deserved," she said stoutly.

"Goddamn it, Garnet! It was obligation. Twist it any way you want to, that's still the basis of the trouble between us, and you know it."

"And we both know our being together like this is wrong, Brant. We might have committed adultery."

"It's not wrong," he said quietly, moving closer to

her again. "And...it wouldn't have been adultery," he rushed on. Oh, Lord, this didn't seem the place to tell her, but it was the chance he'd been looking for all along. He *had* to tell her sometime, and he guessed the time had come.

"Garnet," he began, "it wouldn't have been adultery because..."

His voice trailed away as he caught sight of her little face staring up at him quizzically. Looking away from her, then back again, he plunged ahead.

"I should have told you that day at Great Oaks, but I couldn't manage it. When you showed me your husband's picture, I knew. I tried that day and I tried again since then."

A chill was beginning to engulf her, and she continued to stare at him, unblinking, her mind fighting him even as she listened.

"Your husband is dead, Garnet. What everyone has been trying to tell you is true," he said as gently as he could. "You're a widow."

"No," she whispered. "You're lying." But even as she said it, she knew he wasn't lying.

Very slowly, she lost her color, but her eyes never left his face. After several horrified moments, she whispered, "How do you know?"

And then he had to tell her all of it. He did, brutally forcing himself to say everything he wished he didn't have to say, until he finished with, "He and the other reconnaissance scouts were shot trying to escape. I swear that if they hadn't tried to run, we would simply have taken them prisoner. I didn't want them shot, Garnet. I never wanted to shoot anyone, ever, during the whole goddamned war."

She seemed suddenly to have been struck deaf. Her face, gone white and still, appalled him. He had driven a knife into her heart, he realized that. In another moment she went limp and would have collapsed had he not caught her in time.

Garnet woke on a bunk, Brant gently slapping her cheeks. She lay as still as a corpse, only her eyes alive, accusing.

"Are you all right?" he asked anxiously.

She didn't answer. She didn't have to. Her expression was eloquent enough.

"Say something, Garnet. Please."

It was like waking from a ghastly nightmare to discover an even more hideous reality. "If he's dead," she quavered, "why wasn't I notified by the army?" He could barely hear her.

"Apparently his papers were lost. I don't really know. But the war records were badly muddled on both sides, Garnet. It's understandable, considering the enormous amount of work. That's always the way in war."

Slowly Garnet sat up and rose from the bunk, refusing his proffered hand, as if it were bloody. She stood up, her whole being filled with bitter hatred. "Murderer," she whispered hoarsely. *"Killer!"*

"Garnet, I tried to explain the circumstances to you. What else could I do? Let spies escape? Garnet, I didn't kill your husband. I killed an enemy soldier."

"But he—he was just a boy," she stammered, sobbing then. "You said so yourself."

"He was a *soldier*. And *I* was a soldier. He had his orders. I had mine. That's war, Garnet."

"So is this!" she cried, and, in one swift, vicious motion, she pulled the pistol from his holster and would have shot him point-blank, except for his quick reaction in knocking her hand away.

The bullet went into the floor, and Brant wrested the gun from her before she could aim again. She threw herself at him, clawing, screaming. "Damn Reb! I hate you! I'll hate you till I die!"

She whirled away then, suddenly running to the buggy and grabbing the reins before he could stop her.

"Hey!" Brant yelled frantically, as she started off. "Stop, Garnet, stop! That's the wrong way! Go east, not west! Garnet!"

He stood yelling in the doorway, watching her careen crazily across the prairie toward the sun. Her wild, reckless driving could mean an accident. Running as fast as he could, Brant headed for the ranch to get a horse and go after her.

Chapter 15

SWEAT speckled the roan gelding's hide, and saliva frothed from his mouth. He ran as wildly as a mustang, and Garnet was terrified. She pulled on the reins as hard as she could, making her gloveless hands raw. She had forgotten her bonnet too, and her unpinned hair fluttered in the wind. Finally, she managed to bring the horse under control and to a comfortable trot.

There were no mileposts or landmarks out there to guide her, not even wheel tracks. A backward glance revealed no sign of the camp site. Panic rose.

The position of the crimson sun told her she was still headed westward. But that was all she knew. Without a compass, she might wander for days in the desolate wilderness! Bleached skeletons, mostly animal, were scattered over the prairie, and she had even passed a human skull, with hollowed eye cavities and teeth.

Would the horse find his way home? No such luck. He plodded along, the buggy lurching over rocks, chaparral, and dry arroyos. Hawks and vultures circled, their spread wings casting ominous shadows. Rattlesnakes were probably nearby. Jackrabbits abounded. Deer and antelope ran in the distance. Nightfall would bring prowling wolf packs. In her deepening terror, she blamed Brant Steele entirely.

Thirst reminded her of the water canteen under the seat, and she wished there were enough to share with the slobbering horse. She was sipping gratefully from the canvas-covered container when suddenly she saw several structures in the distance. A mirage? Hysteria? Seth said people often had peculiar symptoms on remote plains, and that some lost their minds.

But, no, she wasn't hallucinating. It appeared to be an old Spanish mission. The iron cross atop the bell tower was clearly visible, and the church was the tallest edifice in a complex of adobe ruins. The sun-baked clay was chipped and crumbling, yet serene, as if its whole purpose in this wild and wretched land was to instill hope and tranquillity.

Despair of finding the place occupied enveloped Garnet until she saw a small green vegetable patch in the compound. There was also a donkey and a wood-wheeled cart. Someone must live there. She tethered the horse and climbed, trembling, out of the buggy.

A bald, brown-robed figure was kneeling in the chapel, tonsured head bowed over a breviary. Absorbed, he did not glance up and seemed not to hear her.

She tried to pray, but her mind was still seething with hatred for Brant Steele. She did not belong in this sacred place with its saintly images and the Crucifixion depicted on carved plaques lining the walls. But a respite might calm her. Then, perhaps, resignation would follow.

The monk rose, genuflected before the altar, and moved quietly down the aisle before the darkly varnished oak benches. He paused in surprise at the last pew. He had dark skin and darker eyes, and he spoke with a Spanish accent. "May I help you, señora?" he asked. "You seem ill, or distressed."

Garnet nodded, her gaze fixed on the ebony rosary beads attached to his cord-bound waist, the string so long the cross nearly touched his sandaled feet. He resembled a painting of Saint Francis of Assisi. "I'm lost, sir."

He smiled at her. "I'm Father Marcial Angelino— padre to my small flock. And no one is ever truly lost, my daughter, except by choice."

"You don't understand, Father." She rushed on. "I meant that I—I don't know where I *am*. I ran away from someone, and now I'm lost."

"I see. Were you fleeing your spouse?"

"No." Garnet glanced at the statue of the Madonna, wondering what her own mother would think of her. "I—I almost killed a man, Father."

His thick black brows arched. "Almost, señora? Is he badly injured?"

She shook her head. "No." She shrugged. "It's a long story, which actually began over five years ago. I don't wish to bore you with it, Father."

"I would not be bored, señora." A sweep of his hand indicated a black-curtained cubicle. "And believe me, there is no confession I have not heard. But that is your choice. May I inquire where the incident occurred?"

"Somewhere on the perimeter of the Duke Ranch. Do you know it?"

"Ah, *sí!* Some of the Mexicans working there are among my flock."

Garnet was greatly relieved. Her guardian angel must have guided her there.

"Thank Heaven!" she cried with clasped hands.

"Then you can tell me how to get back? Or how to get to Longhorn Junction?"

"*Sí*, señora. But the sun will soon set, and you could not find your way at night, even with a moon. You had best remain here until morning. I'll prepare a pallet for you in the sacristy."

Garnet hesitated. "My relatives will be worried about me, Father. We were attending a barbecue at the Duke Ranch when I left for a drive with the foreman. My name is Mrs. Garnet Lane, Father. I live with my uncle, Seth Travers."

"No doubt a search party will be organized, Señora Lane. You will be safe here and easy to locate. Any of the Dukes' vaqueros could direct a posse to Mission San Juan."

"I guess you're right, Father."

"Well, I have offered my evening vespers," he said. "Would you care to share my dinner?"

"I'm not hungry, but I'd enjoy a cup of tea, thank you."

"So would I, señora. Unfortunately, I have none— nor coffee, either. The best I can offer is a brew of wild mint. I subsist mostly on vegetable soup and bread, and some donations of food from my people. Sometimes they bring me goat's milk and cheese. They gave me that *carreta* and burro for transportation. My parishioners are very resourceful," he added proudly. "The sacrificial wine is fermented from algeritas and mustang grapes. The communion hosts are often bits of tortillas, and I bless the burnt wood-ashes for benediction incense. Come, señora. It grows dimmer in the chapel, and I have no candles to spare."

Garnet walked beside him into the vestibule, where he dipped his right hand into a font of holy water and crossed himself. She wondered how he could endure that coarse, heavy garment in summer, and if his sockless feet got cold in winter. Was the personal discomfort a kind of voluntary penance?

As with all early Franciscan Texas missions, religion was only one of its reasons for being. San Juan had served its colony as fort, school, clinic, refuge, and wayfarers' station. The site had been selected for its convenient water supply, a spring-fed creek ingeniously viaducted into the compound via the ancient Roman canal methods—for every Latin missionary monk was also an architect and engineer, as well as a scholar and practical physician.

"We must tend to the horse, Señora Lane, and stable him for protection. I have lost several goats and a cow to the night predators, and I fear for the poor donkey every day. Tethered creatures are easy prey."

Only the strong and cunning survive, Garnet thought. Denny was dead because he had not been clever enough to outwit his captors.

"Do Federal troops ever pass here, Father?"

"Occasionally, on their way to an outpost. Why don't you visit with my pets a while? I have a possum, a squirrel, a gopher, and several birds hopping about with wing splints."

"And a darling kitten!"

"That's a bobcat cub whose mother died near the mission. I heard it crying. My little menagerie are all Nature's orphans."

"May I play with them, Father?"

"*Sí*, señora. The cub's eyes are open now, and it likes to nibble fingers and toes. They are all delightful company."

The picture of Saint Francis came back to her as Garnet entered the courtyard. Later, at sundown, a flock of doves flew to Mission San Juan to roost in the belfry. Much later, lying on her pallet in the sacristy, Garnet heard their soft cooing. Soon the marvelously relaxing herb brew lulled her into a deep slumber.

A tolling bell woke her before dawn. Still dressed except for her shoes, Garnet scrambled for them in

the dark and then opened the door. The monk, sur-
rounded by his pets, was holding a burning broom-
weed torch.

"Good morning, Señora Lane. You slept well?"

"Like a rock, Father. But it's still dark! Do you
always rise so early?"

"Always, but earlier than usual today," he explained. "I heard a cowhorn on the prairie just now
and answered it with the bell. I think someone is
coming for you."

As the galloping hoofs neared the mission, he extended the improvised torch. "Come, hold the light
for me while I open the gate."

"Is that wise, Father? He may be unfriendly, a
felon fleeing the law, perhaps."

"Or a lost stranger?" he asked significantly. "I
turn no one away, señora."

"I know, Father." Garnet sighed, suddenly recognizing the rider and his mount. She had hoped for
almost any rescuer but this one.

He jumped from his horse and doffed his hat. *"Buenos días,* Padre! I'm Brant Steele, from the Duke
Ranch. I trust this reckless young lady wasn't too
much trouble to you?"

"None at all, my son. I enjoyed her company."

Brant glanced at Garnet, whose purple eyes blazed
with anger. "Your family are wild with worry, my
dear, and a brigade of cowhands are out beating the
brush for you." He offered the monk his hand. "Thank
you, Padre, for keeping her here. I'll hitch up the
buggy and drive her home."

Garnet's eyes beseeched the priest, betraying what
he had already guessed. "This is the man I told you
about, Father."

He nodded.

"I would prefer to wait for someone else, Father."

"That may be many long hours, señora, even days."

"I don't mind," she insisted.

"Fasting and sleeping on the floor?" His tone was

persuasive. "For your own sake, let Señor Steele escort you back to your loved ones, Señora Lane." He was sure that the young man wasn't dangerous.

Father Angelina smothered the torch in the dirt as a bright pink glow illuminated the eastern sky. "Isn't that a glorious sight? You can travel a fair distance while the morning is still cool, my friends."

When the equipage was ready, Garnet sought to outwit Brant. "I can drive, if you'll lend me your gloves. Why don't you ride ahead?"

She failed. "No, my horse has been toting me and my saddlebags most of the night. I think he would rather trot behind us."

After the padre's blessing, Garnet turned on the seat to wave. Then she complained bitterly to her rescuer. "I prayed never to see you again! Why did you have to be the one to find me?"

"Perhaps because I hunted the hardest. You gave me a hell of a scare, Garnet, and I ought to paddle you."

"I hate you!" she cried. "I hate being with you!"

"Not really, darling. You only think so."

"How dare you call me darling!" she raged. "I should have killed you!"

"You tried." He smiled ruefully. "Fortunately, you're a bad shot."

"Take me home, Brant. And after that, I never want to see you again! Is that clear?"

"Quite clear. But meetings between us are inevitable. The Dukes purchase supplies from your uncle, you know."

"You also patronize the saloon."

"Why not? Miss Lee seems to enjoy my company."

"And you hers?"

"Very much. She's a *pleasant* person."

Garnet averted her face, staring to the far right of the rolling, rugged prairie.

"Talk to me, Garnet. Tell me you understand what happened to your husband, and that you realize I had no choice whatsoever. What would you have done if you'd been me?"

"Why should I ease your conscience?"

He took a deep breath, then told her the rest of it. "I have a few of his things in my haversack. You might want to have them."

"You ghoul!" she gasped, aghast. "Robbing the dead!"

Brant winced. "That wasn't my purpose at all. His ring and watch would certainly have been stolen. I wrapped Private Lane's things in his kerchief, intending to send his effects to his family eventually— but I found no address."

He had placed the scarf and two items wrapped inside it in his pocket, knowing he had to give them to Garnet then. She had been told the truth and she needed only to receive her husband's possessions. Beyond these duties, there was nothing left for Brant to do. He had explained as best he could: If she didn't see his side of things, he couldn't make her.

Slowly, he handed over the scarf. Her eyes were riveted on it, and she held it in her lap for a long time, never once looking away from the tiny bundle. She stared at the yellow silk neck scarf with the initials *DRL* embroidered on one corner, her farewell gift on which she had tediously labored a whole week. Very slowly, she reached inside and took out the sacred wedding band and beautifully engraved gold Swiss watch. As she held them in her hands, she suddenly wanted to yank Brant's pistol from its holster again.

Sensing her thoughts, Brant shook his head. "Garnet, killing me wouldn't solve anything."

"I owe it to Denny...and to myself," she said in a dry voice.

"If others feel that way, there will never be anything but slaughter. Please, Garnet."

She wouldn't let him off so easily, but she couldn't

think of anything to say, so she changed the subject. "What did you tell my relatives?"

"I said the horse started limping, as if it had thrown a shoe, and I got down to investigate, and while I was dislodging a stone from the hoof, something spooked him into running away with you still in the rig.

"After the long trek to the ranch, I was nearly lame myself. All the men volunteered to search, riding off in all directions. The vaqueros suggested Mission San Juan, and I could only hope you weren't confused enough to continue going west—toward Indian territory and Mexico. I guess Providence does watch over foolish females, after all."

"I didn't care about anything when I left that shack yesterday, and I still don't," said Garnet. "I'm only sorry that I worried Aunt Jenny and Uncle Seth. Weren't they suspicious of the injuries on your face?"

Brant gingerly touched the lacerations from her fingernails. "Why, I ran into a low-hanging mesquite branch."

"There are many thorny things out here," Garnet remarked laconically. "And not all of the horns are on cattle, either! Yours are just invisible."

"Well, Jenny and Seth seemed convinced."

"You're probably an excellent liar."

"Will you betray me?"

"Why should I make a diabolical villain into a hero?"

"Then we'd better end this conversation, my dear. I rode all night. I'm weary and saddle-sore, and I don't need any more battles. But I will tell you again what I said in the bunkhouse, Garnet. I love you. I love you more than I've ever loved any woman. Sometimes I think I always will."

What could she say to that? She turned away, gazing out to her right, and kept silent until they reached Longhorn Junction.

Chapter 16

GARNET had just opened the bureau drawer where she kept the tintype of her husband when Jenny entered. Tears glistened in Garnet's eyes and her voice was a mere whisper. "Denny's dead, Auntie. Brant Steele killed him."

And Garnet told her aunt the story.

Since Denny's death was what Jenny had suspected all along, the news did not surprise her, except that a bizarre fate had saddled Brant Steele with the terrible deed.

"I can't see Brant Steele anymore, Aunt Jenny. If he dares to come here, I'll refuse to speak to him." She sat down on the bed, gazing forlornly at the tintype. It had continued to deteriorate despite all her precautions: A network of hairline cracks was spreading over the darkening image—the prelude to obliteration. Garnet clasped it to her heart, vowing that at least the memory would never vanish.

Jenny embraced her. "At least you know now, darling. Is knowing so much worse than wondering?"

"It's as if a part of me has died, too," Garnet murmured. "And I'm not sure I can live with the dead part, Auntie, or even if I want to live at all."

"Those are the emotions of the bitter cup. But it'll pass. You'll survive."

"I'll have to dye my clothes," she said tonelessly.

"You don't need widow's weeds, Garnet. That's just a symbol. You can mourn in your heart, as you've been doing for a long time now without realizing it. But you mustn't grieve forever, Garnet. Above all, you must not do that."

Twilight deepened to dusk, purpling the last of the evening shadows. Whippoorwills called plaintively on the prairie. Mrs. Mason was leading her milch cow home from the square, chatting with a neighbor who was shooing her small flock of clucking chickens to their coop. Seth Travers bade the ladies good evening and proceeded somewhat unsteadily to the Mercantile Mart.

Jenny, busy at the stove, smiled a little at his condition. "I gather you boys had more than one drink?"

"We shared a bottle, Jen. Brant Steele had a heap of sorrows to drown."

"I know, Seth. Garnet told me."

"Poor girl! I pity them both, Jen. But Brant *had* to do what he done in the war. You understand that, don't you?"

Jenny nodded. "But Garnet doesn't want to understand. She says she never wants to see him again, and I'm afraid she means it."

Seth braced his hands on a chair. "The Duke Ranch is my best customer, Jen. I can't offend the foreman when he comes to order. Besides, I was a Confederate, like him. Except for my age, I'd have been fighting the Yankees too. Garnet will just have to avoid Steele, if that's how she feels. But, Jen...that poor man is in love with her."

"Ever since they met," Jenny agreed, sighing. "He'd be so good for her, too. Right for her. Maybe she'll forgive him one day, but we can't force anything. I'm worried about her, Seth. She's still in shock, some sort of daze. It could mean a serious setback, maybe a total collapse."

"Now, Jen, don't borrow trouble. Lemme set the table," he offered, as Jenny took dishes out of the cupboard.

"With those shaky hands? No, I'll do it."

"Yeah, I'd drop every one. Forgive me, Jen. I ain't been this drunk in years. Not since the day we heard about Appomattox, now I think about it. Steele said that was his last big drunk, too. But alcohol didn't seem to affect him much today. The more red-eye he gulped, the more sober he got. That gal finally made him stop."

"Miss Lee?"

"Yep. I reckon she'll console him tonight, if he lets her. Any fool can tell she's crazy about him, which don't make Sully Voss none too happy." Seth paused, puzzled. "I wonder how her monkey lives without bananas and coconuts?"

Jenny was ladling a tureen of beef stew. "Lollipop eats food people eat."

"Is our little girl gonna take supper with us?"

"I'm not hungry," Garnet said quietly from the doorway, and Jenny wondered how much of the conversation she had overheard. "Have you any black dye in stock, Uncle?"

"Why, I—I don't think so, honey. Real dye is hard to get these days, being mostly imported from Europe. And there was such a demand for it during the—the last five years..." Seth paused, swallowed. "Ladies around here make their own dyes from roots, leaves, bark, and berries. During the fabric shortage they invented some fairly nice colors for butternut homespun, too—some as good as store-bought."

"I need only black, Uncle. Perhaps I can find a packet or two in the inventory tomorrow."

"Sit down and eat something," Jenny urged.

Garnet shook her head, retreating to her bedroom sanctuary.

To Jenny's disappointment, Garnet insisted on dyeing her clothes black. From a combination of donated ingredients, black hawthorn predominating, they made a dye. India ink could not have been more effective.

"I don't like it," Jenny told Seth, after the somber clothes were hung on the line to dry in the first mild norther of autumn. "All the while I was helping Garnet I had this strange feeling..."

"What feeling, Jen?"

"That she was really making her own shroud."

Brant Steele came into Seth's store a couple of weeks later. Without preamble, he asked, "How is she?"

Seth frowned. "Saddest little creature I ever seen. Jenny says her health's gone back to where she was a year ago, and Doc Warner don't quite know how to handle her. Talking to her don't help. Maybe if she went home...but winter's fixing to set in up yonder."

"I don't suppose—"

Understanding, Seth interrupted. "No, son. At least, not yet. She made that clear. I ain't even gonna tell her you were here. You got a order to place for the ranch?"

Brant nodded, giving Seth a list. "Can I buy you a drink at the saloon?"

"No, thanks. My head's still fuzzy from the last one. Tell me, Mr. Duke still planning to drive them cattle north next spring?"

"Yes. It's a seller's market."

"How far you taking 'em?"

"Wherever he can get the best price. Probably to Kansas, Chicago, or Missouri. No definite agreement yet."

"Duke better pray the herd don't develop Texas fever before the end of the trail," Seth said. "Then other states would quarantine the longhorns at their borders and kill the healthy stock along with the sick ones, to be sure their own breeds were safe. But I reckon you know that."

"Yes. I've been talking to Mr. Duke about crossbreeding. Importing some English Herefords, East Indian Brahmas, or Angus from Scotland, and trying to breed out this longhorn weakness. Get more tender beef that way, too. Other ranchers are doing it now."

Brant's eyes kept wandering to the living quarters. Jenny came out once to greet him and offer a cup of coffee, but there was no sight of Garnet. He lingered another half hour, making conversation, hoping to see her, then finally gave up and left.

On the way to the Silver Spur, Brant brooded bitterly. Wars, duels, honor—did a man ever really have the duty or the right to kill another? That poor green boy, playing soldier, bewildered, frightened, shot in the back like a coward while running to freedom. Killer, Garnet had called him. Murderer. Maybe she was right.

"Why the long face, darling?" Lacey asked him. She placed a glass of whiskey in his hand. "Good stuff, and not stolen. Voss gave it to me, plus a big pay raise."

"Tame as Lollipop now, eh?" The monkey was licking his reward sucker from the evening's final performance. "Eating out of your hand?"

"No, he's still an overbearing, arrogant, insufferable gorilla," Lacey said. They were in her room. Slipping into an emerald satin negligee and matching mules, she told him her news. "A fella that owns two saloons in Dallas was here last week, offering me my pick of them. Seems my name's getting famous in Texas. Voss raved about rustlers and raiders and ordered him out. Then he doubled my salary and offered a long-term contract, which I refused. All I got to do to keep him in line is threaten to vamoose. But it might be different if he knew everything."

"About us? Hell, Lacey, he's known all along."

Lacey removed the pins from her hair. He liked it loose, and she always relished the feel of his hands in it.

"True—but Voss thinks I'm just fooling with you, amusing myself, and that when the novelty wears off, I'll turn to him."

"Well?" he sighed.

"Don't hurt me, Brant. Don't make me suffer because of her."

Brant scowled and sank lower into the chair. "Leave Mrs. Lane out of this, Lacey. She's apart from us."

Lacey did not agree. Indeed, she considered Garnet Lane the reason for their troubles. But she knew that tone in his voice, that warning. A little provocation, and he'd walk out of the room—and possibly out of her life.

Changing her tone, she said, "I been thinking about changing my act, spicing it up a bit. Been practicing with Lollipop, and he's just about ready with the new routine. I split a couple of tutus down the side and sewed on ribbons to be released on cue." She waited for his reaction. Brant slouched deeper in the chair, stretching his long muscular legs in the tight brown canvas breeches. "I'm gonna shave myself and wear a flesh-colored chiffon fig leaf," she continued. "I'm gonna ride in bareback on a gilded pony with my hair on fire. I'm gonna—goddamn it, Brant, you haven't heard a word I've said! And you couldn't care less if I stripped to the buff or laid every saddle tramp in the territory!"

Tossing her hairbrush on the floor, Lacey exploded in one of her rare tantrums, throwing herself across the bed and beating the mattress.

Brant straightened, sitting with his knees spread, pondering the faded carpet between his scuffed, spurred boots. Lacey wept as if her heart were being wrenched out of her breast. Finally, he rose and went to her.

"Play-acting, Lacey? I never expect hysterics from you."

"Why not? Are they reserved for ladies only? I have feelings too, and you're trampling on them, Brant." She was lying on her stomach, sobbing into the pillow, but at his touch she rolled over and gazed up at him with wet, supplicating eyes. "You're killing me, Brant."

"I kill everybody. I have a fatal charm."

"Forget that, can't you? For tonight?"

She extended her arms to him, and Brant moved to lie on top of her.

Later, she said, "Don't go. Spend the night, unless you intend to wake up early to attend the chautauqua."

"Very funny, Lacey."

"I'm serious. That circuit evangelist is gathering folks at the waterhole for another fire-and-brimstone revival tomorrow. There'll be preaching, repentance, and baptisms. You read the Bible, Brant?" she said.

"My mother read a chapter every night after supper. It was her children's bedtime story."

"My folks never believed in anything but money," Lacey reflected. "Hucksters out to fleece suckers." She gave a wistful sigh. "I like to hear church bells ringing, especially cathedral chimes."

"You're getting sentimental, Lacey. Booze and sex always does that to you," Brant smiled.

"And that's forbidden, too. Temperament, sentiment, religion—all taboo for women like me? Oh,

I'm not pretending to be the sad whore with the heart of gold. Hell, I'd rather have a poke of gold."

"No, you wouldn't, Lacey. Stop it. You're not a whore at all."

"There's degrees of prostitution, sir, any respectable matron could tell you that, although many are just legal mistresses. But I'm not bucking for a cactus-covered cottage on the prairie, Mr. Cowman, even if you were offering it. A hut, a horse, and a herd might be enough for some men, but women usually crave more. I bet that's one thing the Widow Lane and I have in common. And I'll tell you something else. If ever she marries again, her spouse will be the cuckold of a ghost!"

Brant buckled on his holster without even glancing at her. "You finished jawing, ma'am?" he asked.

"No!" she cried, bolting toward him. "You know I didn't mean any of that! I'd live in a dugout or a hollow log, learn to rope and brand, eat dust and die for you—if only you'd ask me, need me, love me. Want me for your own, Brant!" She waited for the words, horribly aware that her emotional flood had only embarrassed him. There was a long silence. Then Brant, his face tight with pain, whispered, "Good night, Lacey. Pleasant dreams."

"Thank you. And give her my regards."

"Her?"

"That little shadow who'll be riding the lonesome trail with you, cowboy," she replied.

He didn't try to deny it, not to his devoted lover, much less to himself. There would have been no point, since neither of them would have believed him. He only wished there weren't such pain in Lacey's voice—or that there was something he could do about it.

Chapter 17

LACEY put up a scraggly cedar branch on the marble-topped table in her room, draped it with a silver-sequined ruffle from one of her costumes, and hung some candy suckers and trinkets on it for Lollipop. For Brant she put mistletoe—which grew on the mesquites—everywhere. There was even a sprig in her hair.

"You've got the spirit, all right," he said, kissing her as he came in the door.

"You know something, Brant? I'm twenty-five years old, and I never once spent Christmas in a real home. When I was a kid, it was a tent pitched in the woods or along the road wherever the medicine wagon happened to be camped. When I went on circuit as a trouper, it was a boardinghouse."

"That's awful," Brant commiserated sincerely.

She nodded. "Could be sadder, though. I knew a girl in a fancy parlor house, so fine the patrons had to produce references and be screened by the madam. She told me the saddest place in the whole world is a brothel during holidays. The customers, even the biggest bastards, always stay home with their families. They help decorate the tree and play Santa Claus, shoot fireworks on the Fourth of July, go to church on Easter. That's how they compensate for the infidelity. I bet you wouldn't be here now, either, if you had a family. Did you come to town to see me, or were you hoping to see *her*?"

"Lacey," he sighed, "I came to wish you a Merry Christmas."

"Merry Christmas," she murmured.

Lacey opened a decanter. "Lucky thing cheer comes in bottles." They touched glasses, but there didn't seem to be anything to toast. Lollipop was playing with his new rattle, chewing on it like a teething baby. Watching him, Lacey's eyes clouded.

"Let's rent a rig and go to San Antone, Brant. We can come back tomorrow." There was desperation in her voice.

"What for?"

"It'd get us away for a while."

"But it wouldn't change anything, Lacey. It'd all be the same when we returned. The only way to escape is to make it permanent. If you want to be rid of Voss and the Silver Spur, really rid of him, you'll have to leave Texas."

"Would you like me to go? You'd like to be free of me. I'm a habit you can't break. You walk out, but you always come back. And then it starts all over again for me, the longing, the frustration and despair. Now it's Christmas, folks are going to church and giving presents and being happy, and I'm blubbering in my booze. Believe me or not, Brant, I never loved a man before, not really, and I wish to God I didn't love one now. It's too much pain. Someday I'm gonna go, and travel a lot farther than San Antone. What'll you do then?"

"Wait for you to come back."

Lacey stared into her glass. "Don't be so cocksure, mister! Don't you realize having me around is your life insurance?"

He laughed. "Did Voss tell you that? Don't believe it, Lacey. He's the biggest coward west of the Mississippi! That's why he never wears a gun, so he can't be challenged to draw it. Big-mouthed, fat-assed coward!"

"Maybe, but he's got some brave bulls in his pay. One word from me and you'd be dead."

"Then you could bury me on boot hill and wear black."

"Mistresses don't mourn publicly, lover. That's for wives—ladies like Mrs. Dennis Lane. I wonder if she'd mourn the man who made her a widow."

Lollipop dropped his toy just then, and it rolled under the bed. He scampered after it, chattering.

"You make as much sense as he does," Brant remarked.

"He understands me," Lacey replied with a catch in her voice. "In that respect, he's smarter than some people I know."

Brant stood, lifting his hat from the bedpost.

"You just got here! I haven't given you my present yet."

"I've already had that present, honey."

"Well, it's a gift you can give over and over. That's what's so wonderful about it."

"Yeah."

Lacey gripped his arms. "Darling, please?"

"Don't stampede me, lady. And for Christ's sake, don't beg."

"Oh, Brant, you're not tired of me, are you? You still like me? I'm still good for you—and fun in bed?"

"Goddamn it, Lacey!" He stormed from the room.

Brant went into the Silver Spur and took a table by the window, where he could watch Seth's store.

"Mind if I sit down?" he heard Sully Voss's voice.

"It's your place," Brant replied coolly.

Voss dropped his bulk into the opposite chair. "What're you drinking?"

"Coffee, if there's any made."

"I sell liquor."

"I've had my quota for the day."

"Why'd you come in here, then?"

"To warm myself at the friendly Yule log," Brant said cynically. "If you haven't noticed, it's damnably cold outside, fixing to sleet or snow."

"Miss Lee ain't performing today. According to her, it ain't decent to dance half-naked on the birthday of Jesus Christ. Strange, three hundred and sixty-four days a year her act is art and don't seem to bother her, but on Christmas it's suddenly offensive."

"Humor her," Brant suggested.

"I been doing that since she arrived," Voss muttered. "Never humored a woman in my life as much as I have her. Ain't she told you that? You see her often enough—just come from visiting her, in fact. One of my boys seen you."

"How many spies do you use, Voss?"

"Some of them are friends, not spies."

"Men like you don't have friends."

"Cocky, ain't you, cowboy? I know you Southerners are quick to duel, and I reckon you're a fast draw. But there's faster ones around here."

"You're scaring me."

Laughter rumbled in Voss's heavily jowled throat, shaking his bloated belly. "Steele, you got a skirt protecting you. A frilly little tutu—though I'm damned if I know what she sees in you."

"Why don't you ask her?"

"I did. She says you remind her of her brother."

"She doesn't have a brother."

"I know. That's what chaps me." Voss surveyed Brant shrewdly. "You don't provoke easy, do you?"

"Not with my back as a target. You want to arm

yourself and go out on the square, face to face, that's fine with me. I refuse to start any trouble on your premises—and let your hired *pistoleros* drill me into a sieve."

"Smart." Voss studied his rival with hooded eyes. "When you taking the Duke cattle out?"

The question irked Brant. "After spring roundup, as you surely know. Nobody drives cattle north in winter unless they're loco."

"Well, I reckon I can bide my time until then," Voss muttered, patting his gold-buttoned vest. "Hey, Steele, what's so interesting out there? You keep watching the square like you expect to see Santa and his reindeer."

"Have you heard about anybody in town being sick?"

"Just that Yankee widder. But that's nothing new—she's sick most of the time. About the only place she goes now is to church and the doctor. Seth Travers says she'll be going back East come spring, if she's still alive then. I reckon she'll be catching a stage just about the same time you hit the trail, cowboy."

Bert Warner emerged from the living quarters of the Mercantile Mart, and, without another word to Voss, Brant left the saloon.

"Hold up a minute, Doc!"

Bert Warner paused, shivering in his inadequate dark suit, his breath white in the frosty air. "Yeah?"

"I saw you go in there. How is Mrs. Lane, Bert—and don't tell me about your ethics. I'm not asking anything very personal, just how she's doing."

"How do you think? I can't cure her any more than that charlatan who sent her out here could cure her."

"But why *not?*"

"The kind of medicine she needs can't be found in a pharmacopoeia. Once I prescribed *you* as a possible treatment, but you only made matters worse, you big dumb cayuse!"

"She had to know the truth, Bert."

"Not the whole truth. I think it was a mistake, but that's not my business. What are you doing in town today, anyway? Don't they celebrate Christmas on the ranch? Or couldn't you keep away from Voss's mare? A wonder you don't have the clap by now."

"The lady is not in that profession, Bert."

"Sure, sure, pure as spring water."

"You been tippling cactus juice, Doc? That's a thorny tongue you got. Let's forget Miss Lee, shall we? How can I help Mrs. Lane?"

"Try to bed *her* for a change, make *her* desire love. And life," the doctor advised bluntly. "That's what she needs now, Steele. She has to want to live!"

Brant blew on his ungloved hands, his fingers numb with cold. "She won't see me."

"Well, I tell you this much, she's not strong enough to throw you out. And if you need a reason to visit her, I'll give you one. Come on home with me. I have to mix an elixir for her. You can take it over there."

Brant watched in the office while the doctor worked with mortar and pestle, grinding ingredients into a fine powder, which he then liquefied with whiskey, measured into a marked bottle, and labeled with his directions.

"Looks potent, Doc."

"I wish it were an aphrodisiac," Bert said. "But you don't find that kind of formula in the *Medicus Familius,* and I don't know how to invent a good one."

"You really think that's all she needs?"

"Not all, no. If I did, I'd be tempted to slip a little Spanish fly into that. But it all begins with sex. Women tend to equate physical and mental emotions, and some can't distinguish between them. They think to desire a man is to love him, and vice versa. Here!" Warner thrust the concoction at Brant. "Try not to destroy this opportunity. You may never have another one. I'm a doctor, not a cupid."

*   *   *

Garnet's elders welcomed Brant like a long-lost son, feast and all. Seth pumped his hand and slapped his shoulder. Jenny embraced him and bestowed a maternal kiss on his cheek, saying warmly, "How nice of you to stop by, Brant! We didn't expect you in town today. Seth says we may get some nasty weather. Have you had dinner? There's a stuffed turkey roasting, and I baked two pumpkin pies. Take off your coat and come sit by the fire."

Brant removed the bottle from his fringed leather jacket. "Dr. Warner sent this for his patient."

"Good. Give it to her. I'll be in the kitchen, making some soup for her. Maybe you can persuade her to dine with us later." Jenny's voice quivered with anxiety. She ushered him to the sickroom and shoved him inside. "You have a visitor, dear."

Garnet was sitting up in the single bed, pillowed against the wagonwheel-spoked headboard. She was wearing a white flannel nightgown sprinkled with pink rosebuds. The high-necked, long-sleeved garment was somehow more seductive than Lacey's sheerest chemise. Her soap-and-talcum sweetness was more alluring than any cologne. Her long fair hair was tied back from her small oval face with a pink satin ribbon. Jenny kept her looking pretty and presentable, even when Garnet protested.

"Merry Christmas!" Brant called to her, then went over and handed her the bottle. "A gift from your doctor."

"More tonic? I've taken enough to make a dry ditch run! Is this some Indian mixture? He must have exhausted all orthodox remedies by now."

Brant stood by the bed, nervously shifting from one foot to the other. Her frailness and pallor shocked him as deeply as her haunted eyes.

"You're supposed to take one tablespoon immediately."

"I'll take it later...maybe," she said, setting the

bottle on the bedside tray beside others. "Thank you for delivering it, Mr. Steele."

"Don't treat me like a stranger, Garnet," he said hoarsely. "I wanted to visit you before, many times, but I knew I wasn't welcome."

"What makes you think you are now?"

"May I sit down?" he asked wearily.

"I don't see how I can prevent your being seated if you wish."

He pulled up a chair and reached for her hand, but she tucked it under the covers. "I have a contagious lung disease," she said in a taunting voice.

"Is that the doctor's diagnosis, or yours?"

"I've seen consumptives. They waste away. Some have dreadful coughs, but not all. The coughers have galloping consumption and go quickly. The chronic cases linger. Mine is chronic. You'd better go, Brant. You're exposing yourself to consumption."

He smiled. "Concerned for me, Garnet? I thought you wanted me dead."

"I did, once."

"And now?"

"It doesn't matter anymore, one way or another."

"It does to me, Garnet."

"Guilty conscience?"

"I'm worried about you."

"Oh, Brant, you're not fooling me! I know why you're here. Dr. Warner sent you. He thinks your medicine might be more effective than his, but he's wrong."

Facing the window, she contemplated the bleak gray sky. Harsh prairie winds laden with ice crystals rattled the pane and invaded the cracks. Garnet thought of the warmth and comfort of her home in Avalon, fires blazing in nearly every room, and all the decorations. Seth had chopped down a wild native cedar tree and some hollylike algerita branches, with which Jenny had done her artistic best, but Garnet missed the spruce and traditional greenery, the bright ornaments and bayberry candles. She sighed.

"Please go, Brant. I don't feel like having company."

"I won't bother you, Garnet. Just let me stay in the room for a while."

"You'd be keeping a premature wake, nothing more."

"That's suds and self-pity," he exploded impatiently. "I told you once you were a coward, Garnet, and I'll tell you again. You're willing yourself to die, because you lack the courage to live. Life challenged you, and you'd rather surrender than fight. I'm inclined to believe Dennis is better off dead than saddled with such a meek little molly."

Her hand shot out from the quilts with amazing energy, aimed for his face, fell short, and caught his forearm instead.

Brant grinned. "Missed again, honey. Bad aim. You need practice."

"You spoiled my aim last time."

"You want to try again?" He offered her his pistol.

"Loaded?"

"Always," he nodded. "If that's what you want, Garnet, if killing me would make you happy, then go ahead. Maybe I deserve it. Maybe that's what every soldier deserves for doing his duty—not medals, but bullets." He thrust the revolver at her, handle first. "Take it, Garnet. Shoot me."

Garnet stared at the gun. A cold chill swept her suddenly and she shivered, murmuring tremulously, "Put it away, Brant." Her voice was stronger as she said, "You shouldn't be wearing it in the house. Aunt Jenny doesn't approve."

Brant sheathed the weapon and waited, gazing at her with open yearning. "I'm still deeply in love with you, Garnet. I want to marry you." He leaned forward to kiss her, but she drew back fearfully.

"You'll catch the sickness," she lied hastily.

Sensing her emotions, which were attuned to his own, he said, "Then we can waste away together, my dear. Get married, go to bed, and never get up."

"Is that all you ever think of?" she admonished. "Going to bed!"

Her directness betrayed her thoughts and belied her languid pose. Brant had always admired her exquisite, passionate violet eyes. He nursed a romantic notion that they would glow deep purple in intense desire, but just then they were a glacial blue.

He pled his case softly and as eloquently as he could. "Intimacy can be pleasant, Garnet, for two people in love—and I've already proposed marriage."

"You want a sick wife? A woman who couldn't bear you children, or would die soon?"

"You're obsessed with death."

"It's the fever."

Brant felt her forehead gently. It was cool, satin-smooth. His hand longed to linger, to stroke her face, throat, breasts, all of her. "You don't have any temperature, Garnet."

"It comes and goes, with chills between. There was a girl in Avalon with lung disease, and so I know the symptoms. She died. I shall die, too. I know it. I feel it, and I'm not such a coward as you think, Brant. I dream of death, and sometimes I even sense its presence. It's not an old man with a long white beard and scythe. I envision an angel taking my hand, leading me over a great mountain into a beautiful, peaceful green valley...."

"My little ingenue," Brant said, smiling poignantly. "I've seen that drama in the theater. I'm impressed with your performance, Camille, but not convinced. I've seen consumptives, in the war and before. Their cheeks were rosy with fever, not lily white, and they spat up blood and often passed out from pain and weakness."

"That'll come later."

"No, it won't! Listen to me, Garnet. You're going to stop pampering your sorrow. Stop worrying your family and jeopardizing *their* health. You're going to rise from that bed, marry me—and have a bunch of kids!"

"I'd rather die," she declared.

Brant merely laughed and strode to the kitchen door. "If the soup's ready, Miss Temple, bring the patient a big bowl. I'll see that she eats every delicious spoonful."

"I will not, sir!" Garnet muttered furiously.

"Yes, you will, darling, because I won't leave until you do. So the length of my stay depends on you."

Her eyes smoked in fury. "You're a skunk, Brant Steele! And a rattlesnake and a coyote—and I'll spit the broth all over you!" she threatened.

That delighted him. "My, my! Since when do genteel ladies spit? But no matter, I'll keep refilling the bowl—and that's a huge kettle of soup. Later you'll have some Christmas dinner, at the table, even if I have to carry you to the kitchen and tie you in a chair, or hold you on my lap and force-feed you like a baby. Jenny worked very hard preparing a festive dinner, and we're all going to enjoy it—with grace before and afterwards."

Jenny brought the soup, glanced apprehensively at the quarreling couple, and rapidly retreated.

"Damn you," Garnet raged, as Brant tucked a towel under her chin. "I don't need a bib!"

His wry grin reminded her of her ungracious threat. "Just a precaution, my dear."

Garnet blushed. "Aunt Jenny forgot the croutons. Would you get some for me, please? And a napkin."

"Of course. Anything else?"

She hesitated. "A bowl for yourself, if you like."

"Thank you. I would."

When he returned and sat down, Garnet asked wistfully, "What was Christmas like on the plantation?"

"A grand celebration, lasting through New Year's. Many parties, visitors, and house guests. The slaves received gifts and had their own parties. All holidays were jubilations at Great Oaks. Before the war, I mean." He paused, hoping she would not dwell on his last unfortunate phrase. "I'm sure you enjoyed Christmas in Connecticut, didn't you?"

Her expression was transformed then, and Brant knew he had lost her attention. He sat silently, listening to the sleet hissing against the window.

PART THREE

Chapter 18

ONE morning toward the end of January, Garnet
refused the breakfast tray Jenny brought to her,
insisting that she felt well enough to go to the table.
She wanted no more meals in bed.

Delighted, Jenny went to tell Seth. She praised
Dr. Warner's medications, while Seth credited his
own time-tested elixir of sulphur and sorghum. Garnet smiled, convinced that the real cure was simply
a surfeit of idleness and boredom. Tired of resting,
weary of coddling, she wanted an occupation. Could
she work in the store?

"Certainly," Jenny answered promptly, cueing
Seth. "Uncle Seth was telling me recently that he'd
like some help."

"That I was," Seth agreed. "You can start right
now if you like, honey."

The last freight Conestoga from the Texas Coast
had brought in some bolts of calico, gingham, chal-

lis, dimity, and white nansook for underwear. It
gave Garnet pleasure to make a lovely display for
the yard goods, the solid colors grouped in a spec-
trum and the floral prints in a bright arrangement
of their own. She checked the selvages for the trademark of the Ashley Mills, which loomed and shipped
thousands of yards of material over the country and
abroad, but these had come from another New England textile mill, one of her father's competitors.

Her talent for artistic arrangement showed also
in the trays of thread, racks of ribbon, braid, and
laces for trim—items long absent from Southern
markets. Good commercial buttons of brass, glass,
shell, or mother-of-pearl were still scarce, however,
and seamstresses continued to improvise with covered acorns and berries, tiny pebbles, and hand-
carved wooden buttons.

Garnet soon became familiar with the tastes of
the female customers. She offered suggestions from
the fashion books and patterns her mother continued to send, and the women praised her assistance
to the proprietor. Sales of feminine apparel increased because of Garnet.

"By golly, you got a natural sales ability!" Seth
complimented her happily. "Truth is, I had trouble
moving some of them unmentionables. Now I got
to order more."

A potbellied stove kept the Mercantile Mart fairly
comfortable in bitter weather, but there was no
cracker or pickle barrel, considered standard equipment in the general stores of New England. Nor
did the customers linger long after buying their
things. Seth explained:

"Pioneering folks got too much to do to fritter
away time gabbing or whittling, even in winter.
They use their spare time to mend harnesses, fix tools,
repair their homes and outbuildings—and figure
out how to keep going with the odds against them.
Frontier settlers can't afford the luxury of sitting

around talking, not in any season. They got to maintain constant vigilance against the elements, the animals, and sometimes the Indians. Why, just staying alive out here is a challenge unknown to most Easterners," Seth continued. "Your generation, anyway—and even your parents', for that matter, they were born in civilization. In the West, you got to work and scramble to survive at all."

"I don't mind," Garnet mused with surprising understanding. "I've had my fill of leisure for a while."

"Heartening to hear you say that, child. Now, if you'll unpack that box there, you'll find a rainbow of rickrack braid that'll put stars in the ladies' eyes."

"Mine, too?"

"You always had stars in yours, sweetheart. They was dim for the past few months, but they're beginning to shine again...brighter than before, I think."

"Do you, Uncle?"

"I do. So does your aunt. And someone else, too."

Garnet did not pursue that.

Garnet was especially friendly to the members of the occupation forces, though their blue uniforms still struck pain in her heart, swift and piercing as a bayonet. Eleanor had written that the Civil War Monument was nearing completion and would be dedicated on the next anniversary of either Appomattox or Gettysburg. Naturally, Private Dennis Robert Lane's name would be included. Garnet hoped passionately to be home for the ceremony.

Jenny always managed to have a pot of fresh coffee and a pound cake or gingerbread on hand when Brant's wagon arrived. Loading the wagon was followed by hospitality in the kitchen until the conniving cupids suddenly remembered urgent tasks and left. Their conspiracy embarrassed Garnet and made her cross with Brant, as if it were all his doing.

"Mighty glad to see you up and about," he told her one afternoon, smiling complacently. "I said you'd leave that bed, didn't I?"

Improved health had rekindled Garnet's spirit, always a trifle too pert for her mother.

"You also told me I'd marry you," she said tartly, "but that's one mistake I'll never make."

"How do you know it would be a mistake?"

"Some things are only too obvious," Garnet replied, moving toward the stove, wishing she dared raise her skirts to warm the backs of her legs. "And don't imagine you had anything to do with my getting better. I got up because I was bored, and mostly because I realized it was my only hope of returning home. I don't crave spending the rest of my life in Texas!"

"What's wrong with Texas?"

"What's right with it?" she parried. "A land where every man totes a gun? With savages lurking in the wilderness? You must be loco!"

That amused him. "A little, perhaps: *poco loco*."

"Texas terrifies me."

"Life terrifies you, Garnet, because you haven't grown up. You're still hiding, like a timid child hides from goblins. You live in a dream world."

An indifferent shrug dismissed the subject, and Garnet concentrated on removing a bit of lint from her dress. Every stray thread seemed to gravitate toward the black fabric, and she was always brushing at herself. Widow's weeds were impractical in the dusty store, and even more so in the everlasting dust blowing off the dry prairie.

"Shouldn't you be riding the range or something?" she asked archly.

"Trying to get rid of me?"

She didn't deign to answer.

He gazed at her closed expression for several

moments and then asked abruptly, "What does your hasty retreat to Connecticut hold for you, madam?"

"A future without you, sir."

Brant frowned, watching as she unpacked bolts of fabric. "That sheer blue stuff would compliment your coloring nicely," he said hesitantly. "Make a pretty dress."

"It's Swiss *voile,* the best fabric we have, and I expect you'll see it soon on some ladies in town."

"I'd like to see it on you."

"Well, you won't." She turned her back and began arranging and rearranging the spools of thread.

Although summarily dismissed, Brant lingered. What was it about this wisp of a woman that intrigued him so? She was lovely, but he had known equally lovely ladies and certainly far more agreeable ones. Her fragile fairness was, in fact, eclipsed by Lacey's blatant voluptuousness. They were as different as sunlight and shadow. Lacey exuded vigor and sensuality, while Garnet suppressed hers, yet her temper could match any woman's. It was possible that her essentially passionate nature might surpass Lacey's.

Brant ached with wanting Garnet, sometimes as though he had been kicked, and the thought of possessing her wrenched him. Something had to make her his.

"When are you going to remove those weeds, Garnet?"

"I'll go into secondary mourning after a year. That's gray."

"And how long will you wear gray?"

"A year or more. Perhaps forever."

"Why not sackcloth and ashes?"

"I'm mourning, Reb, not atoning."

"Gray is for ghosts, Garnet, and black is for shrouds."

She gazed at him eloquently, her eyes the color of wild violets. *"His* shroud was blue."

Brant gasped, but he controlled himself. She would never allow him to forget. "Give me the credit voucher," he muttered, "so I can sign it and get out of here."

Chapter 19

HAVING learned early in her engagement at the Silver Spur that the door on the improvised dressing room did not insure privacy, Lacey dressed at the hotel and timed her arrival to the last possible moment. Never truly eager to go, she was morose that evening. Near-naked as she was in the costume, even her heavy wool cloak was little protection against the bone-penetrating winds. Reluctantly, with her shivering little partner tucked inside the thick folds of her cloak, she set off resentfully to earn her living.

When these maudlin moods struck her, Lacey blamed Brant Steele for everything. If not for him, they could both be in New York now, living in civilized comfort, while she performed in respectable establishments and studied for the legitimate theater. But he did not love her.

What was she to him? He didn't care what happened to her, what kind of spectacle she made of herself, how much of herself she exposed. There was little concealed by the flesh-colored satin fig leaf fastened around her hips with a string, and the two tiny silver-sequined cones pasted to her sassy nipples only emphasized her full breasts. She was advertised as "The Luscious Lacey Lee, the Wickedest Wench West of the Mississippi!" And Sully Voss was becoming a real problem. Fending him off required continual cunning.

That she continued to address him formally and to repulse his advances with threats of leaving infuriated Voss. He had taken refuge in cynicism. He felt foolish before his men, imagining that they joked among themselves about his inability to bed the bitch, especially since Brant Steele had no difficulty. Each time Lacey spurned him, Voss promised himself it would be the last rejection. She would surrender the next time, or be damned sorry.

The usual roar of applause greeted the star's entrance, and Lacey did not have to study the faces to know their minds: Before the night was over, every man present would rape her in fantasy. Pretending to be unaware of their lust was a feat requiring more acting skill than some Shakespearean actresses possessed.

The piano player struck the opening chords of her theme as the proprietor moved to center stage and made his introduction, much like a carnival barker hawking a flamboyant freak.

"Gentlemen, cowboys, and the rest of you! The Silver Spur is proud to present its stellar attraction, 'The Luscious Lacey Lee, the Wickedest Wench West of the Mississippi!'"

During the boisterous applause, someone yelled, "You forgot Lollipop!"

Voss grinned. "How could anyone forget the little creature who makes monkeys of us all? Here they are, fellas, the two of 'em!"

Cringing a little, Lacey unfastened the gaudy rhinestone clip at her throat. A flunky appeared to take the cloak. Lollipop, clinging to her svelte waist with both paws, his head nestled on her warm bosom, blinked at the lights and then bestowed his preliminary kiss and hug. Male response to the animal's show of affection swayed the rafters and rattled the windows.

As Lacey performed the repertoire chosen for that evening, she scanned the audience for Brant. Between acts she visited the tables and let customers buy her watered-down drinks at exorbitant prices, and touched the shoulders of gamblers to bring them luck. She kept a shrewd account of the bogus liquor sold and demanded a percentage of the sale, plus a gratuity for the slightest favor to any gambler, whether he won or lost.

Lacey had never had so much money or so few expenses, and her savings mounted steadily. She knew she could quit this iniquitous den any time— and if the leer in the boss's eyes got any worse, it might have to be that night. His nostrils flared like a coyote's sniffing a female scent. Where was Brant? It was *their* night.

Her final show was at eleven o'clock, and Lacey ignored the hoarse cries for more. Grabbing her cloak from the rack and tucking Lollipop inside, Lacey ran. She almost managed to reach the Longhorn Hotel before Voss, huffing and puffing, caught up with her.

"Hey, there, honey, not so fast!"

"It's cold out here, Mr. Voss."

"Mr. Voss, Mr. Voss!" he mimicked. "I told you a hundred times, the name's Sully."

Lacey continued on her way, Voss now stomping laboriously beside her as they entered the hotel lobby. "Good night, sir."

Winded, gasping for breath, he grinned, trailing her up the stairway like a determined hound. "How about a nightcap?" he ventured.

"After all that slop in the saloon?"

"You didn't drink any of it. You never do. You toss it into the handiest spittoon when the suckers ain't looking—and I don't blame you. Straight, that red-eye'd be poison, which is why I dilute it with water. Considerate of me, ain't it?"

Lacey purposely fumbled the key in the lock, to warn Brant if he was inside. Finally she opened the door. The room was empty.

Lacey lit the oil lamp. "Satisfied?" she asked as Voss checked the closet.

Voss muttered, "He must be sick tonight. Or maybe his horse threw him."

"You hope."

"Yeah. Nobody I'd rather see crippled or dead than Steele."

"Please go, Mr. Voss. I'm tired." Lacey sighed.

"Stood you up tonight, didn't he? Tell me, what magic charm does Steele have?"

"The kind you wouldn't understand, sir."

"Love? Shit, there ain't no such thing."

"May I please retire?"

"Not alone, baby."

"Get out," Lacey ordered icily.

Voss scowled. "You been here over seven months now, Lacey. You know I'm hot for you, but you keep on giving me the boot. What do you want? Name it, and it's yours."

"I want to be left alone," she answered wearily.

"By all men—or just by me?"

His whiskeyed breath reached Lacey clear across the room. "Well, since you narrowed it down that way..."

"Steele will never marry you, Lacey."

"That's not news to me."

"I might consider marriage."

She laughed. "I'd rather marry Lollipop."

"Oh? Does he know more tricks than I do?"

"You got a vile mouth, Mr. Voss, and vulgarity doesn't appeal to me."

"I bet I could, if you'd let me," said Voss.

Lacey took a deep breath. "A gentleman never forces his attentions on a lady, so show me how genteel you are by leaving now. I want to undress and go to bed."

"*Lady?* You can't get much more undressed, honey."

"See? That's what I mean about you, Voss! You think I don't know I'm practically naked? But you have to remind me, humiliate me with cheap remarks. Get out of here, you slimy polecat, before I holler for help!"

"But your boyfriend ain't round, that night clerk downstairs is in my employ, and those drunken cowboys riding my bar gals in the other rooms here are too busy to bother with you."

"Why don't you take one of those bar girls, Mr. Voss?"

"Already took 'em all," he said, edging toward her. "Laying the boss is part of the job."

"Not for me," Lacey declared, stepping back. She was not afraid of him, not really. Nobody touched Lacey Lee if she didn't want them to, not since her stepfather. "Don't come any closer, sir."

"Peppery, ain't you?" Sully grinned, ignoring the angry warning. "That's good. I like my women hot, and I think you're chili pepper."

As he grabbed and tried to kiss her, Lacey struck him across the face, her long nails raking his cheek, and tried to lift her knee to his groin. But Voss was beyond reason. Why had she not seen it before? His eyes glittered. He was transfixed. The devil would force her!

Lacey had retreated as far as she could go, her back against the bureau. She felt among the items on the cold marble surface until she found hard steel—the scissors she had earlier used to trim some ravelings from her tutu. Picking it up, she held it firmly behind her back and warned again, "Sully, leave me alone! I mean it."

Clutching her bodice in his big hands, he ripped the flimsy garment away and pressed his bloated belly against her quivering body, stimulated by her shaking. His impassioned guttural moans revolted Lacey, and fear sickened her with shocking swiftness.

Lollipop, in a frenzy, jumped up and down on the bed, uncertain whether to attack, watching for a cue from his mistress. But Lacey was intent on Voss, and the animal acted on instinct. He lunged several times at Voss, clawing at him and chattering hysterically.

Lacey did not want Lollipop or herself hurt. Swiftly, and with an amazing calm, she aimed forward the steel scissors poised in midair, glinting in the lamplight, before plunging them into Sully's chest. His eyes widened in sudden, surprised horror, but he made no sound. He continued to grin idiotically, so that for a terrible moment Lacey feared she had missed her mark. Now surely he would kill her. With sick relief she saw the crimson stain spreading slowly on his ruffled white shirt bosom and then on the brocaded weskit. A low, guttural moan escaped him at last, and he crumpled at her feet, a ghastly grin frozen on his face.

Lacey knelt beside him, frantic for a pulse or heartbeat, but was too nervous to detect either. Lollipop was issuing curious noises, glancing frantically from his mistress to the man on the floor. Lacey gazed at her victim like an astonished hunter at a dangerous animal fought and killed in self-defense.

Sully's eyes had rolled back in his head, half-closed, only the whites visible. His upper clothing was moistly red and the carpet beneath him was becoming saturated. She turned his face sidewise to allow the gurgling blood to flow out, lest it strangle any remaining life. Then she took Lollipop and her reticule of stashed cash, blew out the lamp, and cautiously checked the corridor. She slipped out in the dark-hooded wrap, monkey and cash beneath the cloak.

Cautioning Lollipop to silence, Lacey hurried down the back stairs and stood in the windy moonlight behind the building. Where to go?

The next stagecoach would not pass through until tomorrow afternoon, and by then the chambermaid would have discovered Sully. A posse would be hunting her by then. She might be hanged—possibly without benefit of a trial, if erratic frontier justice prevailed. Or she might rot in jail awaiting the circuit judge. Would she ever be able to locate an attorney to take her case?

A number of saddled horses were still hitched to the rails in front of the Silver Spur, but she was hardly an expert rider. Why hadn't she at least taken the precaution of dressing decently? Her chances of finding refuge in a good Christian home were practically nil.

Oh, God—she had to get out of town, far away, and very fast! Luckily Voss's bodyguards were still drinking or gambling.

Lacey moved stealthily through the shadows until she reached the Mercantile Mart. Would Jennifer Temple help her? She rapped gently on the back door, clutching at her cloak with the other hand. Although quivering with cold, Lollipop sensed that it was not a time for complaining chatter.

Lacey tapped again, rattling the knob urgently, and finally heard movement. Candlelight flared in the windows, and she wished she could blow it out.

"Who's there?" Seth called through the closed portal.

"It's me, Mr. Travers. Lacey Lee. I got to talk to you and Miss Temple right away. Please?"

Seth opened the door. By then Jenny was up too, and Lacey could hear Garnet asking questions. Soon all three were in the kitchen, staring curiously at their unexpected midnight visitor with the squirming bulge under her cloak.

Observing the respectably clad ladies in their flannel nightgowns and modest wrappers, Lacey despaired of either much sympathy or help. Swallowing to moisten her dry throat, she apologized for disturbing them and began a rapid explanation.

"I came to you good people in desperation, not knowing what else to do! When they find him, the sheriff will be on my tail, and—"

"Find who?" Seth interrupted, poking up the coals in the stove. "What've you done, woman?"

As she explained, Seth shook his white head gravely. Jenny gasped. Garnet was most surprised of all by the man's identity, however. She had thought that Brant owned Lacey's Saturday nights.

Seth replaced the poker on its rack. "We sure got to help her."

"Of course, but how?" Jenny asked anxiously. "We'd be accomplices, Seth, and guilty under the law."

He shook his head. "She was defending her honor, Jen. A female's got a right to defend her honor."

"No offense intended to you, Miss Lee, but who would believe that?"

"Most anybody in their right wits. Think about it, Jen. If she was willing to submit to her attacker, would she had to do what she done?"

Remembering her own recent episode, Garnet felt an ironic empathy. "That makes sense, Auntie."

"I suppose," Jenny sighed, "although the sheriff may have a different opinion. And there'll be Voss's brutes to reckon with, too. We can't hide her here."

"Definitely not!" her niece echoed.

"Well, not for long, anyway," Seth said. "But if I could get a message to the Duke Ranch—"

"Oh, no, sir!" Lacey cried. "That's the first place

they'll look for me! I was hoping to get to San Antonio somehow, and onto a stage."

Seth shook his head. "Naw, that's too logical, and therefore it's risky. The law is aware of every stage route and schedule in this state. They'll be watching the stations in and out of San Antone, you can bet. Pull down the shades, Garnet. Brew some coffee, Jen. We got some serious thinking to do."

Crucial moments were ticking away and Lacey stared hypnotically at the swaying pendulum. The striking gong startled her ... once, twice, thrice, like death knells to her ears. If she was still there at dawn, she would be trapped—and doomed!

"Please, Mr. Travers, time's wasting, and I'm gonna be a sitting duck!"

"Easy, gal. There's still customers at the saloon, and the hotel'll be packed as usual tonight. Folks around here know my Saturday-night carousing is long over. Even if I could sneak you away in my buckboard without being noticed, I can't figure any safe place, except maybe the Mission."

"The Mission?" cried Jenny and Garnet together, astonished.

Seth nodded. "The best refuge is often the most unlikely one—and it may be the only one in this case."

Lacey said skeptically, "I ain't never even met the padre. He's a holy man, and I'm a sinner dressed like Eve when she was thrown out of Paradise!"

"Yeah, that's a problem," Seth acknowledged, adding, as Lollipop peeked out of the cloak, "Only you can't blame your monkey like she blamed the snake. Get some blankets, Jen, and pins if you got any. If not, sew her and the critter up in that wrap. The padre's used to people baring their souls, but not their flesh. I'll go hitch up the rig."

Jenny offered to lend one of her gowns, although aware that it would be too snug over Lacey's kettledrum breasts. Garnet's clothes would not fit at all.

"Thank you kindly, Miss Temple, but I hate to involve you folks with borrowed clothing," Lacey said reluctantly.

"We already are involved," Jenny told her firmly. "Come into the bedroom, and let's see what we can do...."

Chapter 20

CONCEALING so much sensuality would have been difficult even with a tent. The best they could hope for was not to accentuate it. Lacey's bosom was much larger even than Jenny's, and the gaping bodice was about to pop. They simply could not deliver her to the Mission San Juan in that condition.

"Is that the best you can do, Auntie? She still looks...bumpy in...places."

"That's because she *is* bumpy in places," Jenny said. "Dear, you'll just have to keep your cloak on."

There was the sound of Seth's boots trodding across the bare floor, and then his hoarse, cautioning whisper. "Never mind the preparations, ladies."

Jenny poked her head out of the bedroom. "Why?"

"We can't leave yet, Jen. There's a couple of drunks sleeping in the hayloft, which means I can't hitch up the rig now. They might remember too much when they wake up."

"Mother of God," Lacey murmured. "It'll be dawn in a few more hours—too late! What should I do, sir? Give myself up?"

"That would be foolish." Seth paused, frowning. "I got another idea."

"It better be good," Jenny muttered.

"She can hide in the root cellar."

"They always search root cellars!"

"Yeah. But see, I got two of 'em! One outside, and one under the store that nobody knows about. After the Indians left this area, I used it as a tornado shelter. The trapdoor is under a counter. Of course, you'd have to keep the critter quiet while anyone was in the store. We could give you a signal, maybe drop something heavy on the floor."

"And how long do you imagine we could keep her down there?" Jenny questioned. "Months?"

"We'll cross that creek when we get to it, Jen. We done promised to help her—and Seth Travers don't go back on his word."

Lacey felt wretched over the dissension she might cause in this peaceful household. "It's all right, folks. I'll just have to face the music and dance."

"At the end of a rope?" cried Seth. "And us too, maybe, as accomplices. Don't count on your sex to save you, honey. No law against hanging women in this country. Didn't Mrs. Surratt die on the gallows with the rest of the so-called conspirators in Lincoln's assassination?"

Lacey's hand went involuntarily to her throat, vividly feeling the knotted noose.

Garnet paled, and Jenny admonished Seth. "No need to be macabre, Seth! We just have to wait now for further developments, and try to act normally. Garnet and I will go to church, as usual. Your absence shouldn't occasion much curiosity, considering your attendance record."

"Can't deny that, Jen. I ain't never claimed to be

real religious." And as the community roosters began crowing, he decided, "Prepare the shelter."

When the heavy counter was moved and the trapdoor opened, Lacey gazed into a dark, cold, musty hole in the earth, only slightly larger than a grave. Spiderwebs were strung across it and dirt filtered through the rotting shoring boards. A rickety ladder served as stairs.

Although accustomed to cramped spaces, since she had lived most of her life in a medicine wagon until the age of thirteen, Lacey had never lived underground or in total darkness.

"Any rats down there?" she asked tremulously.

"Nope. I try to keep varmints under control," Seth answered kindly. Jenny and Garnet fetched food, water, and blankets. "But you can't burn no candle. The light would shine through the cracks—and also use up the oxygen faster. It won't be comfortable."

"Yes, sir, but I'm mighty grateful."

"Time enough for gratitude later, if it works."

Lacey hoped that Lollipop would not be afraid of the dark prison. Could she calm him with candy, cookies, and cuddling?

Seth then instructed the other women, "Drop them covers down yonder. I'll stash the water jug and the vittles. Then you better go fix some breakfast, if we're gonna stick to our regular routine. Chimneys of the early risers will soon be sending smoke signals."

"May I help?" Lacey pleaded, hoping to avoid the black pit just a while longer.

"Afraid not," Seth said regretfully, understanding. "Better stay in here, gal. They'll fetch us some hot grub. You keep a eye on the hotel and be ready to scat, pronto." Soon they heard the heavy iron skillet placed on the hottest stove-lid, and then the sizzling of frying bacon and eggs. "Don't that smell good?"

Lacey nodded, though she was actually nauseous.

Morning sickness? No, fear. Pregnancy had never been one of her worries. Brant had wondered about her apparent sterility until learning of her stepfather's brutal rape before puberty. He well understood her almost maternal attachment to Lollipop; a monkey might be the only "baby" she would ever have.

Seth urged, "Cheer up, gal. It ain't the end of the world."

"It might be for me, sir." She sighed. "If so, would you kind folks adopt my poor little pet? Or try to find a good home for him?"

Seth cleared his throat, embarrassed. "Yeah, sure. He's cute—and better trained than some youngsters. Jenny can sew him some more rompers. Them fancy pants got to be his Sunday suit. Does he always wear that little hat?"

"Mostly on stage."

Jenny and Garnet exchanged worried glances. Seth was making commitments they might not be able to keep. The tough frontiersman had a heart of mush!

"Perhaps Mr. Steele would like to have your pet?" Jenny suggested.

"He's too busy on the ranch," Lacey said. "Besides, Lollipop prefers women. He always liked you, Miss Temple. Your niece, too. He's real affectionate."

"Yes—well, I think we'd better dress for services," Jenny decided, as the capuchin kissed his mistress's cheek. "The first bell will sound soon. Come, Garnet."

Later, as the second bell was beckoning the faithful, commotion began at the Longhorn Hotel. The clerk dashed outside, followed by the Mexican chambermaid and some sleepy-eyed, partially garbed guests—cowboys still buttoning shirts and pants, troopers in rumpled uniforms, half-clad saloon girls.

"Get back inside," Jenny ordered Garnet, "and lock the door, quickly!"

Seth had already seen and was helping the fugitive down the ladder. Sacks of grain and boxes of merchandise were then piled on top of the trapdoor. He hurried to the living quarters. "We got to stay in here. It's Sunday, remember, so the store ain't open except for emergency purchases. Maybe Garnet should go to bed and act sick—that wouldn't look suspicious, and it might mean privacy."

"Good idea," Garnet agreed. "I won't even speak if any searchers enter the house. But what if it doesn't work?"

"It has to work," Seth declared emphatically, and her aunt nodded vigorously. "Go on, honey, do your part."

The window shades were raised for better surveillance. Dr. Warner was rushing toward the hotel with his old medical satchel. A small crowd, mostly churchgoers carrying hymnals, had already gathered on the square.

"I better go out there," Seth decided, "or folks might wonder why we ain't curious, too."

"Hurry," Jenny urged, "and bring back the news before I die of suspense."

Twenty minutes later Seth delivered some disquieting, complicating information. "Voss is still alive, but barely conscious because of blood loss. The Doc's with him now. No one doubts who done it. One of Voss's boys went for the sheriff."

"If only we could tell Brant."

"No way yet, Jen. None of the Duke Ranch fellas camped here overnight. The Silver Spur's customers were soldiers and transients, doubling up in the hotel rooms and taking turns with the gals."

"No need for details," Jenny interrupted, hastily. "Are those bums still in the hayloft?"

"Yeah, I'll have to wake them."

The bell clanged another notice and worshipers moved toward the church. The circuit preacher would have a ready-made sermon subject this morning, Jenny mused, on the Wages of Sin!

Stupefied by alcoholic slumber, the drifters had to be shaken. "Hey, you guys! The sun's up, time to be on your way!"

They sat up slowly, finally rising on wobbly legs, scratching and brushing hay from themselves. Seth was unable to distinguish the colors of the squinted, bloodshot eyes in the leathery faces.

"Mornin', mister. I'm Jerry Smith, and my pardner here is Harry Jones. We's travelin' light." They nodded like puppets, grinning, and stuck out rough hands.

Although the names were obvious aliases, Seth responded hospitably. "Pleased to meet you, boys. I don't mind strangers borrowing my barn to rest in, but I like to be asked first. I got rules about smoking, since I was burned out once by careless men passing through. Where's your mounts?"

Jones answered, "Still hitched to the saloon rail, far as we know."

"I take it you ain't heard what happened to the owner of the Silver Spur last night?"

Smith grimaced, pressing his temples. "From the feel of my head and belly, I hope the bastard got killed. He must cut that rotgut with lye-water."

"You're pretty near right on both scores," Seth told him. "Voss serves slop—and he got a scissors stuck in his chest."

"Had to be a female," Jones nodded sagely. "Probably one of his own bar belles." He nudged his partner, winking. "Reckon it was the one we tried. She was a feisty skirt, that's for sure!"

"You best go fetch your horses," Seth advised, "if they ain't been stolen by now. You must've been skunk-drunk to forget your horses in this country!"

"God almighty, Harry—how could we done that! Damn fools, us! Come on, let's git the hell outta here!"

"Too late," the other muttered, as Voss's top gun approached. "Here comes trouble! Will you tell him we was in your barn all night, mister?"

"Howdy, Travers," Roscoe Hamlin called. "These saddle tramps friends of yours?"

"Nope, they just camped on my property overnight, without my permission. Guzzled too much redeye to ride out."

"Yeah, I saw 'em in the Spur, eyeing the Wickedest Wench in the West. And she sure lived up to her name. I reckon it's useless to ask you hoboes if you know anything about it?" he asked, peering at them.

Jones responded, "Naw, we was dead to the world."

"So's that bitch gonna be, real soon," Hamlin said.

"Can we leave?" Smith asked. "If horse thieves ain't snatched our mustangs?"

Hamlin grunted. "If you get your asses out of Longhorn Junction and never return. Scum like you give any town a bad name."

"Yes, sir. Thanks to you both." They donned filthy slouch hats and moved quickly off toward the square.

Hamlin's attention then focused on the owner of the Mercantile Mart. "Sorry, but I got to search your premises."

"Go ahead."

Picking up a pitchfork, Hamlin scaled the loft ladder and stabbed viciously into the loose hay, muttering, "I'd like to stick that slut like she done Voss!"

"Does he pay you that well?"

"He pays enough, and I'll have to find another income if he dies."

"You mean, like work for a living?" Seth gibed.

Scowling at the barbed humor, Hamlin tossed the tool aside and leaped down into the stable, narrowly missing some fresh manure. "Mind if I look inside your house and store?" he asked in a challenging tone.

Seth shrugged, trusting that Jenny was prepared. "I could demand a warrant, Hamlin, considering you ain't no duly elected or appointed lawman. But I got nothing to hide. Just try not to alarm the ladyfolk. My niece is feeling poorly. I better let them know," he added, pounding loudly on the rear door, "in case they ain't dressed for company. You know how women are."

"Yeah, hellcats, most of 'em—and that Lacey Lee is a real she-panther."

Jenny admitted them, affecting puzzled surprise. "Visitors so early in the day, Seth?"

"Mr. Hamlin wants to inspect the premises," he informed with a barely perceptible wink.

"Surely not in the room where Garnet lies ill?"

"I seen females in bed before, ma'am."

"I'm sure of that, sir. But I assume you will respect a *lady's* privacy," Jenny said emphatically. "Please do not disturb Mrs. Lane if she's asleep." Jenny opened the door quietly.

As the stranger entered, Garnet pulled the covers over her face so that only her modesty-outraged eyes were visible. Her dismay was genuine.

Hamlin doffed his hat. "Beggin' your pardon, ma'am. I won't be long."

"I should hope not!" Jenny declared angrily.

Soon, satisfied, Hamlin proceeded to Seth's room, commenting, "Might have better luck in here, eh? The whore prefers men's quarters—although she'd have to be mighty desperate to pick yours, wouldn't she?"

"Insulting bastard, ain't you? In my day, I was a better stud than you ever were, Hamlin—and sure as hell more of a ladies' man! Just get on with your snooping."

Convinced that their subterranean guest had been properly warned, Seth accompanied Hamlin to the store.

"Being a customer, you know the layout," he said, speaking loudly, "including the location of the stockroom. Ain't much attic, but you're welcome to gander it."

"I will, and I ain't deaf," Hamlin muttered, poking behind the counters and into the bins and barrels.

"I'd appreciate it if you wouldn't purposely spoil my perishables," Seth said, curbing his temper. "Apples ain't easy to get—and you know what one rotten one does to the whole barrel!"

"Where's your root cellar?"

"Outside, by the kitchen. Didn't you see it?"

"Thought that was your storm shelter."

"One and the same," Seth said. "It ain't locked. When you finish in here, go look."

"Naw, it's too obvious for a smart cookie like her to hide in."

Hamlin frowned in puzzlement. "Wonder how she skipped town, if she did? We can't find no missing buggy or horse."

"She's got good legs."

"For dancing, not walking the road in fancy slippers."

"Maybe someone gave her a lift."

"To San Antone? That's the logical direction, and one of the boys is already headin' there. But I ain't leavin' no stone unturned here, neither. Her and that critter sure couldn't get too damned far without being spotted by someone!"

"True."

"You got any clues, Travers?"

"None."

"Well, Sheriff Foster and his deputy should be here before long. You gonna join the posse?"

"Sorry, I can't. Got to protect my delicate ladies. Don't do much strenuous riding no more, anyway. There'll be plenty of young, strong volunteers, I'm sure."

"Except for that Louisianan."

"Brant Steele?"

"Who else? Lacey's his doxy, you know."

"Is that right? Then Voss was trespassing on another man's property, wasn't he? That's a hanging offense in Texas, like horse-thievery."

Hamlin snorted. "A whore is anybody's property!

But her stud will probably defend her, being one of them 'gallant Southern gents.' When he finds out, that is."

"But you ain't sending no one to tell him, eh?"

"The law can do that, with a warrant for her arrest. *If* she fled to the Duke Ranch and *made* it through ten miles of brush, which I doubt. Well, thanks for your cooperation, Travers. I might be back again."

"Any time, Hamlin."

Chapter 21

LACEY felt like a prisoner in a dungeon, doomed not only to death but to eternal damnation. In pondering her life, she could find little of worth. Her childhood had been a wretched gypsy experience in which a gaudily painted medicine wagon comprised her whole world. Her parents had made no effort to conceal their hatred for each other, or their lack of love for their daughter. She had witnessed ugly passions generated by desperate desires and deep frustrations. Then came the horror with her stepfather and its terrible consequences. And now this horror.

What surged through her just then, more horrifying than the thought of her fate at the hands of Voss's men, was the understanding that he had not been dead when she left him. Should she have called for the doctor? That would have meant being captured, of course, but she might have saved Voss's life. She'd meant only to stop him, not to kill him!

Would she have that sin of omission on her soul forever?

After what seemed like a journey to eternity and back, Lacey heard the coded tapping on the trap-door—the signal that it was safe to leave her limbo temporarily. Seth's kind voice filtered down.

"You can take a breather, honey."

She emerged with Lollipop still licking his cherry-flavored sucker. The monkey's exemplary behavior in the recent crises convinced her that he was more human than animal, and that he had at least some understanding of their predicament.

"I recognized Hamlin's voice," she said, "but I couldn't understand much. What did he say?"

"Nothing in your favor, I'm afraid. And he may come back, alone or with the law. Main trouble with that hiding place is it's under my business—and I got to open up early tomorrow."

"Does that mean I can't leave it?"

"Not during the day."

Her face blanched. It would be like living in a grave. She might as well be dead.

"Is it so bad?" Jenny asked kindly. "People used to live in caves, Lacey, and this won't be forever."

"But what if it is? What if I have to hide like a ferret in a burrow for the rest of my miserable days?"

"Try to look on the bright side."

"There ain't no silver linings to my dark clouds," Lacey lamented. "None I remember, anyway."

"Things change," Jenny consoled. "People tend to forget that."

"Whether Voss lives or dies, I'll lose. I never win. Once I spun the wheel of fortune at a carnival, and it broke and fell on the ground. And the clairvoyant claimed her crystal ball cracked when I gazed into it. That's the story of Lacey Lee, or Elvira Schwartz."

"Pardon?"

"That's my real handle, folks—the one I was born

with. And will likely die with, too. Christ, there ain't
even no one to put a stone on my head!"

"Oh, now, Lacey—that's not like you. You're usually so spirited. You do have a few friends, perhaps
more than you realize. Isn't that right, Seth?"

"You bet! Now I better go on out and ask some
more questions, like everyone else," Seth decided.
"Damn, I never seen so many folks on the square at
once since the last public hanging! Be on your guard,
girls."

Half an hour later, Seth announced, "Your stars
are changing, Miss Lee—getting lucky!"

"Lucky?"

"Well, call it a mixed blessing. The hotel clerk
watched the Doc patch up Voss and claims it's only
a bad wound. A little higher and you'd have gotten
his jugular, and a mite lower would have hit a lung.
He's weak, but there's a fair chance he'll live. He
ain't made no charges against you, so legally you're
free."

"What does that mean?" Lacey asked suspiciously,
unable to conceive of forgiveness in Voss's cruel nature.

"I'm afraid it just means Voss doesn't want the
law to take over," Seth said ruefully. "He wants his
men to get you."

"Oh, Jesus!" Lacey tensed and clutched Lollipop
closer. "He wants to deal with me himself! Is he
offering a reward?"

Seth nodded regretfully. "It's a hefty one, too. Five
thousand in gold! The bounty hunters will be out
beating the bushes faster than you know it."

"Can he do that?" she asked anxiously. "There
isn't any law out here? No courts? Don't I get a chance
to tell what happened?"

"You don't understand, Miss Lee. The sheriff
couldn't take you into protective custody without a
warrant, or hold you without formal charges. Voss
is claiming it was an accident, that you and him

was...wrestling playfully, and somehow he knocked your sewing kit off the bureau and fell on the shears. Long as he sticks to that, ain't nothing Sheriff Foster, the Texas Rangers, or even the United States Marshal could do."

"So it's open season on me?"

"The law of the West. Men like Voss helped to create it. They shape it to their own advantage. I'm mighty sorry, ma'am, and I got to change that remark about your stars. If you was *really* lucky, you'd have stabbed him in his black heart."

"I guess I should pray for his death, shouldn't I? I been praying for him to live. But if *he* does, then *I* won't."

"Appears the Lord is listening to you," Seth surmised. "Who knows why? I never could figure a reason for rattlesnakes myself, but I reckon the Creator has some purpose for them."

Her piteous expression moved Seth to pat her shoulder. "It ain't all that bleak, ma'am. Just stay alert. And that goes for all of us," he admonished Jenny and Garnet, "I can't tell you this too often, girls!"

Lacey soothed the whimpering monkey. How much bleaker did Seth Travers think it could possibly get?

Chapter 22

BY midafternoon the citizens were off the streets and the town appeared normal, but Lacey could not enjoy the respite. She had become a trophy, hunted for gold, and she and her benefactors had to maintain constant vigilance.

A dark, ugly memory suddenly surfaced—her family's van being stopped on the road by mounted white men seeking runaway slaves. The shrill yapping of their bloodhounds echoed in her ears, and she asked tremulously, "Do they use hunting dogs around here, Mr. Travers?"

"Not on the prairie," Seth replied. "You only need hounds to tree game in the woods. Besides, it takes some of the sport away to chase down and corner your prey like that."

Prey! That's what she was now! And she did not think Sully Voss would exercise sportsmanship in running her down. "That reward," she murmured, swallowing hard, "does it state the terms of capture—dead or alive?"

Seth hesitated. "Alive, honey. But that wouldn't prevent rough treatment by Voss's scum or the bounty hunters in the process of delivering you."

Lacey understood all too well. She would be at their mercy. And what could she expect from men like Roscoe Hamlin, who had lusted for her as much as his boss did? She tried to send Brant a mental message.

"When do you expect Mr. Steele in town again, sir?"

"He should be picking up supplies in a few days."

"A few days? Oh, Lord, I can't wait that long. I got to leave after dark."

"No, you don't, gal. You got to bide your time here till we can figure out a safe escape. Voss might still develop a killing infection. If not, maybe Brant will eliminate the reward by eliminating the offerer. That's your best hope."

"But how can he help me if he doesn't know?"

"Don't worry, ma'am. He'll learn somehow. Too bad that little dickens doesn't know how to find the ranch. Lollipop could swing his way there on the trees," he finished.

"Yeah, too bad."

Soon Lollipop tugged at Lacey's skirt and hitched at his satin rompers. "He wants to be excused," she explained. "But he's trained to use a chamber pot."

"So Jenny told me—and damned if I ain't inclined to agree with that Darwin fella about our ancestors. There's a receptacle in the ladies' bedroom, and I don't think they'll mind him borrowing it."

"I'll clean up after him and empty the pot tonight," Lacey promised.

Hearing, Jenny shook her head. "No, Lacey, I will. You might be seen."

Garnet was reading in the rocker near the bed,

still in her flannel nightgown and wrapper, prepared
to jump under the covers if a stranger came in. But
it was difficult to ignore Lacey's ministrations to
Lollipop as she gently coaxed him onto the crockery
jar that served during illness and nocturnal emer-
gencies. Jenny had made a chintz cover for it, and
Garnet reminded Lacey to replace it.

"Sure, soon's I wipe him and button his rompers."

"Why bother with the clothes? Aunt Jennifer and
I have seen him naked before. Shouldn't you take
care of his costume instead of letting him wear it?"

"I remember when he was shipwrecked and trek-
king through that Louisiana jungle," Lacey reflected. "Lollipop lost his wardrobe, too, and he was
embarrassed until I got him some new garments in
New Orleans."

"Really?" Garnet refrained from commenting that
the monkey was more modest than his bold mistress,
whose incredibly scanty costumes left very little to
the imagination.

"Uh-huh, he even likes to sleep in a nightshirt
and cap, which I tie on his head like a baby's bonnet."

Unwillingly, Garnet wondered if Brant Steele had
any such preferences in bed. Denny certainly had,
even during lovemaking. Their marriage had been
consummated partially clothed and in total darkness, and Garnet had never seen a totally naked
male. Were they all the same physically? No doubt
Lacey could enlighten her, but Garnet was not going
to bring the subject up. Indeed, she was dismayed
by her own curiosity.

Lacey interrupted her thoughts. "May I talk with
you a few moments, please?"

"What about?"

"Can't you guess?"

"Yes, and I'm not interested in discussing it," Garnet said abruptly.

Her unwelcome guest sat down, uninvited. "I'm

gonna speak my piece, anyway. There's nothing serious between Brant and me—at least not for him.
He's in love with you, Garnet. God, if you only knew
how much! I'm jealous of you, and he and I quarrel
about it."

"Why are you telling me this, Lacey?"

"Believe me, I wouldn't if I saw any chance for
me," Lacey admitted. "But I don't, and I may not be
around this place—or any other one—much longer.
You could have a terrific man just by crooking your
little finger, lady. Why, he's suffering for you!"

Garnet rocked angrily. "Don't treat me like a fool.
I can imagine the kind of games you play together!"

"And that's all it amounts to for him, Garnet. Sex
games, as natural to humans as to animals, and the
males of both breeds are instinctively more aggres-
sive than the females. If the mate a man craves isn't
available, he'll turn elsewhere. Blame the Creator
if you must blame someone, but it wasn't an apple or
a snake that made Adam and Eve sin in the Garden
of Eden. It was the instinct breathed into them along
with life."

"Miss Lee, excusing Brant Steele is playing Devil's advocate. Is that allusion beyond your ken?"

"I apologize for my ignorance, ma'am. I never had
much schooling. But can't you ever forgive Mr. Steele
for what happened to your husband?" Lacey plunged
ahead in the face of Garnet's silence. "You're making
a mistake, honey—a mighty big mistake. Pride and
revenge are sorry comforts on a cold night. If you'd
just melt that ice in your heart and let some warmth
flow through you..." She paused, shrugged. "It's chilly
in here. Shall I poke up the fire in the stove?"

"No, thanks. I can do it."

"I'm glad you recovered from whatever ailed you,
Garnet. You seem much stronger now." She shook
her head. "Maybe this crazy climate *is* good for the
health, after all. You still heading back East in the
spring?"

"God willing."

"Must be nice having a home and family waiting for you." Lacey sighed wistfully. "I envy you, Garnet—in more ways than one. I got nobody waiting for me, not anywhere."

"I'm sorry." Garnet realized an unexpected sympathy. "But we'll do our best to help you, Lacey. Uncle Seth and Aunt Jennifer are very kind and helpful."

"They are indeed," Lacey nodded. "And all three of you are far out on a cracked limb for me already— I pray it don't break off and hurt anyone."

"So do we."

Lacey waited, but Garnet had nothing further to say. "Well, I reckon I'd better get back to the kitchen," she said, taking Lollipop's hand. "Your uncle warned me not to wander too far from my cave."

Her first full night in the shelter was even worse than she had feared. The covers were inadequate, the darkness was abysmal, and Lollipop whimpered in her arms, terrified. Hideous nightmares invaded Lacey's intermittent sleep, and the monkey's twitching muscles indicated similar experiences. Lacey warmed him in the blanket bunting and crooned him back to sleep, over and over, until at dawn she heard Seth opening the store for business. His lamplight shining through the floorboard cracks thrilled her, and the smoke from the Buddha-bellied stove was sweet incense. She eagerly awaited the familiar foot-tapping and friendly voice.

"Hey, gal! You awake?"

"Yes, sir!"

The trapdoor was lifted and propped open, and the two prisoners climbed unsteadily up the ladder. "No telling when the first customer will come, so we're gonna feed you and the critter early. Jenny's cooking now. Garnet helps me in the store, and she can check

the town's doings through the windows. Wonder if
Voss is still kicking."

"I—I suppose we'll learn soon enough." Although
she had been unable to intervene for his life, Lacey
could not bring herself to beseech his death, either.

"Good morning," Jenny called, bringing food. "Did
you rest well, Lacey?"

"Fine," she fibbed. "Lollipop too."

"Well, eat heartily."

Seth and she ate on a counter, Lollipop on the
floor. They were finishing when Garnet appeared,
ready for work. She had learned to protect her dresses
with aprons, which Jenny fashioned in bright colors
and prints and feminine styles to relieve the stark
widow's apparel which her niece obstinately continued to wear. Today's apron was a ruffled pink challis
with wide strings tied in a fetching bustlelike bow.

Jenny's seamstress skills brought requests from
the local ladies to design and sew for them, even
urgings to establish a dress shop. The idea intrigued
Jenny, although she knew she would be accompanying Garnet back to Connecticut in a very few
months.

Seth, who did not relish the prospect of living alone
again, dreaded their departure. He longed for some
way to postpone it. Despite the risks, he even enjoyed
protecting Miss Lee. It made him feel needed.

"My, don't you look pretty!" he praised Garnet's
fresh, fair beauty.

And clean and neat, thought Lacey, embarrassed
by her own unbrushed hair and teeth, and her rumpled clothes tainted by the animal's gamy odor. Always fastidious, Lacey was greatly distressed. But
she had no time to dwell on it. Seth hustled her down
the ladder as Garnet signaled to him from the window and the jingling portal bell announced the first
customer of the day.

Mrs. Bessie Barker was the town gossip. Very little went on in the entire county of which she was not aware. "Mornin', Seth, Garnet. Y'all heard the latest about Mr. Voss?"

"Nope," Seth answered. "Ain't been out yet."

"Well, looks like the sinner's gonna cheat the grave diggers out of their fee." Bessie plopped her market basket on the counter, preparing to stay for a long visit. "Doc Warner done a good job on hemstitching him together, and Felicia Perez says he's gulpin' beef broth by the gallon—even ordered fresh blood from the butcher's to help get back his strength. I expect he'll heal fast and be runnin' that Babylon waterin' hole again soon, more's the pity."

"Reckon the Almighty just ain't ready to summon him yet," Seth ventured tentatively, testing for more news.

"The Almighty? Hah! When his time comes, it's Satan he'll be reportin' to!" the old lady piously predicted. "That brazen hussy, too."

"Judge not, lest ye be judged," Seth murmured. "Ain't that what the Bible says, ma'am?"

"It also says the wicked shall be punished!"

"You need anything today?" Seth asked, tired of her.

"Some more knittin' wool, if you got it—the same shade as that shawl I started last week."

Garnet smiled. "I'll help you, Mrs. Barker. Autumn brown, isn't it? I think we still have a few skeins."

"Same price?"

"Yes, ma'am. But the next shipment from the Northern wool mills will be higher. Merchandise continues to cost more since the war."

"Damn Yankees!" she swore testily, forgetting Garnet's home. "They're all growin' fat fleecin' us poor Southerners. Too bad we can't establish some mills and factories in the South, but they got all our money. Worse even, some of our young girls are marryin' Yankees."

Garnet suppressed any comment, placing the brown yarn in the basket. "Need any other notions, ma'am?"

"A packet of large-eyed needles, please. My sight's failin', though I still see what's goin' on well enough."

"And hear," Seth murmured.

Unaffronted, Bessie cackled like one of her laying hens. "You bet your boots, Seth Travers! Nothing wrong with these old ears! That Mexican chambermaid told me Miss Lee left all her fancy costumes behind. How far could she get without clothes?"

"Farther than some women with them," Seth suggested smoothly, tongue-in-cheek.

"No doubt!" Bessie retrieved her basket. "Put this on my bill. Good day, folks."

Later, making the entry in the ledger, Garnet observed, "Her account is already in arrears, Uncle."

"I know, honey. But her only income is from selling eggs. She's waiting for her late husband's Confederate pension. That might just be a long wait. Reconstruction is tough on the losers."

Garnet sighed. "It's hard on some winners, too. I wonder if our cellar guest heard that about Voss?"

"I heard," Lacey called, raising the trapdoor slightly. "Couldn't miss that foghorn voice. She could be the town crier."

"She *is*, when you think about it," said Seth. "Bessie Barker invented the grapevine communication system in this area. News travels faster by her mouth than the telegraph wires. That's why we got to be extra careful."

The bell tinkled again, and Lacey retreated fast. More customers came in, were served, and departed. All discussed the exciting drama and mysterious disappearance of the suspect, but nobody had more than the basic information.

Roscoe Hamlin purchased his daily supply of plug tobacco, cut off a portion with his penknife, and hung around the store, chewing and spitting into the cuspidor, spattering the floor frequently.

"Sloppy aim for a top gun," Seth commented.

"I shoot bullets, not quid juice. You want a demonstration on that row of lamp chimneys on yonder shelf?" He grinned, patting one of the pistols in his double-holstered belt. "I'm ambidextrous, you know."

Seth glanced at his educated great-niece for help.

Garnet obliged. "It means he's as skillful with his left hand as with his right."

Seth grunted, unimpressed. "Just don't try proving it in here, Hamlin. And aim your mouth better. I don't want to clean up your spit."

"Your womenfolk too fine to scrub floors, Travers? I notice they empty slop jars—oftener than usual this morning. Somebody have the flux last night?"

Hamlin ruminated his cud and spat again, ringing the rim of the old brass spittoon. Then he removed one of his revolvers and spun the magazine. "Seems lots of folks got that ailment since yesterday. Not surprising. A thing like that bitch done to a leadin' citizen is enough to scare the shit out of anyone."

"Curb your foul tongue!" Seth commanded, as Garnet's face reddened. "There's a lady present!"

"Wasn't she sick in bed yesterday? Fast recovery—or was it just one of them delicate female times?"

Jenny rustled into the store, outraged. "Sir, you are an unspeakable boor! And because we allowed your unauthorized invasion of our privacy yesterday does not permit you to stay here and insult us now! Shouldn't you be minding Mr. Voss's business?"

"You're right. I humbly apologize for my rudeness, ma'am. This affair's got me real testy. I'm forgettin' my manners. But my temper's nothin' compared to my boss's. He's sittin' up and walkin' some already. Voss always was strong as a bull, and right now he's madder than one with a cocklebur under its tail. You never heard such roarin'! Why, I thought he was gonna kill the maid when she spilt some of the fresh blood the butcher brought him. And he wouldn't pay Burly Matthews or drink any of the blood until Burly swore it didn't come from a steer."

Jenny felt nauseous and was afraid her niece would faint. She knew patients with severe anemia were sometimes treated with raw liver or even animal blood, but hearing about it was revolting. "We don't care to hear any more about it," she said firmly.

"Well, anyhow, Voss wants Miss Lee real bad. If she ain't found pronto, the reward will be raised to ten thousand bucks. Handbills with a description of her will soon be posted everywhere in Texas and even beyond."

"That's for criminals wanted by the law," Seth said. "I thought Voss wasn't charging her with a crime."

Hamlin grinned slyly. "Nope, he's callin' her a missin' person about whose welfare he's concerned. Good thinkin', ain't it?" He sauntered toward the door. "Adiós, all."

"Animal," Jenny muttered.

"Dangerous one," Seth agreed.

"You think he has her scent?"

"The monkey's, maybe. We better burn a sulphur candle."

"Camphor mothballs would be just as effective and less suspicious," Jenny suggested. "Puncture a box on the shelf and scatter a few on the floor over the trapdoor. Why is Roscoe Hamlin staying in town, anyway?"

"So Voss won't renege on any promises," Seth surmised. "That jackal will take the lion's share of the reward, no matter who delivers the prize. Meanwhile, he'll pocket some of the saloon's profits. Business won't be so good without the star attraction, but there'll still be plenty of patrons. The Silver Spur's the only watering hole for miles. Come Saturday night, Hamlin will be busy—and we'll have to make hay while the moon shines."

Sweet Jesus, Lacey prayed, shivering in her cloak. How much longer could she endure the strange, awful limbo?

Chapter 23

"I DON'T feel so damned good," Voss complained, as the doctor examined the wound. "Puked up my breakfast this morning, and I think I got fever."

Bert had already noticed signs of infection, including several ominous red streaks radiating from the wound. "You've developed some proud flesh, Mr. Voss."

"I always had proud flesh, Doc."

"It will have to be treated promptly."

"Treated how?"

"Well, medicine has failed. Cauterization is indicated now to prevent further spread of the poison."

Fear and bewilderment invoked fury. "Are you sayin' I might die from a little puncture? What the hell kind of medic are you? Men had gangrene in the war and lived."

"Limbs were amputated, or organs were removed," Bert explained. "Surgery isn't possible in

201

your case, and I can't see any advantage in waiting. I'll get some hot coals from the blacksmith—unless you feel strong enough to go to his forge with me. I have the necessary equipment in my bag."

"The iron? What if I say no?"

"It's my duty to warn you of the possible consequences, Mr. Voss, but the choice is yours. I never force anything on my patients, not if they're conscious and capable of making decisions."

"But you said the wound looked all right Sunday!" Voss accused angrily.

"That was several days ago. Things change, sometimes rapidly, and often for the worse. Unfortunately—"

"Unfortunately for me," Voss interrupted, "you're a goddamn quack! If I die, it's murder on that whore's head, and my boys will see that she hangs for it!"

"I was there when you gave your deposition to Sheriff Foster," Bert reminded him. "You declared it an accident and your own fault, remember?"

"I *lied*. I want to punish her myself. But she tried to kill me, and that's the truth, Doc. You got to tell the law that. You got to!"

Bert shook a couple of aspirins from a bottle, and handed them to Voss with a glass of water. "Swallow these, Voss. They'll help to lower your fever. Cauterization will probably keep the infection where it is." He waited while Voss gulped the aspirin. "Shall I send for the coals?"

Voss thrashed on the mattress, causing virulent blood to ooze through the fresh bandage. Pain stabbed his chest and he groaned.

"Lie still," Bert cautioned. "The more you move, the greater the risk of proliferation."

"Forget the medical yammering and fetch the blacksmith," Voss muttered. "Just one warning, Doc. If that hot iron don't cure me, you're gonna be wearin' a brand on your face!"

Dr. Warner had heard similar threats from sol-

diers on battlefields and cowboys on ranges, while
the irons heated on campfires. A strong-armed assistant would be needed to restrain Voss, and he
would have to find someone.

"I'll be back as soon as possible," he said, stepping
into the hall, where he spoke in Spanish to the Mexican chambermaid who doubled as nurse.

Felicia Perez nodded. "*Sí*, Señor Doc! I lock door,
not let out. Voss bad. Loco," she added, tapping her
head significantly. "But I no touch him. You bring
man help you, *por favor?*"

"I'll try, Felicia," Bert said, frowning.

The Duke Ranch supply wagon was just rolling
into town, the foreman at the reins. "Whoa!" Brant
commanded, halting the mule team.

Jumping off the seat, Brant hailed Dr. Warner
and removed a list from the pocket of his fringed
rawhide jacket. "Morning, Bert. Another order for
you to fill. I'll pick it up after I see Seth."

"I've got some healing to do first, Brant. You folks
at the ranch heard about Sully Voss, I presume?"

"Yeah, the vaqueros brought the news from Mission San Juan Sunday. The padre was saying Mass
when one of Voss's boys burst in and took over the
pulpit to announce the reward for Lacey Lee. A couple of parishioners wanted to shoot him for spitting
into the holy-water font on his way out of the chapel,
but Father Angelino forbade them. Not many folks
praying for Sully Voss's recovery, Bert."

"I suppose not, but even so, the high price on her
head makes the bounty hunters salivate."

Brant gazed at him intently. "Do you have any
clues to her whereabouts, my friend?"

"No. I practice medicine, not law, and I'm on my
way for a scuttle of live coals now."

"To sear a gangrenous wound?" Brant guessed,
long familiar with the treatment because of his time

in the war. "Well, sizzle him good, Doc, without the morphia. He deserves it."

"I could use some help with him, Brant, and his men are out on the hunt. How about you?"

"That would be a real irony, Bert. Your patient is living on borrowed time, anyway. If he survives, someone'll kill him soon enough anyhow."

"And his hired guns? Roscoe Hamlin is operating the saloon now, but I think his main interest is in the reward. A man could do a lot with ten thousand bucks, which is the new ante. Buy some land, maybe even reclaim the old family plantation."

"I gave up that dream long ago," Brant said grimly. "And I wouldn't betray my worst enemy to Sully Voss for all the stolen Confederate gold—much less for his tainted ten thousand Yankee dollars. That's blood money, worth the same to me as thirty pieces of silver."

Bert Warner smiled and clapped his shoulder. "I figured you'd say that. I was just playing Diogenes, hunting that elusive honest man. If you locate Miss Lee and need any help, you can trust me."

"Thanks, Doc. Somehow I knew *you'd* say *that*. Shall we go get those coals now?"

It infuriated Brant to see Voss in Lacey's bed, but no more than it incensed Voss to see his despised rival.

"What the hell are you doing here?" he demanded, glaring at Brant.

"I requested his assistance," Warner explained smoothly as he and Brant lifted the bucket of live coals to a convenient stand. Bert inserted a special instrument into the coals.

"To hold me down? I ain't no scared kid, and Steele better keep his distance."

"Gladly," Brant agreed. "Watching you suffer won't hurt me a bit."

Voss paled, his bravado receding as the iron was tested with a few drops of water.

"Not hot enough yet," the doctor decided. "The tip's got to turn white."

"Spit on it next time," Voss muttered.

"Allow me," Brant offered. "Are you sure you can take it, Voss? A hot iron can burn worse than carbolic acid. But then, I've always thought rapists should have both applied to their genitalia—along with a castrating knife."

"I never raped that bitch!" Voss bellowed.

"Only because she stopped you!" Brant controlled a violent urge to smash the bastard. "If you come out of this, Voss, you better start wearing a gun."

"Break it up!" the doctor ordered brusquely. "You can fight some other time." Another test of the iron showed that it was ready. "You want a whiff of ether, Voss?"

"Naw, just a big slug of whiskey," he growled, reaching for the bottle beside the bed and uncorking it.

Voss gulped rapidly, spilling some sour-mash bourbon down his chin and into the raw wound. He might have screamed, except for Steele's presence.

"Better bite on something," Bert advised. "So you don't chew up your tongue."

Scorning the towel Brant held out with a deprecating gesture, Voss muttered, "Get on with it, Doc."

At Warner's nod, Brant grabbed both of Voss's arms and held them hard behind his back. He wedged one knee between his shoulder blades, immobilizing the man.

Voss cringed, then bellowed in agony as the smoldering rod seared the festering flesh. The room was quickly filled with a putrid odor. The few seconds of treatment seemed interminable to the victim, who raged deliriously before the instrument was withdrawn. Bert plunged it into a pitcher of cold water, where it steamed and sputtered. Spitting bloody saliva from his mouth, Voss yelled, "You goddamn sons-of-bitches! I'll get you both for this. I better live! You hear me?"

Brant drawled, "I reckon the whole county heard your bawling, brave bull. You made more noise than the youngest calf under the branding iron. Biting a bullet would have saved your tongue, you know. And whether you appreciate it or not, Bert and I did you a great favor."

Voss's thick, sore tongue made him gag by then, and Dr. Warner knew that a depressor would be necessary to admit air to his lungs. Removing a teaspoon from his bag, he warned, "Either this, or I'll have to slit your gullet and stick in a reed for breathing."

Virtually helpless and in awful pain, Voss surrendered. Nothing could surpass the torment he had endured, but he refused to ask for painkiller while Steele was there.

"Think you can manage alone now, Doc?" Brant asked wearily.

"Yes, and thanks. I'll fill the Duke Ranch drug order soon as I can get to my pharmacy. I still have to clean and dress the wound again. The fingernail scratches and teeth marks are mostly superficial, but that little wildcat really fought him. The monkey too, I guess."

Brant looked hard at Voss and said, "Yeah, and he'll rue the day he tangled with her—especially if he doesn't cancel that reward."

His words hung in the air long after he had gone.

Chapter 24

SETH TRAVERS was working on his ledgers when the foreman of the Duke Ranch arrived. Unpaid bills from the previous year had brought him close to bankruptcy, but he steadfastly refused either to dun his customers or to refuse them further credit—even though some owed him two years or more. Balancing his books was a precarious feat, like walking a tightrope over a canyon. And though the reward money could have solved his problems swiftly, Seth never gave it so much as a fleeting thought.

The smooth, rich timbre of Brant's baritone voice thrilled Lacey in her cold, dark seclusion almost as much as if he were making ardent love to her. Oh, how she missed their lovemaking! The thought of never lying with him again nearly induced an emotional hemorrhage.

Garnet, searching the stockroom for a piece of fabric for a customer, emerged clasping the bolt of cloth in her arms. Her eyes flashed toward Brant, then shyly away.

"Good morning, sir."

Brant smiled, sweeping off his Stetson and laying it on a counter. "The top of it to you, ma'am! You're looking better every day."

"Feeling better, too," she responded, as Señora Galvan examined the material. The cloth was an Ashley Mills product, and Garnet was very proud of its fine quality and the distinctive trademark on the selvage. "Tissue gingham, señora. Soft as silk."

"Sí, madama," she agreed. "Muy bueno! I buy for my daughters, Lola and Juanita. Many yards."

The garbled Spanish-English conversation amused Brant, although he knew Garnet would be embarrassed and resentful if he commented on her newly acquired Texas lingo and mannerisms.

The sale was completed, including the appropriate spools of thread and a couple of paper patterns, and Señora Galvan left happily.

When the three were alone, Brant addressed Seth. "I heard about the excitement here Sunday and saw some of the posters around town. Anything new?"

Seth nodded. "Give me a hand with these sacks and crates, Brant. My niece will keep watch."

Brant had solved the mystery before Seth's signal to the fugitive brought a cautious lifting of the trapdoor. In a moment, Lacey's eyes gazed up at him pathetically.

"My God!" he exclaimed. "How long have you been down there?"

"Since it happened," she answered. "I didn't know what else to do, Brant. These kind folks took me in — and now we're *all* in a jam."

"Jesus," Brant swore softly. He ought to have killed Sully Voss long before. Instead, he had probably helped save the bastard's worthless life.

Seth said, "I saw you and Bert carrying a pail of hot coals to the hotel, Brant. To burn out the wound?"

"Yes. Voss'll probably live."

Lacey trembled. "Lord have mercy, I'm doomed! Lollipop, too. Voss will dash his brains out, because he bit and clawed him. Both of us fought that beast, tooth and nail. But he's strong and wary, and I never could kick him where it'd do the most good. The scissors were my only chance."

"I know, Lacey. I'm just sorry Voss isn't dead and in hell where he belongs."

The monkey was quite subdued now, hiding his face against his mistress's bosom. "You got to forgive the way we look and smell," she apologized, embarrassed. "It's close quarters down here."

"Never mind that," Brant said gently. Garnet averted her eyes from what appeared to be a lovers' reunion. "Lacey, don't despair. We'll get you out of this somehow."

"I been praying you'd come, darling."

The passionate endearment seemed to humble Brant, for he pressed Lacey's hand and uttered consoling words. The tenderness irked Garnet, who sharply announced that someone had just stepped out of the Silver Spur. Then she gasped, "It's Roscoe Hamlin—and he's coming this way!"

Instantly Lacey retreated and Brant and Seth replaced the obstacles over the trapdoor. When Hamlin entered, both men were leaning on a counter, feigning study of the long Duke Ranch list. "I don't believe I got all this in stock," Seth said before looking up. "Oh, hello there, Roscoe! You run out of chewing tobacco? Lemme check the case. Brown Mule, right?"

"Yeah, but I still got a few plugs left." He shifted the quid in his mouth so that one cheek bulged like a grotesque boil. "I noticed old man Duke's wagon out front and just wanted to thank his ramrod for helpin' the Doc with Sully."

"No thanks necessary," Brant said, scorning the proffered handshake. "I was obliging the doctor, not the patient. That should have been your job, Hamlin."

"I was busy in the saloon, checking stock and such. We're running low on booze. The new shipment better get here before Saturday. There's only three casks of red-eye whiskey left."

"Dilute them with twice the usual amount of branch water," Brant suggested smoothly, "and you'll triple your slop stock and your profits."

Hamlin's grin revealed large, darkly stained teeth and several gaps in the scurvy gums. "I reckon we won't be havin' the displeasure of your company no more, Steele, now the queen of the saloon entertainers is gone?"

"Depends on the new entertainment," Brant lied.

"Well, the other gals are practicin' new acts, but I got to admit they lack...talent. Betty Lou sings like a caterwaulin' cat, and Sue Anne dances about as gracefully as a hobbled heifer. I'm gonna have to advertise in San Antone and Dallas for somebody new and special, if that runaway witch ain't found soon. That's the real purpose of the generous reward. Sully don't want to harm her—just force her to work for him till she's old and ugly."

"Which would be the ultimate punishment," Brant surmised. "No doubt she'd prefer to die."

Hamlin laughed, spewing thick brown spittle in the region of the cuspidor. "Maybe—but why should Voss make it easy for an attempted murderess? A few lashes with a whip now and then would keep her in line. Ain't that how you Dixielanders controlled slaves? I bet you flogged your share of darkie bucks on your plantation and fooled with plenty of your black wenches."

Brant's anger was instantaneous. "Another effrontery like that, Hamlin, and I'll demand satisfaction!"

"You challengin' the top gun in the county to a duel?"

"How long since you've tested that reputation, top gun? Ten years? You're over forty and your hands have the liquor shakes. You've been bluffing on past performances, if not downright lies, which you pay others to talk around."

"Oh, that's good!" Hamlin goaded. "But my nigger remarks didn't rile your Southern blood, Steele. Your dander's up over Lacey Lee. I reckon you miss what she's been giving in bed. I don't blame you."

"Choose your weapon, Hamlin."

"I'm wearin' it. Unless you figure to use one of them French duelin' pistols?"

"Name the time and place," Brant growled.

Garnet glanced anxiously at Seth, who raised a calming hand. "Hey, now, fellas, take it easy. No harm done. You can settle this peaceably."

Hamlin scoffed. "Afraid I'll spill his guts on the square, Travers?"

"Nope, afraid he'll spill yours," Seth temporized. "Don't you realize, you old braggart, that Steele's got you bested in age and experience? He's younger by at least a dozen years, and he was in the Confederate cavalry. You ever heard of a trooper—especially one of ours—who couldn't shoot fast and straight?"

Hamlin hitched up his twin holsters, which hung below his heavy paunch, and endeavored to inflate his sagging chest. His challenger was tall, slim, broad of shoulder and narrow of hip, with a firm jawline and keen, clear eyes. He always seemed alert, with no hesitation in his movements.

Hamlin's dewlaps quivered. He waited, hoping the peacemaker would interfere again, or that Mrs. Lane would protest this barbarous means of settling male disputes. Obviously Steele would not withdraw his challenge, and for Hamlin to renege would brand him a coward. He spat again, wiped his mouth, and muttered, "Let's get it over with, Steele."

"Hold on, Hamlin!" said Seth. "This is gonna be done fair and square, or not at all."

"What're you, his second?"

"I'm talking rules and regulations, Roscoe! Honor, too. No tricks. No cheating. I seen you duel before, and you got the scruples of a bandit in ambush. But if you jump the count this time, I swear I'll blow your head off myself. I want witnesses and the Doc present. And you'll be allowed one gun only, like your opponent. That's the correct standard. Savvy?"

Beneath the floor, Lacey struggled to suppress a cry of caution to Brant, and in her anxiety she clutched Lollipop so tightly that he squeaked in protest.

Hamlin spun on his heel, eyes darting suspiciously. "What was that?"

"What?" asked Seth nonchalantly.

"I heard a squeaky noise."

"Your dry bones creaking and quaking," Brant scoffed, beckoning him toward the door. "Come on, top gun!"

The principals were quickly outside and striding toward the square. Seth grabbed his hat and coat and shotgun. Astonished at the rapid movements, Garnet cried, "The hot-tempered fools! Stop them, Uncle!"

"Can't honey. It's gone too far. Neither man could stop now without losing face."

"That's better than losing your life! This is insane! They'll kill each other."

"That's the object of a duel, girlie. Stay inside, if you can't bear to watch. I got to go now."

Garnet beseeched her aunt, who was standing, stunned, on the kitchen threshold. "They're going to fight on the square, Aunt Jenny!"

"I'm sure Brant is capable of defending himself, Garnet. Seth will see that it's an honest contest— and so will I," Jenny declared, removing a loaded rifle from the gun rack and rushing outside.

Garnet was wringing her hands despairingly, when Lacey's muffled voice called, "Garnet, go tell your uncle to search Hamlin! He carries a concealed gun—a derringer—usually in a special sleeve-pocket. Sometimes in a boot instead. He'll cheat!"

In her haste, Garnet tripped on her long skirts, nearly stumbled, and finally reached the square. She saw that her message was unnecessary.

Aware of Hamlin's treacherous ways, Seth was making a ceremony of frisking both contestants. Locating Hamlin's hidden weapon, he scowled and tossed it aside.

"You're a disgrace to Texas, Roscoe Hamlin!"

"I forgot about that little toy," he shrugged.

"Like hell you did!"

Jenny had summoned Dr. Warner and John Bream, the blacksmith, as witnesses, and soon other folks, mostly male, converged on the square. Accustomed to impromptu gun battles incited and generally decided by the fastest draw, a formal duel was a curiosity. Wagers were made on the outcome.

"Five bucks on Hamlin," one old-timer gambled.

"Ten on the Louisianan," said another.

A third gambler offered to cover them both.

Seth clarified the rules again. "All right now, you fellas will start back to back, take ten paces, turn, and fire on the count of three. Bream, can you count that high without stuttering?"

"I—I ain't sure," the blacksmith stammered.

"I'll officiate," the doctor volunteered. "Will either contestant be satisfied when blood is drawn?"

Brant deferred to Hamlin, who growled, "Shit, no! It's him or me. And we're using pistols, not swords, Doc!"

"So be it. Gentlemen, take your positions!"

Garnet shivered. She had forgotten her wrap, and the north winds whipped her black gown above her ankles and fluttered the ruffles of her petticoats. She tried to catch Brant's attention, to convey her best wishes with a look, but he was intent on Hamlin. All her grievances against him suddenly vanished, and she prayed fervently for his safety. As if in a trance, she watched as the men touched backs and began the formal forward pacing. Then they turned and faced each other, arms akimbo.

"One!" Bert counted.

Pistols were removed from holsters.

"Oh," Garnet murmured, "I feel faint, Auntie."

"Shh," Jenny cautioned. "Don't distract Brant."

"Two!" the physician shouted.

Weapons were raised and aimed. But the third command, "Fire!" was not completely issued before Roscoe Hamlin fired—and missed.

"Trigger-jumper!" Seth yelled, cocking his shotgun. "Yellow-livered coward!"

Brant had already shot the pistol out of his antagonist's tremulous hand, wounding several knuckles. But instead of seizing what was by then his rightful advantage, he lowered his weapon and allowed Hamlin a chance to retrieve his.

"Pick it up, top gun!" he called. "I hear you're ambidextrous! Prove it now!"

"Why, he's daring him!" Garnet gasped, and was sternly rebuked again by Jenny.

Grasping his revolver in his jittery left hand, Hamlin aimed and squeezed the trigger. His vision was blurred by fear and fury, and the wild bullet barely grazed Brant's fringed jacket sleeve. Simultaneously, Brant returned fire, knocking his gun to the ground again.

"Is it still you or me, top gun? If so, where do you want it—in your heart or your head?"

Speechless with humiliation, Hamlin ambled slowly off, dripping a trail of blood all the way to the Silver Spur. He could not bring himself to glance up at the hotel window from which Sully Voss had surely witnessed his shameful defeat.

Assured that Steele was unscathed, Dr. Warner went to attend the loser.

Brant sheathed his weapon. Only then did his

grave eyes seek Garnet's eyes, which glistened with tears of relief. He did not speak, and Garnet was so immobilized that Jenny had to help her move along to the Mercantile Mart.

Seth was saying, "You should've sent Hamlin to boot hill when you had the chance, son."

"I think he's fairly harmless now, sir, besides the fact that he may end up with a few stiff fingers on both hands. His pride will suffer the most."

"Yeah, and lots of folks will be grateful to you for plucking that old rooster's tail feathers. In your place, he'd be strutting and crowing. Believe me, he'd have plugged you in a vital spot if he could. I wanted to shoot him for jumping the count, and I don't see how you could restrain yourself when he did."

"I expected it, Seth. I was prepared. Men of his caliber don't know the meaning of the *code duella*. His temper and his nerves defeated him."

Seth indicated the grazed fringe on Brant's raw-hide jacket sleeve. "He could've clipped your right wing, though. Don't be so danged modest about your victory, man! Let's celebrate with a jug."

"One drink will be enough," Brant smiled. "Voss's top gun may be out of commission, but others are looking for Lacey. We have to get her away somehow."

Dismayed that his primary concern was once again Lacey, Garnet said sarcastically, "Congratulations, Mr. Steele, on sparing a drunken lout's life! Would that you had been so gallant, so compassionate with your young war prisoners!"

Stung, he did not reply.

But Jenny was shocked into reprimand. "How unfair, Garnet! Apologize to Brant."

"I will not!" She set her chin obstinately as they all stepped onto the porch and entered the store. "You can come out of your hole, Miss Lee!" she called loudly, making her feelings clear. "Your hero is here!"

After the cases were moved aside, Lollipop scooted

up the ladder, his mistress swiftly behind him. Lacey embraced Brant and covered him with kisses. Picking up her exuberance, the monkey chattered and danced around as if they were on stage.

"Oh, my brave darling!" Lacey cried. "I died a thousand deaths hearing the shots!" Then she saw the torn fringe. "Are you hurt?"

"No," he replied, sheepishly disengaging her. "But Doc Warner has another patient."

"You should have killed Hamlin!"

"My sentiments exactly," Seth concurred, fetching whiskey and glasses. "Don't worry, though. Roscoe won't be much use to anybody as a hired gun now."

"Good!"

"Good?" Garnet echoed jealously from her position at the window. "Do you enjoy having men spill blood over you?"

Jenny intervened diplomatically. "The ladies will have coffee and cake. Come, Garnet, help me serve."

Her niece followed reluctantly, anticipating another scolding in the kitchen.

"You're behaving shrewishly, Garnet. If you can't curb your jealousy, at least try to control your temper."

"Jealousy?"

"Of course! When will you stop lying to yourself? You were just as concerned about Brant as Lacey was, and you should have shown it. It would have meant so much to him, Garnet, to know you cared for his safety. Instead, you insulted him—and wounded him. Seth was astonished, and I was appalled."

"I'm sorry, Aunt Jen, but what difference does it make? Brant was fighting for Lacey, not *me*. It was Hamlin's comments about *her* that provoked him."

Jenny, slicing a sponge cake, sighed. "You can't be that obtuse, Garnet! Surely you realize the challenge was a ploy to maneuver Hamlin outside before the monkey could betray us all?"

Garnet went silent, feeling naïve and stupid. How could that obvious tactic have escaped her?

"I—I guess I'm not very bright, Auntie."

"Just blind sometimes, dear, and too stubborn for your own good. Brant Steele is a true hero. He's quite a man, Garnet. I doubt you'll ever meet another one to compare."

"You're always singing his praises, Aunt Jenny. Maybe we should blow a trumpet before rejoining him?"

"I would, if one were handy," Jenny smiled, indicating an old cowhorn on the wall. "Shall we try that?"

"Oh, you're impossible!" Garnet chided, smiling as she filled the sugarbowl and cream pitcher. "Pour the coffee and come along, before Uncle Seth gets tipsy congratulating our Southern cavalier!"

Chapter 25

BRANT remained in town the rest of the day to discuss Lacey's crucial situation. Hating her close confinement, Lacey welcomed the respite, and the monkey was exuberant over his freedom. Watching him run to Brant for kind words and comforting pats on the head, Lacey realized that she was more enamored of this heroic man than ever. She sensed a definite change in Garnet's attitude toward Brant, too.

The genteel Connecticut Yankee was observing her former wartime enemy with far more admiration than before. And there was yet another emotion in her expressive eyes, one which the experienced Lacey recognized as genuine jealousy.

Garnet obviously desired a successful escape for their guest, so desperately, in fact, that she sanctioned proposals formerly regarded as too difficult or too risky.

"What's wrong with Uncle Seth's original idea of taking her to Mission San Juan?" she asked firmly.

"Too suspicious at night," Brant replied. "A bounty hunter might challenge us on the way."

"Shoot him before he has a chance!" said Garnet, astonished by her ruthless remark.

Brant gazed at her curiously. "Are you serious?"

"Well," she relented, abashed, "I mean, you wouldn't have to wound him any more than you did Roscoe Hamlin. Just put him out of business."

He disagreed. "On the contrary, we might have to silence anyone chasing us permanently, my dear. And what if there's more than one? Some bounty hunters form posses, and others hunt in packs as indiscriminately as coyotes. No. But I have another idea that might work."

Lacey's eyes glowed hopefully. "What?"

"A mock funeral."

Her jaw dropped.

"I said 'mock funeral.'" Brant rushed ahead. "It's a method of smuggling contraband and was frequently used by Southerners, both military and civilian, during the war. The enemy usually honored a funeral procession—and we managed to transport some high-ranking officials to safety. Of course, there were always some actual corpses around to confuse them."

The explanation rekindled Garnet's anger. "It didn't succeed with your President Jefferson Davis, when he tried to leave your flaming, defeated capital in a hearse! The coward was captured just outside of Richmond and now he's in Fort Monroe prison, waiting for his trial. I hope he's found guilty of treason and hanged!"

"We're all aware of that, dear," Jenny soothed. "But I'm not sure I understand, Brant."

Seth explained. "It's fairly simple, Jen. All we need is some cooperative folks and a fake-bottomed vehicle to haul the coffin."

"Empty coffin?"

"No, a live body."

"It sounds diabolical," Garnet remarked.

"Not to me!" cried Lacey, "I think it's a heavenly idea!"

Seth deferred to Brant. "Tell 'em, son."

"Well, we have the necessary vehicle at the ranch," Brant began. "It's used on cattle drives to carry extra arms and ammunition, money, and other essentials. And there's always a spare coffin in the carpenter shed. Several small holes can be drilled in it to let air in."

Lacey's throat had become dry and tight. "Me? In the coffin?"

"No, you'll be stowed in the false bottom. I'll ask one of the vaqueros to be the corpse. The lid of the box will be nailed down, but only until it's delivered to the padre for burial."

Jenny frowned. "It seems complicated."

"Not to Mexican Catholics," Seth said. "They call their cemeteries *campos santos,* which is spanish for sacred ground. They believe that, in order to save their souls, their bodies must be buried in earth that's been consecrated by a bishop. The only sacred cemetery in this area is the one at Mission San Juan."

The scheme still seemed too bizarre to Jenny, and Garnet was just as dubious. She asked, "Will there be a mock burial too?"

"Only if we have to have one—and the grave will have to be prepared for that. People survive burials in coal mines, don't they? Our 'victim' will be rescued as quickly as possible. He'll be sleeping comfortably, in a trance which will look like death, should anyone be suspicious and ask to view the body." Observing their puzzled expressions, Seth continued, "He will dose himself with a hypnotic drug used for centuries by Mexican Indians in medicine and in their religious ceremonies."

"Oh, Lord," Jenny sighed. "How little we know of this strange land!"

"And not much time for learning right now, either." Seth addressed Brant. "Who did you have in mind? Julio-Bear?"

"Yes," Brant nodded.

"What an odd name!" Garnet exclaimed.

"He's a half-breed," Seth informed. "But that's another tale, which I'll save for later. We'll let Brant handle it from here on. He's had more experience with this sort of thing during the war."

"Camouflage and trickery?" Garnet murmured.

"Survival," Brant said seriously, then turned to Lacey. "Do you understand your role?"

She nodded. "I'll be in a real-life drama."

"Lollipop will have to be sedated, of course. Julio-Bear will know what to do. We'll try to make it comfortable for both of you, but it won't be easy. If you'd like some sedation too, I'm sure Doc Warner will have something."

Lacey saw an opportunity to test her theatrical ability. "No! I want to be awake. But even if this works, Brant, what then?"

"The padre and Julio-Bear will figure something," he answered confidently, standing abruptly. "First we have to get you to the Duke Ranch. Would you prefer to go in a sack or an empty barrel?"

Lacey chose a barrel, afraid that a flexible container might injure Lollipop. "It's gonna be a tight squeeze, though," she said, as the men decided on a flour barrel. They helped her into it, then handed in the monkey.

Brant grinned, advising, "Don't breathe deeply until we're out of town. Lucky it's an extra-size barrel, or your 'baby' would have to travel in a nail keg. Get him some food, Garnet. Candy and dried fruit, if you have any."

Garnet quickly found a fresh apple, two slices of bread, and three flavored suckers for the monkey.

Then Seth brought a hammer and nails from the hardware section, ordered Lacey to scoot down inside the barrel, and fastened the lid loosely. The two men carried the stowaways to the wagon and loaded on crates and gunnysacks of supplies, while Garnet and Jenny reconnoitered the town.

"Any spectators?" Brant asked under his breath, before boarding the wagon.

"Just the cow and chicken owners," Garnet replied, "and they're not watching."

"The funeral procession will leave the ranch early tomorrow morning," Brant said. "If you folks want to join it, be there by eight o'clock." He tipped his hat, picked up the reins, and the mule team started off. "Adiós."

The setting sun cast shadows across the wagon and the wintry square. Soon the prairie cattle would begin their mournful twilight lowing. Sober citizens were already in their homes, preparing for supper, and in the saloon, the girls prepared for the evening patrons.

The temporary boss of the Silver Spur sat morosely near the plate-glass window, gulping whiskey and contemplating his wounded hands. Voss would surely demote him and maybe even fire him. Sully had no sympathy for failures. His hireling knew that as surely as he knew his injuries would always affect both his shooting and his fighting, making him practically useless as a bodyguard.

Worse, his premature firing had branded him a coward in front of witnesses. Even the barmaids shunned him already, and their whispering and giggling infuriated Hamlin.

"More liquor," he shouted at Sue Anne.

"Soon's I shine these glasses," she drawled, employing the dishcloth as leisurely as she dared.

"I want it now, you slut!"

She obeyed, but Roscoe knocked the bottle of diluted red-eye to the floor, where it crashed. "You know I don't drink that slop!"

"Sorry, but Mr. Voss sent word to conserve his private stock, Mr. Popgun—I mean *Top*gun. We can't serve you the best no more. Whyn't you go talk to him at the hotel? He may have new orders for you."

"Yeah? They'll keep. I'm still in charge here, so get your lazy ass back to work! Bring me some Tennessee sour-mash, and then clean up this mess."

Sue Anne smiled cynically and sauntered back to the bar. "After I finish what I'm doing," she said, picking up a glass.

Betty Lou emerged from the improvised dressing room in one of Lacey Lee's costumes. "How do I look?"

Roscoe scoffed. "You ain't got the face, figure, or talent for that dress. Neither of you tarts could draw flies, not if you stripped naked and smeared yourselves with honey."

"Same to you." Betty Lou thumbed her nose and raised her finger to him.

Hamlin drained the rest of his drink. He still hoped to hang around the Silver Spur long enough to fill his saddlebags with money. Sully Voss was too obsessed with finding the Wickedest Wench in the West to trail Roscoe Hamlin. Or so Hamlin hoped.

Brant had liked Julio-Bear from their very first meeting, and he knew the Dukes trusted him absolutely. His story was familiar to every native in the county.

Disowned by their respective families because of their interracial marriage, Julio-Bear's parents had gone into the wilderness to live as best they could. By a fish-filled stream, they built a teepee from deer hides. Taught by his Indian father, Red Bear, their son learned to hunt and fish early. Animals were trapped for their pelts, which were cured and sold or traded at a downriver post reached by canoe. His Mexican mother fashioned garments and moccasins from skins. The family slept on buffalo robes, keeping warm with them in cold weather.

They were a happy, loving family until the terrible summer day when three desperate men discovered their camp. War paint disguised their faces, but the desperadoes were not Indians. Nor were they Mexicans, although they spoke Spanish. They shot his father as Red Bear reached for his bow and arrow, then took turns raping Julio-Bear's pregnant mother. The boy, rushing to help her, was hurled against a tree and left for dead.

Barely conscious, Julio-Bear heard her screams and pleas as if in a horrible nightmare. A kick to her swollen belly finally silenced her. The teepee was robbed of its small cash horde, and the desperadoes rode off with the family's most valuable pelts across their mounts.

Julio-Bear buried his parents in the pit recently used to hold the pelts, covering them with leaves and fallen limbs to discourage scavengers. Afterwards, he sat for hours on the river bank.

He was thirteen, the age at which a pure-bred Indian would be put through his manhood trials. His Catholic mother had taught him much of her religion. She had also told him about the many Spanish missions in Texas and the kindly monks who would help people in need regardless of who they were. The orphan prayed that he would be able to find refuge.

"After weeks of wandering, wanting to die, I found Mission San Juan," he had told Brant. *"Mi madre,* she was so good—a saint. I never realized men could be so cruel to women. Even now, I sometimes hear her crying and begging them not to hurt her and the baby. The padre knows passages in Scripture to describe those beasts. He tried to help me forget with prayers."

"And education?"

"Sí. There were other converts at the mission, and

we all worked—men, women, children. We had schooling, too—lessons every day except Sunday. We learned in two tongues, though I don't speak so good English. But I love God and religion, and the statues of the saints in the chapel inspire me. They endured so much for their faith. My mother was a martyr to men's brutality."

"Many woman are, Julio," Brant said, thinking of the women cruelly violated during the war, especially the pretty young virgins. "Some of the atrocities I've seen would make me ashamed of my sex and the entire human race."

Once again, the two of them were in serious conversation. Brant apprised Julio-Bear of the trouble they faced.

"You know what those fiends did to your mother. Well, I want to spare Miss Lee a similar fate, Julio, and we need your help."

His dark, compassionate eyes and solemn brown face remained immobile as Julio-Bear listened raptly to the plan, nodding in agreement, apparently convinced that it could work. "When do we start?"

"At dawn, Julio. Do you think we can count on the other vaqueros to be our escorts?"

"Oh, sí! Two will ride ahead to notify the padre and dig the grave in the campo santo."

"Thank you, Julio. Now we'd better get some sleep."

"But, Señor Brant—the lady should be here already. And the monkey too, so we can prepare them."

"They're on the ranch now, my friend, having supper with their host and hostess." He smiled at Julio's perplexed look. "That flour barrel I brought back from town didn't contain flour...."

"Ah!" Julio grinned broadly, enjoying the coup. "Very clever, Señor Brant."

"Mr. Seth Travers and his relatives are our friends in this, Julio. And so are the Dukes."

This didn't surprise Julio-Bear, who had always been treated very well by the people he considered his new family.

"*Buenas noches, amigo.* I see you in the morning."

Chapter 26

EVEN as she dressed, Garnet was dubious about attending the mock funeral. Curiosity was an incentive, for she still could not imagine the travesty could be accomplished without mishap. But she also wanted to observe Brant's reaction to what might actually be his final parting with Lacey Lee. She would not admit her curiosity to her aunt and uncle, both of whom were determined to ride in the cortege from the Duke Ranch to Mission San Juan in order to lend assistance.

"Seth has the buggy ready, Garnet. Get your cloak and bonnet," Jenny urged. "If we're not there on time, they'll leave without us."

"I'm hurrying as fast as I can, Auntie. But won't people wonder why we're attending the funeral of a person we don't even know?"

"Except for us, only Dr. Warner is aware of the 'dead' man's identity and this plan," Jenny said.

* * *

The Dukes greeted Seth and his family with warm handshakes and an invitation to their hearty beefsteak breakfast. The breakfast would have to do them for the day. "Heaven knows, the poor padre can't afford to feed us," said their hostess, "no matter how long we must stay at the mission. He lives on donations and what he can produce, you know—and I've prepared a couple of baskets of food to give him."

Garnet ate more than she had expected to of the heavy, greasy fare. Washing it down with steaming black coffee that almost scalded her delicate throat, she marveled once again that so many Texans did not use cream or sugar. Cows, according to Seth, were more for meat than for milk, except for infants and sick folk.

Alma Duke was oddly garbed in a long hubbard of coarse black fabric, black leather boots, and heavy gloves. A Mexican mourning *rebozo* was draped over her head. Two female servants, similarly dressed and toting the covered baskets, were to ride in the back of a buckboard driven by their mistress. The master's gout and lumbago were acting up again, despite Dr. Warner's medications, but he refused to indulge what he called trifling ailments. Throughout the preparations, the demeanor of all the ranch employees was perfectly natural. No one would have suspected the drama going on at the Duke Ranch.

The pine coffin, bare except for a small hand-carved wood cross and some wild cedar greenery, was already loaded onto a large, false-bottomed wagon. Garnet assumed that Lacey and the sedated animal were also aboard in their places. Brant, busy, merely nodded good morning to Garnet before announcing that everything was ready. Realizing that he intended to drive the hearse, Garnet said unexpectedly, "It's rather crowded in the buggy with my folks. May I ride with you, Mr. Steele?"

"Certainly, if you like," was all he said, but his surprise was obvious.

At his signal, the mounted vaqueros formed an honor guard and the rest of the mourners followed. Only a few men remained to tend the ranch, and they stood with bowed heads, sombreros held over their chests, as the procession passed.

"Do they know the truth?" Garnet whispered to Brant.

"Most do, except for the range riders."

"Won't the others be suspicious when Julio-Bear is resurrected?"

"Probably. He'll certainly command respect—perhaps even reverence—until they realize he's not a ghost. Apparitions do sometimes appear to Catholics, you know."

"But what if Sheriff Foster or his deputy should drop by the Duke Ranch in our absence?"

"No reason for that, Garnet. The law is not searching for Miss Lee."

"Maybe not, but the bounty hunters are."

A cautious glance reminded her that Lacey was awake in the compartment. "Any betrayer would have to deal, not only with the Dukes, but with the angry spirits of Julio-Bear's ancestors. I think we're safe."

Garnet tucked her cold fingers under her wrap and tried to keep her teeth from chattering. "Why couldn't the sun be shining? Gloomy weather is an ill omen."

Brant laughed softly. "That's *gris-gris* talk."

"What?"

"Voodoo superstition. Many Louisiana blacks and some whites believe in voodoo. Some buy charms to ward off bad luck. Occultism is medieval, Garnet. Or do they still practice witchcraft in New England?"

"How should I know? I'm a Christian. But everything out here is strange and frightening, Brant.

What we're doing now, for example! It's weird, and I'm very nervous—but Aunt Jenny isn't."

"Good for her! I'm glad to have her on our side. She's very steady in a crisis."

"Gibraltar," Garnet agreed. "Like Father Angelino. I trust he's prepared for this?"

"The padre was warned, Garnet. You don't embark on a project like this without considering every possible contingency. I learned a great deal from my commanding officer, who believed that if anything could go wrong, it probably would. He was an intelligent man. So is the padre."

Garnet shuddered. "There's a mystique about that monk and the mission, Brant. I felt it when I was there. And I began to wonder about Catholicism. Do you believe their doctrine about Saint Peter?"

He shrugged. "I'm not a theologian, my dear. And why this sudden interest in religion?"

"Maybe I have a doomsday premonition about all this. Some of us should be reciting our *mea culpas*." She paused, twisting her hands under her wrap. "It was a dark day when I met you, Brant Steele! Nothing but disasters, with one or two exceptions."

"Like saving your life?"

"Don't remind me all over again. Aunt Jennifer does it often enough and, of course, considers me ungrateful. I'm *not* ungrateful!"

Brant did not reply. He was watching the lead guard, about a hundred yards ahead, who had just signaled an alert. "Brace yourself," he warned. "This could be another calamity."

A cavalry troop was galloping toward them, waving the American banner. Halting his company and the funeral procession, the officer called, "Captain Vance Morely, United States Army. Your name, sir?"

"Brant Steele, formerly of Louisiana."

"And of the Confederate Army?"

"Correct."

"What's your destination?"

"Mission San Juan."

Through her ninon veil Garnet observed the blue uniforms and yellow neck scarves, seeing Denny's face on every young trooper. Once again, hatred for his killers rose painfully in her breast.

"I presume there's a corpse in that box, Mr. Steele?"

"Inspect it yourself, sir, if you have no qualms about disturbing the dead."

"My mission concerns a massacre," Morely said, surveying the others in Brant's party. "A wagon train was attacked some forty miles west of here. There were no survivors, and more bullets were found in the dead than arrows. Guns are being smuggled to the Indians by various means—including coffins."

"We're aware of that, Captain. And I repeat, you are free to examine our cargo. The folks in the vehicle immediately behind own the Duke Ranch. I am their foreman. We are going to bury an employee who died suddenly of a strange, deadly malady. Father Angelino is expecting us, but we will wait for your inspection."

Morely appeared both embarrassed and afraid of contracting the fatal disease. After a few tense moments, he said, "That won't be necessary, sir. I'll accept your word. Forgive me for detaining you, but it's my duty."

Brant's salute was more habit than respect. "I understand, Captain. No offense. May we proceed?"

The captain nodded curtly, then gave his troop a signal. They moved on, leather creaking, harness jangling—sounds familiar to a former cavalryman. Brant's face tightened grimly as he remembered charges he had led against such horse soldiers, and the furious battles in which the bloody ground had been littered with fallen, screaming mounts and dead and wounded in both uniforms. What madness!

Garnet interrupted his reflection. "You're a cool one, Brant Steele! And smug, too. You fooled the Yankees. That pleases you immensely, doesn't it?"

"Not especially—although it wasn't the first time, Garnet. Beguiling the enemy was a vital skill during the war."

"And no doubt you possess a devilish penchant for it!"

They had traveled less than a mile before there was an even more ominous interruption. A pair of stragglers appeared from behind a clump of chaparral. Garnet's hands gripped the wagon seat. They were wearing bedraggled buckskins and scraggly beards, and smelled worse than their lathered horses. Reigning their mounts near the hearse, one of them challenged, "Funeral, eh?"

Brant eyed the man silently. Garnet quivered. Again she was grateful for the veil which hid her fear.

Angered by Brant's silence, the man's partner demanded, "You deaf, mister?"

"No, but you must be blind. Our mission is obvious, isn't it?"

He spat on a wheel. "Mind if we look at the body?"

Mr. Duke spoke up gruffly. "Not if you can identify it and yourselves beforehand. State the name of the deceased, declare your friendship, and we'll open the casket."

"We can't do that, old man."

"Then what do you want?"

"Oh, maybe money and jewelry."

"We have neither," Brant stated flatly. "Go find a stagecoach or train to rob."

"Hell, there ain't no trains in this part of Texas, and damned few stages! Besides, we're peaceful fellas. From Laredo. Heard about a big bounty offered by a saloon-keeper. We'd sure like to collect that reward."

"You and a hundred others," Brant drawled. "But as every scavenger knows, that woman has long since fled the state. If you doubt it, go talk to Sully Voss and Roscoe Hamlin in Longhorn Junction." He jerked his thumb in the direction opposite the town. "It's that way."

"Yeah? I got a feelin' you're tryin' to throw us off the track. How come you got six armed Mexicans guardin' a corpse? Is it the governor?"

"He's important to his family. Those men are his relatives. It's traditional for them to escort their dead."

"Ain't that nice? We're sort of sentimental that way too, ain't we, Brother Josh? My name's Linus. I didn't get your handles?"

"We didn't throw them."

"Well, mind if we tag along and watch the burial?"

"Not if you don't cause any trouble," Brant warned. "If so—" He gestured toward the vaqueros, all of whom were glaring at the saddle tramps.

"Naw, we're just driftin' and ain't got nothing better to do," Josh said.

"No surnames?" Brant questioned.

"Nope."

"It figures."

"You insultin' us, mister? We ain't bastards. We had a real pa—he used to be our partner, in fact. A rattler got him last year. And I still think something fishy is goin' on here. We're ridin' with you."

His brother nodded. The strangers trotted their animals to the rear of the cortege.

Garnet whispered tensely, "They don't believe you."

"They will," Brant assured her, "after the burial."

"Oh, my God!"

The outburst brought Linus forward. "What's the matter with her?"

"She's the widow, you fool!" Brant told him angrily. "Now get back to your place before you're shot!"

"Yes, sir. Sorry, ma'am. We didn't know." He tipped his filthy hat and retreated to the rear.

Garnet raged but kept her voice to a whisper. "Why did you tell him that?" she demanded.

"They're suspicious. Besides, it seemed logical. You're dressed for the part."

"But now I'll have to act it, too," she hissed. "Damn you, Brant Steele! Damn you, damn you, damn you!"

"Silencio, madama. Voices carry on the wind—and curses are unseemly from a delicate grieving lady. Besides, you don't have a Spanish accent. I would advise you not to speak at all in their hearing."

"Do I look Mexican? I have blond hair, violet-blue eyes, and extremely fair skin!"

"So do many Spaniards—particularly the true natives of Spain. Just keep quiet. You may weep, if you wish."

"Did I say it was a dark day when I met you? I was wrong, Rebel. It was the blackest day of my life."

"Sí, madama."

"Stop calling me that!"

"Would you prefer Señora Julio-Bear?"

"I would prefer to bury you, señor, for good."

Unperturbed, Brant reached over to pat her trembling shoulder consolingly, taking full advantage of the situation. Garnet fumed in helpless submission. Someday, she promised herself, someday she would even all her scores with this arrogant devil!

Chapter 27

IT was noon before they reached Mission San Juan.
Father Angelino, waiting for them in the belfry,
tolled the death knell. He went to meet them wearing
funeral vestments. After murmured greetings, he led
them to a prepared grave, like a gaping mouth dug
in the terra-cotta earth of the *campo santo*. Two diggers opened the log gates to admit the hearse.

"Two strangers joined us along the way," Brant
said quietly to the monk, who nodded in complete
understanding.

"Dearly beloved," he announced with beckoning
hands, "the interment will take place before Mass."

The drifters' suspicions increased.

"How come, Padre?" Linus inquired, stepping forward. "I thought you Papists done a lot of prayin' in
Latin and blessin' with holy water and ashes before
the plantin'."

"Burial," the priest corrected. "And you are cor-

237

rect—for usual cases. But this corpse has not been embalmed," he explained, his nostrils flaring suggestively, "and I understand the poor soul perished of smallpox."

"Smallpox? Jesus *Christ!* Why didn't somebody tell us that?" Linus exploded. "Get him in that hole and covered up! You folks should be quarantined! You're spreadin' plague around! Ain't you afeared of gittin' it yourselfs?" he cried, backing away from them. He looked again at the women and saw that they were all heavily veiled. He assumed then that they were concealing pockmarks. "I reckon some of you is immune," he said.

One young Mexican maid, plagued by youthful acne, lifted her *rebozo* briefly—and the drifters moved farther back. "Y'all ought to be in a pesthouse," Josh cried. "Linus, let's ride on!"

"Not so fast," Mr. Duke said, drawing his pistol. "You insisted on attending this service, and you're not taking to the saddle before it's over!"

The rationale behind this escaped Garnet, who was by then utterly bewildered by the entire farce. Perhaps Duke considered it a prevention against later investigations of the grave?

Father Angelino directed the pallbearers to carry the coffin to the site, where hemp ropes were placed beneath its head and foot. The coffin was slowly and carefully lowered into the freshly dug grave as the others stood silently by.

Remembering the numerous floral tributes always available in Avalon, Garnet thought how sad and bleak a funeral was in wintry Texas. Even so, it was probably better than the burial her darling Denny had received. She began to weep in deep sobs and might have collapsed, except for Brant's steadying. Her attempt to shrug him off was futile. Brant was persistent.

The mock wailing of the other females added to

Garnet's sobbing convinced the interlopers that they had been wrong: they were witnessing a real burial.

Father Angelino dropped the first clods of sandy soil onto the coffin. They thumped, disintegrated, spattering the wood like tears. A Latin blessing and the sign of the cross concluded the ceremony, and soon the mourners followed the priest to the chapel. The cowed strangers, ignorant of Catholic custom, bent to drink from the holy-water font in the vestibule.

"Crazy kind of fountain, ain't it?" Linus remarked to Josh, hanging back as the others filed toward the front pews.

"Yeah. Do you mind, mister, if we just sit in the rear?"

Mr. Duke, satisfied that they had been convinced and were intimidated, nodded permission and went up the aisle to join his wife.

"You believe there's really a pox victim in that box?" Linus whispered behind his hand.

"Well, it sure as hell ain't no live whore with a price on her head, brother! She'd have hollered bloody murder when that dirt started fallin' on her."

"You're right. We might as well mosey over to Longhorn Junction and see what we can learn."

Two vaqueros, serving as altar attendants, were lighting candles in preparation for the Mass. Votive lights flickered in small cranberry-glass containers before the graven images, some of which were so artistically painted as to appear alive in the shadowy atmosphere.

"Yeah, this place makes me jittery. It's spooky, with them plaster idols everywhere starin' at us! Notice how their eyes seem to follow you? Come on, we can sneak out quietly, before the priest begins the mumbo-jumbo."

This was the precise action Mr. Duke had expected from them, and everyone up front relaxed considerably. Demons were always uneasy in God's domain.

Lacey held her breath as boots crunched on the gravel past the improvised hearse. Dear Lord, how cramped and aching she was! Lying for hours in the same position had been agony. How often she had stuffed her handkerchief into her mouth to keep from moaning! She was nearly frozen, too, despite the blankets and the tranquilized monkey cradled close to her. She wished now that she too had swallowed some of the magic potion.

Just as it seemed that she could bear it no longer, that she must either scream or go mad, footsteps approached—and Brant's thrilling voice whispered, "Are you still with the living, lady?"

"Yes, but just barely," she called in a croaking voice. "Please, get me out of here."

"Soon as those hombres disappear, honey."

She was, as it turned out, too stiff to move, and Brant had to lift her out of the compartment. Lacey was in his arms, her head resting gratefully on his chest, when Garnet and the others emerged from the church.

Jealous rage assailed her, pricking at her like a devil's pitchfork, and she muttered fiercely to Jenny, "I was right, Auntie. He jeopardized all of us just for *her!*"

"He'd have done the same for any woman in danger, Garnet. For any man, too."

"No! He killed Dennis! You're wrong about him. You always have been."

Jenny sighed, glancing at Brant. "That was war, Garnet. *When* will you ever concede that?"

Shrugging, still glaring at the couple, Garnet turned to Seth and said, icily, "May we leave now, Uncle?"

"Not quite yet, girlie. Brant and me got some talking to do with the padre. Miss Lee ain't in the clear yet."

"She's been a millstone around all our necks," Garnet declared, and, approaching Brant, asked sarcastically, "Well, mastermind? What's your plan now?"

"First the pawn must be rescued," he replied. "Or have you already forgotten the hero of the drama?"

"I haven't," Lacey murmured.

Spades of sod were flying upward from the grave, and soon the workers were prising off the coffin cover. Still in a trance, the shrouded "corpse" was carried into the mission. The box was nailed shut again and promptly reinterred. A stick cross was placed on the loosely arranged earth. Only then were the tips of the long hollow reeds, for air, suddenly visible. Neither the Mexicans nor the Indians were novices at the extraordinary procedures.

Nor was the conspiracy over.

While his compadres supervised Julio-Bear's revival, Brant and Seth huddled with Father Angelino. The mission could not provide permanent refuge for the flamboyant entertainer and her unusual partner. Another subterfuge would be devised, and apparently only those three males would be privy to it.

Mrs. Duke and her maids had departed for the ranch, and the remaining three women were directed to a small chamber containing the barest essentials for human existence: a bucket of drinking water and a gourd dipper, a loaf of bread and some corn tortillas, and several Mexican blankets and serapes. The swaddled monkey was brought to his mistress, who gasped, fearing that he was dead. But the vaquero reassured her.

"Not dead, señorita. Just long siesta. He wake soon, but he no jump and play now. Maybe mañana."

Lacey smiled. "*Gracias,* Tomás. Thank the others for me, too, *por favor?*"

"*Sí*, señorita. I go now."

Jenny indicated the folded blankets on the floor. "Shall we be seated, ladies?"

"What austerity!" Garnet remarked, remembering that it had been the same on her first visit to the mission. "This monk does more than work, fast, and pray. He martyrs himself every day. I wonder why we can't listen to the men?"

"The less we know of details, the better for us," Jenny surmised. "That way, we can't inadvertently reveal secrets. This has been quite an experience, hasn't it?"

"One I could have done without," Garnet complained without thinking.

Lacey's humility and gratitude were poignantly pathetic. "I want to thank you again from the bottom of my heart for everything you did for me. Specially you, Miss Temple, for stitching up this dress and petticoat. Why, I'd be naked without them—and in the house of the Lord, too!"

"A pity He doesn't take better care of His abode," Garnet said, shivering as the frigid wind blew sand and dust through the narrow paneless windows. Guns had been fired from those windows when San Juan was a fort. "Must you hold Lollipop that way? You look like madonna and monkey!"

It upset Garnet that she and Lacey had come to this mission for similar reasons, for rescue, and were indebted to the same men for helping them. Brant Steele was certainly the gallant Southern cavalier, protector of females in distress, regardless of their morals or murderous intentions! But she realized that Sully Voss would never forgive Lacey as Brant had forgiven Garnet. The other woman was in far greater danger from her victim than Garnet would have been from Brant.

"You're awful quiet, Garnet," Lacey said hesitantly. "I hope I ain't offended you somehow."

Garnet huddled in her cloak, wishing she were

anywhere but where she was. "I'm just cold, Lacey.
You could freeze ice in this vault! It was summer my
first time here, and far more pleasant. The thick
adobe walls deflect the sun."

"And there was no price on your head," Lacey
added dolefully. "But you could set one on your
heart...if you cared."

Garnet thoughtfully spread a colorful serape over
her knees, toying with the fringe. "Neither my
heart—nor any other part of me—is for sale, Miss
Lee."

"Sorry, honey. I didn't mean no insult. You don't
know how much I admire ladies like you. Envy you,
too."

"I'm sorry," Garnet relented. "I was just babbling,
Lacey. It's a bad habit with me. Anyway, I'll be returning to Connecticut as soon as winter is over."

"You're lucky. I don't have any idea where I'm
going."

"Maybe north, too?" Garnet suggested.

"Why?"

"The cattle drive. You could be smuggled out of
Texas in a chuck wagon, or even the same wagon
that carried you here, with cowpoke bodyguards."

"Why, that's a brilliant idea!" Jenny exclaimed.
"I bet Brant has already thought of it and intends
to hide you here until after the roundup."

Hope flamed as brightly as love in Lacey's eyes.
"Oh, do you honestly think so? I'd go with him,
gladly—anywhere, any time, anyhow!" She clasped
her hands prayerfully and looked heavenward.
"Please, God, make it happen."

Displeased, Garnet regretted her suggestion. "That
won't be until March, and Father Angelino couldn't
risk his reputation by keeping a single woman at
the mission that long! No, I'm sure they're devising
another plan for you."

Julio-Bear's sudden appearance in the arched portal was as startling as a vision. Peculiar splotches

marked his face and hands, but his strong white teeth flashed in a pleased grin. *"Buenos días, amigas!"*

Lacey placed Lollipop carefully on the floor, stood up, and embraced him warmly. "You've risen from the dead, señor."

"No, señorita. Only from the grave."

Garnet was staring at him in genuine horror. "But you really *do* have the plague! And we've been exposed!"

He shook his head quickly. "No, no, *madama!* We fix last night, Señor Brant and me. If some curious ones had look in the box, they would have seen this." He grinned again. "I hear those two hombres act like scared coyotes when the padre say the cause of my death." He scratched off a dark, simulated scab, revealing healthy red-brown skin beneath. "Clay and sienna, see?"

Garnet heaved a sigh of relief. How many more shocks would she have before this nightmare was over?

Julio-Bear knelt beside the monkey to test its reflexes. Catatonic just a little while before, Lollipop now showed slight reaction. "A few more hours," he predicted to the anxious Lacey. "He behave a little loco for a day or two, señorita, then he be *bueno.* Don't feed him yet. Just give water. He be thirsty when he wake up. *Comprendo?*"

Lacey nodded. *"Muchas gracias,* Julio. You saved my life."

Anticipating Garnet's question, the man shook his head. "Do not ask, Señora Lane. You and your aunt must go soon with your uncle to the pueblo."

"Pueblo?" she repeated.

"Town," he translated. "Señor Brant will get Señor Duke back to his ranch. Most of the others are already gone. Señorita Lee will remain. I say *adiós* now." He waved his hand and left.

"Well! I supposed we're dismissed, Aunt Jen."

Garnet was affronted by their sudden, summary exclusion from the rest of the adventure. Hadn't they harbored the fugitive from the beginning, taking considerable risk? Were they not to be trusted with secrets anymore?

Jenny was on her feet, pressing Lacey's hand. "You've played your role magnificently, my dear, and I hope you continue to do so. I think great opportunities await you in your career. Do you happen to know the legend of Helen of Troy?"

"Greek mythology? Really, Auntie!" Garnet scoffed.

But Lacey surprised her. "You mean Homer? I never read the *Odyssey* or *Iliad,* but Brant talked about them when he was hiding me in the secret compartment. He called the wagon a Trojan horse and said he hoped the trick would work as well for us as it did for the Greek warriors. Is that what you mean, Jenny?"

"Precisely."

"Brant is real smart. He had all kinds of wonderful books in the library at Great Oaks, you know. He hated to sell them to strangers who might not appreciate them. That's why he offered them to your family free, Garnet. You mentioned that your pa loves rare books and manuscripts."

"Papa's a scholar," Garnet said proudly, "usually reading when he isn't working." A tentative pause. "Did Brant tell you that the Trojan War started because Helen of Troy eloped with her lover—and that it lasted ten years before that wooden-horse trick succeeded?"

"Brant and me ain't eloping, Garnet. But I reckon the war between Sully Voss and me could last forever—and he'll prob'ly hunt me for the rest of my days."

"Absolutely," Garnet agreed. "In your place, I'd book passage abroad as rapidly as possible." The ungloved hand she extended was chilled as much by her cool reserve as by the cold temperature of the room. "Good luck, Lacey. And Godspeed!"

"Thanks, honey."

Later, waiting in the buggy for Seth, Jenny admonished, "Your remarks were unkind, Garnet. And unnecessary. Lacey Lee is not a rival for Brant Steele's affections."

"What affections? You're always jumping to conclusions, Aunt Jenny."

"Am I?"

"Definitely! Elvira Schwartz and I are not competitors in any sense. That woman just chafes me and taxes my civility." She tapped her chin pensively. "Do you suppose Brant might really take her along on the trail to Missouri?"

Jenny shrugged. "Missouri or Mars—why concern yourself with their destination? Your own is more imminent, Garnet. Avalon, here we come, ready or not!"

"Why do you say that? Good grief! I'm not going home in shame."

"Who could tell, the way you hide your face in public? Felons on their way to the gallows wear black hoods."

Garnet clutched at her long, wind-whipped black veil, tucking it around her throat like a nun's wimple. "I'm mourning my late husband. And that's that."

"Yes, dear. But must you do it so dramatically? One actress in Brant's life is enough."

"Hush!" Garnet cried, covering her ears. "Just please forget Brant Steele!"

"Of course, dear. As soon as you do."

"I already have."

"And the moon is made of green cheese," sighed Jenny, as Seth joined them.

PART FOUR

Chapter 28

GARNET was putting penny candies into large glass apothecary jars—many-colored jawbreakers, gumdrops, lollipops, taffy twists, peppermint sticks, and licorice whips. The Mercantile Mart had received the largest shipment of confections since the war had curtailed sugar production over five years before, and children and their sweet-toothed elders would soon be delighted.

A small Mexican boy was literally drooling before the counter, and Garnet gave him a couple of free choices. He thanked her in Spanish for the *"dulces"* and ran happily out of the store, across the square, and down a lane to his family's adobe shack.

"You didn't mind, Uncle?"

"No, honey, I'd have done the same thing. Their little faces gazing at those goodies always melt my heart. And Fernando's folks are so terribly poor— they'd starve without the few pesos his mother earns scrubbing floors and doing laundry for the Longhorn Hotel. Not many rich people in Texas now, but I reckon the Mexicans are the worst off."

"And still the wagon trains keep coming—from North, East and South. It doesn't make sense to me."

"It does to the pioneers," Seth said. "They're thinking of the future."

Garnet opened another box of candy. As she worked, she hummed a sprightly frontier ditty, feeling better than she had in months. March had entered gently, signifying an early departure for her.

"Have you been outside this morning, Uncle?" she asked between verses. "It's spring!"

"False spring, child."

"False? It can't be! When Mrs. Henderson was in yesterday to purchase new fabrics, she said the prairie is already in bloom."

"That's right," proclaimed a familiar male voice from the portal, and Garnet glanced up at Brant Steele. "And I've come to prove it to you, ma'am!"

"I'm busy," she said frostily. "Besides, my uncle says the signs are false."

Seth chuckled. "I only meant this old codger ain't ready to shuck his longjohns yet, honey. I never do that till the mesquites bud. Them trees are smart enough to know when winter's really over. They rarely get nipped by late frost. They ain't as impetuous as the prairie flowers."

Garnet replaced the decorative tops on the jars. "The flowers aren't the only impetuous things in this territory, Uncle."

"Get your bonnet and a wrap," Brant said.

"Don't give me orders, sir! I'm not one of your hired hands."

"Please?"

"That's better."

She smiled and went to the living quarters, returning with the clothing. Both black, they had been borrowed from her aunt's wardrobe because the blue taffeta hat Garnet had tried to dye with haw juice was ruined, and so was a straw cloche she had painted with bootblack.

Brant hated the dreary garb, not only because it reminded him of his role in her widowhood, but it detracted from her youth and beauty. Her persistence in wearing black upset him as much as it did her family. "You don't look dressed for the season," he complained.

"Widow's weeds know no season," she replied cogently.

Brant escorted her outside. Garnet pretended to be unaware that the rig and roan gelding were the same equipage with which he had driven her to the bunkhouse last fall, where she had fired his pistol at him in a fit of fury.

They drove westward at a leisurely pace, and he spoke little. The wheels rumbled over a narrow wood bridge spanning a creek.

"Most bridges back home are covered," Garnet remarked.

"To keep the rain off the streams?" he joked.

"No, silly." She grinned. "To prevent the horses from seeing running water, which often frightens them."

"Not in the West. Here they often have to swim through raging rivers with loads on their backs. And wouldn't it be simpler to put blinders on your timid Eastern animals?"

"I like covered bridges," she countered defiantly. "I think they're picturesque."

"And so like dear old New England," Brant drawled.

"I knew we were going to quarrel! We're like flint stones, unable to strike together without sparks. I wish I hadn't come with you. Stop and let me out. I'll walk back."

"Hush," he soothed. "And grow up, will you? I never fancied courting children."

"I'm almost nineteen!" she cried, affronted.

"A mere child. I'm twenty-nine, thirty in a couple of months."

"An old man," she said tartly. "I never fancied old men, except as grandfathers."

"In that case, relax, honeychile. You should be safe enough with this decrepit old fellow."

"I'm not afraid of you, Brant Steele! If so, I wouldn't be with you now. I'm not stupid enough to put myself in jeopardy twice."

"You weren't in jeopardy the first time, Garnet. I had no intention of harming you. *I* was the one in danger."

"I don't care to discuss it," she declared abruptly, turning a haughty profile. "Where's the beautiful scenery you promised me?"

"All around you, my dear, but you have to take off your blinders to see it."

Despite her vexation with him, Garnet could not deny the beauty of the blooming prairie. If it did not compare with the New England countryside in spring, it was only because the landscapes were not comparable—and there was a vastness here that not even the great Connecticut Valley could equal. She caught the strong spicy scent of purple sagebrush, which thrived on the sandy flats as laurel and rhododendrons flourished on the hillsides at home. Bluebonnets rivaled the lupine of her native woods, and Indian paintbrush was reminiscent of the scarlet cardinal flower at the brook's edge at home. Lavender verbenas recalled the wild geraniums in the Avalon meadows. Buttercups and wild daisies were familiar, but she did not recognize the tiny tulip-shaped blossoms, like thimbles of burgundy wine, or the strawy flocked pink stars on short, stout stems, nor the ferny plant with furry amethyst puffs.

"Well?" Brant prompted, as proud of the glorious scene as if he had created it himself.

"It's pretty," she allowed, "if you like flat emptiness, cow chips, and cactus." She would give him no quarter.

"You had to say that, didn't you?"

"I forgot bleached bones."

"Is that a tongue in your mouth, or an arrow?"

"Provoke me enough, and you'll find out. But I'm not just being perverse, Brant. Our Berkshire Mountains and great river valleys far surpass these desolate plains. We have roads instead of uncharted trails, too, and farms and cottages."

"Civilization?"

"Yes. There's hardly a semblance of it here. What's that fuzzy plant with the thistlelike balls?"

"Loco weed. After eating it, cattle literally go crazy. They run around in circles bellowing and pawing, then get convulsions and die. That accounts for some of the skeletons you see. Ranchers lose a lot of stock to loco weed every year. We've lost our share."

"We?"

"The Duke Ranch. Rattlers coming out of hibernation have also killed some animals since spring began, and coyotes have gotten a number of newborn calves, too."

Garnet shuddered. "This is a fierce, cruel land!"

"Until you get to know and respect it," he agreed. "Certainly it's a challenge."

"And you like challenges?"

"Most men do, Garnet. Some women, too. I wish you'd change your attitude toward Texas. Why don't you stay at the ranch while I'm on the trail? Mrs. Duke would enjoy your company—treat you like a daughter. She could teach you a great deal about ranching."

"What for? I'll never need that knowledge. And I'd be even more miserable in that isolated place than in Longhorn Junction."

"Maybe not, Garnet. Maybe you only think so. Try it. Give yourself a chance."

"You sound like Aunt Jenny. She's beginning to

like Texas," Garnet marveled. "I've suspected it for some time, but she only admitted it to me recently. And though she'll go back home with me, she'll probably come back here. Can you believe that? She says Uncle Seth needs her, but that's not the only reason. She must have some Spartan ancestors. I think she actually likes living on the frontier."

"That's not so unusual, Garnet. Many ladies do."

She flicked dust off her black garments. "Probably only because they love some man here. Women are amenable that way, and they see it as their marital and biblical duty. 'Whither thou goest,' et cetera. No woman could really love it here, could she?"

Brant turned the rig to return to Longhorn Junction, and Garnet felt his disappointment. Had she spoiled his expectations? Was she supposed to apologize?

She affected indifference, concentrating on the scenery, just in case—as he had once said—she wanted something pleasant to remember about Texas. The wind was obligingly calm for a change, indeed rather balmy, and the warm sun gave no hint of the cruelty it would inflict come summer. It cast a golden glow over the land, and the spring moon was gilded at night.

"I thought we would ride longer," she ventured with an oblique glance toward him.

"It's just more of the same all the time, Garnet. I don't want to bore you."

Her heart leaped. His handsome, swarthy face was enhanced by the high-crowned, broad-brimmed hat, as was his tall, lean, muscular physique by the Western regalia. His spectacular virility would create quite a sensation in Avalon, and she knew that very well. There were females of all ages who would envy her his company.

"I'm not bored, Brant. And it's just high noon—we can go a few miles farther."

"Really?" He smiled. "That's the nicest thing you've

said to me since we met, Garnet. I was afraid everything about me either upset you or bored you."

"Not *everything*, Mr. Steele. And since we'll soon
be parting forever..."

"Why not be friends?" he finished, chagrined.

She nodded, but still refused to meet his dark,
piercing eyes. "Are we far from the Duke Ranch?"

"Not very. Would you like to go there and pick up
some mounts?"

"I'm not much of a rider."

"They have some gentle horses, and the sidesaddle
is not *de rigueur* out here. Many ladies ride astride,
in Western saddles. There's a big horn to hang onto."

"I'll think about it," she hedged.

"There's not much time, Garnet. We start roundup
in a few days. I'll be busy. My only next trip to town
will be for trail supplies."

She gazed into the remote distance, troubled by
feelings she could neither suppress nor truly understand. She was afraid that he sensed those feelings.
Why should she feel that peculiar distress, that tur-
moil at the very thought of their parting? Why, part
of her was even worried about his safety! What ever
was the matter with her?

"Will you pass through Indian country?" She managed a casual tone.

"Yes. The Oklahoma Territory is thick with them,
especially around the Red River. And there are many
tribes still living on the Central Plains."

"Have you ever fought any Indians?"

"Indians are just men, Garnet, no more savage
than other men when fighting for their survival. Any
soldier would agree. There's no such thing as a civilized war."

Garnet tensed, but didn't pursue it. "I suppose you
still intend to settle in Texas?"

"Are you interested, or just making polite conversation?"

"Both."

"Well, I hope to establish a spread with my earnings from the cattle drive. Mr. Duke is giving me a percentage of the proceeds, in addition to my salary. He'll sell me a part of his land to start—and maybe all of it one day. The Dukes have no living children, and therefore no heirs, and they're getting older."

"So the former planter hopes eventually to become a cattle baron? Rich enough to build a fine hacienda, travel in style, and buy anything he wants, including a wife, if he can't find a local woman to his liking. Well, if you ever happen to be near a hamlet in Connecticut called Avalon, pay me a visit, Mr. Steele."

He frowned. "Why?"

"Don't scowl—it spoils your good looks."

"Stop teasing me, Garnet. Why should I call on you in Connecticut?"

"Oh," she shrugged evasively. "I've never known a cattle baron. I might like to meet one someday."

"You know Mr. Duke."

"Is he a cattle baron?"

"Yep, more or less."

"You'd never guess it to look at his wife. She's as plain as homemade soap."

"Fine folks, though, and wonderful to work for. Aren't you even a little curious about a cattle roundup, Garnet? You missed the one last fall—and this may be your last chance to see one. Come out with your aunt, if not by yourself. I think Jenny would be interested."

"Probably." But she made no promises. And then Garnet surprised herself as much as him when she blurted, "If you want to stop at that—that cabin—while we're nearby, it's all right with me." She waited, tense. "Or did you intend to anyway?"

"I considered it," he admitted slowly, looking straight ahead.

"Did you ever take...*her* there?"

"Her?"

"Your sweetheart."

"Miss Lee was not my sweetheart, Garnet."

"What was she, then, if I may be so bold as to ask?"

"A good friend."

"Indeed?" she scoffed. "And have you heard from your good friend recently?"

"No, but it's only been a couple of months."

"Well, I trust she got away safely and is too smart ever to come back." She paused. "It seems so strange, though, that she could simply disappear without a trace—foiling all the bounty hunters! Almost as if Father Angelino had worked a miracle."

"Oh, I suspect the padre had some assistance other than divine," Brant said laconically. "Some practical experience, too. Churches of all denominations operated underground railroads for slaves, you know. The Catholic institutions in Louisiana were quite skillful. What better disguise than a religious habit? Lacey may be traveling as a nun, for all we know."

The supposition astonished Garnet. "If she plays *that* role convincingly, she could give Laura Keene competition on the stage!"

"That's not inconceivable either." Brant grinned, and Garnet realized that he knew more than he was admitting. Was he still protecting Lacey Lee?

"Oh? Am I underestimating her talents?"

"Perhaps."

"Well, I guess Sully Voss is a most beguiled person! Doc Warner said he didn't even ask the name of the 'deceased' in that pine box, after hearing that he was one of the Dukes' vaqueros."

"And wouldn't have cared, anyway. The bastard dislikes Mexicans, despises Indians, and has no feeling whatever for half-breeds. None of those races was ever allowed in the Silver Spur, not even recognized on the street. Besides, Voss's quarrel now is primarily with Roscoe Hamlin, who ran off with much of his boss's money. The law and bounty hunters are after a real criminal in Hamlin, and the stakes are much higher, too. A twenty-thousand-dollar reward."

"Yes, I've seen the posters," Garnet said. "I still can't see Lacey as a nun, though. Don't they have to shave their heads and bind their—their...?"

"Bosoms? I wouldn't know, my dear. A gentleman never asks. Could you see Miss Lee as a squaw with a monkey papoose?"

"You're joking!"

"No, that was one of the ideas, with Julio-Bear or another Indian as her spouse. Then Father Angelino said that the bishop was sending some sisters from a San Antonio convent to the mission, to discuss establishing a school."

"Why, they arrived in Longhorn Junction that same week in January, Brant, in a black-fringed surrey," Garnet recalled, "and departed immediately, after watering the horse and asking directions. Only the Mother Superior spoke to anyone. We assumed they were under vows of silence."

He smiled. "A teaching order forbidden to speak?"

"Of course not," Garnet murmured, comprehension dawning. "Lacey left with them, didn't she? In one of their habits, with Lollipop in a black carpetbag; I remember now. The curtains were down on the surrey, so no one would notice an extra passenger. How ingenious! I must tell Aunt Jenny. We've wondered."

"Well, it's over now, Garnet. Lacey's safe somewhere, and I think praise is due everyone involved."

"Including me?" Somehow, it was very important that he approve of her performance, too.

"I said everyone, darling."

Garnet looked quickly down at her hands, stilled by the endearment. She was getting very nervous, and she knew that the fluttering of her insides was not caused entirely by their nearness to the bunkhouse. No, it wasn't only Brant who was making her edgy — it was her own increasing warmth, her shockingly unbridled feelings.

She concentrated on breathing slowly and deeply, and she found that, in spite of her nervousness and horror at her feelings, she was eager to reach the bunkhouse, eager to be indoors with Brant. Whatever was the matter with her? she wondered. Or was it her doing? Perhaps Brant had cast a spell over her.

They were silent as he pulled the wagon to a halt by the bunkhouse and helped her down. She averted her gaze, but he understood something of what she was feeling. He understood enough. And when they stepped inside the shelter, he gently but very deliberately took her in his arms and pressed her close. They stayed that way for many moments, neither moving, before he bent down and, as gently as if she were a child, kissed her.

Very briefly, Garnet struggled with herself, but she quickly lost to overwhelming desire, and to discovery. She savored his ardent, probing tongue, relaxing under his boldly wandering hands. A delicious warmth spread through her, flowing like liquid fire. Exquisite manipulations were her first discovery, and, after a time, the igniting of wanton passion in herself was her second.

Garnet knew it would happen. With his assistance, she shed her mourning garments like a butterfly its outworn chrysalis. She lay on the bunk, thinking how odd it was that she had tried to kill him in this room, while now she longed only to make love with him.

And what Brant had told her long ago turned out to be true: Denny had been only a boy. She had known the love of an awkward, naïve adolescent, and this was a mature, worldly man. She and Denny had been timid, scared children indulging in what had seemed forbidden mischief, afraid to fondle each other's nightclothed bodies, to explore, to speak erotic words, to experiment with their own passion.

Not so as she and Brant rushed together in naked yearning, sensual touches, and deep, burning kisses, gladly given and gladly taken. Garnet pulled his head down onto her breast, and he knew instinctively what she craved. He knew, and his mouth and hands told her he knew, and finally her voice cried out to him.

"Yes! That's good! Oh, yes!"

"What's good?" he said, quietly but firmly.

"Playing with my—my bosom."

"Breasts. They're lovely, with sweet nipples—and you like them tasted."

"Yes," she whispered.

She moaned and trembled as he obliged. She kept her eyes closed, dismayed that she could not conceal anything from him. He ventured toward her quivering thighs, encouraging their parting, skillfully exploring her secret female treasures, freeing every desire. She gloried in the exquisite pleasure, in the torment, aching for desperate relief. It came at last, and was the most marvelous and triumphant of revelations.

Eventually, however, she had to look at him, and when she did, he smiled complacently, daring her to deny the truth. And whatever had possessed her all along still did so, for she smiled back, her violet eyes glowing intently and her fair skin flushed. She was radiant, wondrously happy.

"You're beautiful," he said admiringly, continuing to stroke her. "Your eyes are deep purple, just as I imagined they would be in passion."

"I can hardly believe what happened," she murmured. It still seemed a fantasy. "But you were right."

"You're not ashamed, are you?"

"I should be."

"Because you enjoyed love?"

"Well, after all—"

"After all, that's what sex is for," he interrupted. "Pleasure—for both people."

"I—I guess Denny didn't know that," she reflected, reluctant to betray his precipitous and selfish love-making. "We were so young and so...ignorant. We didn't know much about love, and nothing at all about marriage. But that's not news to you, is it? You were aware of that all along."

"Children can only play at love, Garnet."

"And married children merely play house," she said ruefully. "I still had dolls in my room, Brant!"

"Thank God they were only dolls, Garnet. You could have had a child."

"In Avalon, wives expect to become mothers," she said. "But I'm glad I didn't."

"So am I."

After a hesitant pause, she ventured, "Must you go on that cattle drive?"

"It's part of my job, darling, but we'll get married before I leave. The Dukes would love to throw a wedding reception for us at the ranch."

She pondered for a few moments, lying in his arms and gazing at the bare rafters. "We can't do that, dear. It wouldn't be decent."

"What?" he exclaimed, turning to stare at her.

"I was just widowed a few months ago."

"You were widowed over two years ago, Garnet!"

"But I didn't *know* it then."

"What difference—?"

"How would it look? People would think that I— I didn't love or respect my husband."

"That's absurd, Garnet! You mourned him long enough, publicly and privately. He's dead, and we're alive and in love. We've already proved that to each other. Will you let some stupid tradition keep us apart even longer?"

"The situation is so uncertain, Brant. What about the cattle drive? Uncle Seth says it's dangerous."

"I'll come back, Garnet." He smiled. "There are

many miles and obstacles between here and Missouri, I'll admit, but I'm not exactly a greenhorn. Don't worry."

Garnet sighed. "Just the same, I think we should wait, Brant."

"How long, Garnet?"

"A decent interval shouldn't work too much hardship on you," she cajoled. "We couldn't be together on the drive, anyway, so what's the hurry?"

"I want to know you'll be waiting when I return," he said in a determined voice.

"I will be, Brant."

"A promise is not a legal vow, Garnet."

"Don't you trust me?" She sat up and leaned over to look at him closely. "You think I might be unfaithful during your absence? Am I no different from the others? Do they all surrender so easily without a ring?"

Suddenly appalled by what she had allowed to happen, she scrambled off the bunk and hastened to clothe herself, fumbling with her lingerie.

Brant leaped up and caught her shoulders, shaking her slightly. "Stop this nonsense! You're being childish again. You were a woman a while ago— don't go back to being a little girl. I can't wait forever for you to grow up!"

"I'm not asking you to wait! You're free, no apron strings attached. Get dressed, for heaven's sake. What if one of the hands showed up?"

"I'll never understand women!" Brant muttered, releasing her and grabbing his breeches.

"Oh, I think you understand them well enough in bed! It's just outside of bed that you don't."

"Are you going to marry me?" he demanded, buttoning his shirt and tucking in the tails.

"Not yet," she answered, tying on a petticoat. "Maybe never."

He swore under his breath. "Garnet, be sensible!

I'll be gone for several months. We've just made love. Must I explain?"

"You said you were careful."

"That's a precaution, my dear, not a guarantee."

"I'll risk it."

"Goddamn it, Garnet, you're infuriating me!"

"Likewise," she murmured, donning her gown, then fetching her bonnet and shawl. "Will you drive me home, or must I do it myself *again?*"

Fastening his pants, Brant warned ominously, "You got lost the other time, remember? I wouldn't advise a second attempt." He jerked his boots up and buckled on his gun belt, adjusting the Colt .45 in the holster. "And if you decide to shoot at me again, don't miss—because your pretty little ass will be paddled raw!"

"Is that so? Well, if ever I aim at you again, Mr. Steele, I'll score a bull's-eye in your heart."

He looked up, hurt in his eyes.

"You already did, with that remark."

"But not fatal—it only wounded you."

"I swear to God, I never ran into a mustang filly harder to break."

"Hah! You had me saddled pretty good, cowboy! Now you'll have something to yodel about on the trail—how you seduced the proper Widow Lane."

"I ought to slap you for that," he said grimly. Why was she doing this to him?

"Cowmen don't brag?"

"Not this one," he said softly. "Not about you."

They both fell silent, and he followed her out of the bunkhouse. On the ride back, she kept as much space between them as possible.

Brant remained silent until they neared Long-horn Junction, and then he said quietly, "When may I see you again?"

"Why?"

"Good Lord! Why do you *think?* I'm in love with

you, Garnet. And I hope to change your obstinate little mind about a prompt wedding."

"Our quarrel has already decided me, Mr. Steele."

"Garnet, it's a lovers' spat, that's all."

"Speak for yourself, sir."

There was surely nothing to be gained by arguing with her just then, so Brant set his mouth firmly and kept still.

Chapter 29

M RS. DUKE'S invitation was delivered the next morning. "I think it will be interesting," Jenny told Garnet.

"Brant said you would feel that way. How long will you stay, Auntie?"

"A few days, I suppose. But aren't you coming? The invitation includes you."

Garnet was brushing her hair, wondering if it would be too frivolous to pin a black velvet bow in it. "Who cares about a roundup? It can't be anything but cattle and cowboys, neither of which interests me."

"Indeed? Then why did you spend most of yesterday with the foreman of the Duke Ranch?"

"He—he insisted on showing me the blooming prairie, as if it were El Dorado and the buttercups were solid gold!"

"Well, I accepted for both of us, Garnet. We can't

hurt Mrs. Duke's feelings. Just drive out with me—
you can plead a headache when we arrive, and stay
at the ranch house if you prefer. But you really should
take advantage of this opportunity. It's the last you'll
have out here. It'll be something to talk about when
we return to Avalon. Lord knows, the topics of conversation are limited there!"

In spite of herself, Garnet was tempted. A cooling-
off period had made her realize how silly she had
been. Brant had professed his love for her repeatedly,
and if her response to him in the bunk was not love,
then what was it? She blushed, reluctant to face him
again. Such wanton behavior was incompatible with
virtue and most unlike her. She could not reconcile
herself to it. But if she did not go, Jenny might draw
her own conclusions—and Garnet wanted to keep
the shocking secret to herself.

"All right," she sighed. "I'll go for a day and night,
but no more."

As was customary, the drive would be a communal
effort, with several outfits besides the Dukes joining
the drive. More drovers made for greater safety
crossing the Indian Nations. On the other hand, large
herds were prone to stampede, and finding forage
and water for large herds along the route presented
additional problems. Still, the hazards were out-
weighed by the advantages, and neighboring ranchers continued to drive north collectively.

Those who would participate in the venture were
busy organizing their roundups, branding as their
own any calves found with their cows and any mavericks running with their herds. All would soon as-
semble near the Duke Ranch, where trail bosses
would work out the final plans.

Every regular hand had a specific duty, and there
was extra hired help. Brant Steele was supervising
out on the range when the visitors arrived.

Their hostess, favoring her rheumatic knee, limped

out to the buggy to welcome them. "Howdy, folks! Sure glad you came! But mercy, you can't go out yonder in them city duds! The maids and I will fix you up in something suitable."

Suitable, Garnet assumed, was what Alma Duke was wearing: dungarees tucked into boots, a plaid flannel shirt and worn leather vest, bright bandanna, and the tall, sweat-stained hat which was the trademark of Texas cow people, male and female alike.

"Josefina!" Alma called, as they entered the main house. "Lupe! Where are you? I need your help!"

The domestics appeared like genies, smiling and speaking the little English they had learned from their mistress. Soon Garnet and Jenny were transformed. Garnet barely recognized herself in the mirror. The garments all but swallowed her, and she laughed, thinking that she resembled a hobo. Garters above the elbows shortened the sleeves of a faded shirt; the rough denim pants were held around her slender waist by a rawhide belt, and several pairs of heavy knitted socks helped hold the scuffed boots on her small feet. Padding inside the soiled felt hat prevented its falling over her eyes, the thick leather gauntlets fitted her dainty hands only because she wore her wool gloves underneath them. Garnet put on a scarlet cotton bandanna, intended to protect the face during sandstorms or blizzards. Sturdy canvas-and-cowhide chaps to guard against the harsh chaparral were last.

Being larger than her niece, Jenny looked better in her borrowed regalia and sported it jauntily. She coaxed Garnet, laughing, "Don't be shy, sweetie. You look cute."

"Cute? With a false nose and painted face, I could be a rodeo clown! And why must we ride horseback, Mrs. Duke? Couldn't we travel in the buckboard?"

"Not on that rough ground, gal, not unless you want to shake your guts to grits and foul up your female organs. Did Lupe give you a breast support?" At Garnet's nod, Alma Duke, never one to mince words, continued, "Any young woman who rides a horse without support is just begging for the flabby tits of an old cow. And here's some more advice I learned at your age, or younger: If your menses are near, jouncing over rough land in a saddle can bring that nuisance early. I told Lupe to stow some rags and safety pins in your saddlebag, just in case."

Taken aback by her candor, Garnet replied meekly, "I'm sure I'll be all right."

"Females ain't never sure of anything out here, honey. I miscarried on a horse once—didn't know I was pregnant. And Doc Warner claims rough riding delayed my menopause a couple of years, too."

"Are you going with us, Alma?" Jenny asked.

"You bet. Brant would never forgive me—or himself—if y'all got hurt."

This statement convinced Garnet that the Dukes had obliged their foreman by inviting them. Why else would this busy ranch woman want to bother with a couple of Eastern greenhorns? Jenny was a quick study and would learn surprisingly fast. She always craved new experiences. Garnet just hoped that her own presence would not create problems.

A young Mexican groom assisted Garnet into the big Western saddle, fitted her boots into the stirrups, and handed her the reins.

"Mossie's the gentlest mare we got," Alma said, looking on with a careful eye, "and surefooted as a mountain goat. Nothing much frightens her anymore, so she don't spook easy. But if she acts a bit ornery with a stranger, a yank on the curbed bit will settle her down nicely."

"Yes, ma'am."

Jenny was on a chestnut gelding, and Mrs. Duke mounted the piebald stallion she had mastered long ago. "Broke this brute myself," she said proudly, "and taught him everything he knows about working cattle. Rascal always wins the top prizes at the county fairs and rodeos."

Alma took the lead, pacing about twenty-five feet in front, and Garnet imagined that she could handle just as easily the six-shooter strapped around her waist and the rifle in her saddle scabbard.

"Couldn't they find a plainer hat for you, Auntie?" asked Garnet.

"I chose this sombrero myself. I admired the fancy braid and beadwork. Josefina said it's a dress-up sombrero, the kind the Mexicans use for their famous hat dance during fiestas. I'd like to have my picture taken in it."

"I feel silly in this outlandish costume," Garnet said, frowning. "I wouldn't want Mother to see me in it, or see me riding astride, either. It's so indelicate."

"But practical, dear. The horses have to pick their way through brush and rocks—imagine trying to stay on with only one leg hooked over the horn! Mrs. Duke is an excellent equestrienne, isn't she?"

Long before they reached the camp site, they smelled smoke and heard cattle bellowing, horses whinnying, and men yelling. Mrs. Duke rode her frisky Rascal like one of the Furies, quickly disappearing in the dust-and-smoke screen.

Very shortly Brant was galloping toward them on his buckskin stallion, one of the best quarter horses on the Duke Ranch. Brant had broken and trained the animal himself, and Garnet could not help admiring his horsemanship. Words from one of Denny's letters suddenly flashed to mind: *"It seems that all the Rebs can ride and shoot better than our boys. The only way we'll whip them is if they run out of troops or weapons."*

Brant drew rein, swept off his hat, and politely bowed his head. "Welcome, ladies! I'll escort you to the main camp."

He rode between them, surprised but obviously

pleased to see Garnet. She was embarrassed by his nearness and by her bizarre garb. Anxious to make conversation, she said, "I've forgotten your horse's name."

"General," he smiled down at her.

"After General Lee, I presume?"

"Well, not Grant." He grinned widely.

"Why name him for a loser?" She couldn't resist the jibe.

"The general's character and intelligence inspired me," he drawled. "Most militarists, under equal circumstances, agree that Robert E. Lee would have been the victor."

Jenny intervened. "I thought you two had signed a truce some time ago. Let's not breach the peace today."

"Jennifer the Diplomat!" Garnet chided. "She persuaded me to come, as you persuaded Mrs. Duke to send the invitation to us."

"Well, I'm grateful to both of them for your being here."

"Just don't mistake my reason for being here," Garnet said crisply.

"I understand. And don't you fret over any of my foolish ideas," he replied, turning away.

They rode into pandemonium. The chuck wagon formed the center of the camp, and there was bustle all around it. On the outer fringes, men on horseback worked the cattle, keeping them together, while others roped and branded the bawling calves and yearling mavericks.

Mrs. Duke joined her husband in overseeing every aspect, contributing her years of knowledge and her expertise. To the uninitiated, the odors of manure and urine, blood, singed hair and hide fought against the aroma of boiling stew, chili, beans, and coffee.

"I'm sure you ladies would like to rest a while before we eat," Brant said, assigning them to one of the few tents. Garnet immediately retreated and lowered the flap.

Jenny offered assistance to the cook, a grizzly old bachelor, who declined, all in one breath, "I kin manage myself, thankee, ma'am, been doin' it fer years and reckon I'll do it till I croak with a spoon in hand."

Jenny then joined Garnet, who was sitting on one of the two cots. It was a Confederate Army relic, like the tents, *CSA* stenciled on the tent canvas and on the moth-eaten gray wool blankets.

"You won't see much in here, dear."

"I've already seen—and smelled—too much. I wish I had bathed in your lilac cologne and pinned a dozen sachets to my camisole."

"The stench won't be so obnoxious once you adjust to it," Jenny consoled. "At any rate, you can't hide in this tent, Garnet. You must go outside to eat, anyway."

"I have no appetite for the mess cooking in those pots and Dutch ovens! Did you notice the piles of dry cow chips stacked by the tripods? They *cook* over them!"

"Yes, when firewood is low. Trees are scarce on the prairie, you know."

"Oh, Lord! Where's Brant?"

"Working on the range. You'd think he'd been born on it, in a Western saddle and twirling his lariat."

Garnet winced, rubbing the insides of her chafed thighs gingerly. "Well, I sure wasn't! My legs are sore."

"My crotch aches, too."

"Aunt Jennifer!"

"Oh, don't be such a prude, Garnet! We're not in public. That's the part of us that really hurts, isn't it? Our legs haven't been spread so wide for that long in years. Mine haven't, anyway."

Garnet averted her face, afraid her guilt would be evident. Casting about for something to say, she gazed up at the tent. "I bet it leaks. What can you expect of a Confederate product? I feel like a traitor just being here!"

"I don't," Jenny said firmly. "And Brant was kind to provide for us, Garnet. There are only three tents—one for the Dukes, I assume, and one for a clinic. The others, including Brant, will all have to sleep on the ground."

"What are we doing here, Aunt Jen? We're as useless as cockleburs on a cow's tail!"

"True. I envy Alma Duke. It must be elevating to feel as competent as any male. At her age, too, and with rheumatism! I wonder if she's typical of ranchers' wives?"

"God forbid," Garnet cried. "I can't imagine a worse life."

"Alma Duke seems happy. She still loves that old cowpuncher of hers. Her eyes twinkle whenever she talks about him. I bet she wouldn't swap places with Mrs. Astor."

Garnet shook her head in disbelief, cringing as she lay back on the soiled Rebel cot and sighed.

"You'd rest better with your boots off."

"But I may not be able to get them on again. My feet are so swollen."

"I'll borrow some of Mrs. Duke's liniment tonight—if she carries any with her."

"There's more likely a bottle of liniment than one of perfume in her saddlebags. Wintergreen seems to be her favorite scent, next to essence of equine. She sweats like a horse."

"Works like one, too."

Garnet had just dozed off when the cook commenced banging heartily with a rod on an angle-iron. She sat up, alarmed. "What's that?"

"Chow time, gal! We'd better go." Jenny bridged her niece's objections before Garnet had time to voice them. "We mustn't offend our hosts, and we don't want Brant to think the trip exhausted us, do we?"

She didn't miss the gleam of determination in Garnet's eyes.

"And remember," Jenny said, as she straightened her clothing, "we Yankee women are supposed to come from strong Puritan stock."

Jenny left the tent, Garnet trailing reluctantly. Her aunt quickly got involved in an animated conversation with Alma Duke before reaching the chuck wagon, so Garnet went on without her. Her crafty mentor had tricked her again, leading her into the wilderness trap like a blind field mouse to bait.

Brant was waiting at the chuck wagon, holding two tin plates of food. Offering one to Garnet, he said, "For you, milady. Or would you prefer to dine in your tent?"

"Not if I can find a seat out here," she said.

"My bedroll will do," he suggested, ushering her to it. "Sorry we have no better accommodations, Garnet."

"I didn't expect any."

She lowered herself cautiously to the bedroll and took the plate of stew, beans, and sourdough biscuits. A bent tin spoon was stuck in the middle. Brant hunkered down beside her and began to eat heartily. But after a few bites he began to talk. "The strange mulligan is called son-of-a-gun." He was using the polite term. "Ingredients vary with every range cook. But about the only things wasted from a slaughtered beef are the hoofs and horns. All the rest goes into the stew."

Garnet grimaced. "And that'll be your food on the trail drive? All the time?"

"Largely, along with rations of fried potatoes, bacon, and jerky. The vaqueros will eat lots of chili con carne, tortillas, and pinto beans—the latter also known as Western strawberries."

"What are those Mexicans frying in that kettle?"

Brant hesitated. "Cracklings. That's thin strips of

marrow-gut crisped in deep suet. And prairie oysters."

"Oysters? Out *here?*"

He hesitated longer this time. "They're the by-product of castration, which is necessary because longhorns ran wild during the war and overpopulated the plains. It also makes the young ones easier to herd over long distances with heifers. We neutered fifty this morning, and the fellows are feasting."

Garnet set her dish aside and took a deep breath. "And you want to be a rancher! Performing such disgusting surgery and who knows what else!"

"It's routine, Garnet. We did it with the cattle and horses, even the hunting hounds, on the plantation, selecting the best stock for breeding and fixing the others. Mrs. Duke handles a castrating knife as expertly as any veterinarian. Most ranchers' wives are familiar with the operation."

"Could we discuss something else, *please?*"

"Of course. How about you and me?"

"That subject is closed."

"Then what's left, Garnet?"

"Nothing much, Brant. I shouldn't have come."

"Why in hell did you? My hopes flamed when I saw you riding up. Now you've done everything but castrate *me*. Does that satisfy your wish for revenge?"

"How dare you say such a horrible thing to me? You were a gentleman when we met—a Rebel, yes, but a gentleman. Have you lost all sense of decency in this barbarous land?"

"Have you? You're riding roughshod over my sensibilities, Garnet. Your words wound as deeply as kicking hoofs. You hurt me, and you never seem to give a damn! Why did you come? To hurt me more?"

"I told you earlier, it wasn't my idea!" she insisted. "Blame Aunt Jenny."

"Blaming others for one's own actions is not my style, Garnet." He stood up, digging one spur into the earth, angry and exasperated. "Would you like some coffee?"

"That steaming mud they're toping from tin cups? No, thank you."

"Well, tea is not served at roundups, my dear. And I have work to do. See you at supper."

"Don't count on that, Brant."

"Mrs. Duke expects her guests to spend the night."

"Not if I have a choice."

"You don't," he growled, then turned and strode away.

Her eyes followed his tall figure. She could not define her feelings, for they were a puzzling cross between anger and admiration, and bewilderment of hate and affection. Damn him for confusing her! Damn him!

Chapter 30

GARNET became aware of her aunt's shadow, as she blocked the sun between herself and her niece. "Riled him again, didn't you?" she admonished, shaking her head in dismay.

"No more than he riled me! Oh, he makes me so mad sometimes I—I could just spit!" cried Garnet, groping for the ultimate feminine indelicacy. She glanced away at the group of men cantering out to the main herd. "Do you know what they do to those poor, helpless boy-calves after they rope and brand them?"

"Yes. Mrs. Duke told me—and they're called bulls, not boys! Garnet, are you peeved at Brant for trying to educate you about all this?" She realized it must be shocking to someone who knew nothing about ranching, much less some of its harsh practices. "I'm sure he didn't mean to offend you."

Crimson suffused Garnet's fair skin. Only minutes ago, Brant had accused her of attempting to castrate him, and she was still horrified. "It all seems so cruel, Aunt Jen. And savage—especially eating the things!"

"Not to them, Garnet. No more so, anyway, than eating any other parts of the animal," Jenny rationalized. "Alma says bull testicles are believed to promote male fertility and are also considered an aphrodisiac. I gather her husband eats them often, and while they haven't cured his lumbago—"

"That's vulgar," Garnet interrupted sharply, "and I don't want to discuss it any further!"

Garnet did not see Brant again until supper, which was an unappetizing duplicate of the noon meal. She ate in the company of her aunt and their hostess, shunning the unrecognizable ingredients in the stew and pretending to be unaware of the foreman's intermittent glances. Fred the cook and a volunteer assistant washed the utensils and cutlery afterwards and tidied up the chuck wagon as neatly as if it were an indoor kitchen.

Sunset was a spectacular sight on the vast expanse of bright-green grass and brilliant flowers. The western horizon was painted with fascinating blends of saffron, sienna, burnt orange, magenta, and Indian red.

Garnet was awed by the splendor. Her bright bandanna fluttered gently in the evening breeze, and she removed the pins from her pale silken hair, letting it blow freely. She tried to imagine herself on the Connecticut shore, with the winds off Long Island Sound tossing the waves. But somehow the vision was blurred and distorted, and her efforts to capture it failed.

Cowboys not on duty gathered around bonfires and joked, swapping tall tales about past roundups, cattle drives, and their conquests at the end of the long trail. They had their own unique culture, superstitions, legends, myths, even songs. Lonely men, often without family or roots, they drifted like tumbleweed from ranch to ranch, making staunch friends of strangers, as dependent upon one another in danger as soldiers. They brooded in ballads of lament and despaired in private reveries. Most carried a pair of dice, a deck of cards, or both, and a cherished talisman. All carried guns. There were few Bibles in evidence, for the range was their religion. They accepted God as naturally as His creations.

The moon rose, huge, gleaming silver, beautiful beyond any moon Garnet had ever seen. It shimmered upon the land as phosphorescence upon water. There was something mystical and magnetic about it.

But March nights on the prairie were chilly, and the fire felt good. Extending her hands toward it, Garnet was recalling the driftwood bonfires at beach parties and clambakes, when Brant approached with a poncho and slipped it over her head. It swallowed her, and she had difficulty finding the arm slits.

"It's a Mexican cape—very handy in bad weather, and more comfortable on horseback than a blanket or oilskin. Walk with me, Garnet."

"It's dark—and there are rattlesnakes and wolves out there!"

"Panthers, too. And maybe even a few Indians. But the fires keep them all at bay. Cowboys consider it bad luck to let a campfire die, so these will burn all night. Besides, we won't wander far away."

"I was just about to retire."

"It's too early for that," he said.

Garnet stood, vexed by her own indecision. "Am I a puppet, Brant—expected to perform whenever you pull my strings?"

"Is that how you feel?"

"That's how it seems!"

"Not at all, Garnet. I'm well acquainted with your

strong will, remember? There's not much you do without wanting to. That romantic moon affects you the same as it does me."

"I hardly noticed it," she denied.

"No? Then do." Pausing, he tilted her face toward the heavens. "Fabulous, isn't it? Looks as if it's made of diamond dust and quicksilver. Deny it if you wish, but it's drawing us together, Garnet."

"That's lunacy. The kind of moon madness that afflicts rabid dogs...and some people."

He laughed heartily. "Vampires and werewolves? Should I be baying at the moon and fanging your lovely neck?"

"Oh, you monster!"

Suddenly his arms captured her. Her squirming was no more effective than a kitten's as he kissed her firmly on the mouth, lingering until her clenched lips relaxed and she responded. Desperate passion and longing grew, and Garnet expected to meekly surrender on the ground. But she recovered her rampant senses and as much composure as she could manage.

"I'm not a slut, to be taken at your convenience!" she hissed, tearing her mouth from his.

"Good Lord—you think I intended to force you? You have a damned low opinion of me, Garnet!"

"The lowest!" she declared furiously, pushing him away. "I'm leaving now, and if you dare try and stop me, I'll scream!"

Seething with outrage, she fled as swiftly as possible in her clumsy boots, tears brimming. Reaching the tent, she flung herself on the cot, relieved that her aunt was not present. She feigned sleep when, a little later, Jenny entered with Mrs. Duke's liniment in hand.

"Get undressed, Garnet, and I'll give you a massage. Come on now, I know you're playing possum!" Jenny struck a sulphur match to light the tallow candle stub. She lowered the tent flap so the wind wouldn't extinguish the flame. "Sit up, Garnet. I'll help you with your clothes."

"I don't want a rubdown, Aunt Jennifer."

"Suit yourself. Don't complain if you're stiff as a board tomorrow. Alma gave my back and shoulders a good massage and my spine feels better already." She paused tentatively, peering into Garnet's distraught face. "Did something frighten you?"

"Why?"

"Because you're trembling."

"Good night, Auntie," Garnet said emphatically, pulling the shabby covers over her head.

"Still hiding. And you don't even know from what—do you, poor child?"

Coyotes howled at the brilliant moon, calling to mates with a lonesome sound. Cattle lowed. The fires off other camps glowed on the nearby plains. The Duke Ranch force, except for the nighthawkers on guard, were all tucked into blankets or canvas bags. It was a time for solitude and meditation.

The foreman lay in his bedroll, gazing at the glittering sky, which seemed no more distant than the woman he loved and wanted above anything on earth. And would never have.

How in hell could she imagine that only lust inspired him? Condemn him on that flimsy, unfair feminine caprice! How could she? Chastity was in her nature, yet he had known her helpless yearning in his arms. Part of her longed for the joy they had shared, while another, stronger spirit conquered the temptation. If only there were some way to free her! The opposing forces were tearing them both to pieces.

He was still awake when Fred started breakfast at four o'clock. The camp woke before dawn and, as Brant expected, Garnet remained in her tent. Jenny emerged, yawning sleepily.

"Good morning, ramrod!" she greeted him cheerily, in the ranch vernacular Mrs. Duke used for their foreman. The vaqueros called him honcho.

"Morning, ma'am. I trust you ladies slept well?"

"Tolerably, sir. And you?"

"Fine."

"Liar," Jenny challenged. "You didn't catch a wink, much less forty."

He rubbed his unshaven chin ruefully. "It shows, huh? Guess I should have spruced up a bit. But there are few Beau Brummells on the plains—and we'll all have whiskers at the end of the trail."

"I'm sure yours will be dark and handsome," Jenny complimented. "I would like to see you then."

"I doubt your niece would. She already thinks I'm Blackbeard the Pirate."

"Really?" Her brows arched. "Have you behaved like a buccaneer recently?"

"Perhaps," he conceded. "The sun will rise shortly, Jenny. Don't let Garnet miss it."

"Oh, Brant, why don't you burst into that tent like a desert sheik, sweep her up in your arms, and spirit her away!"

He smiled. "That's quite a fantasy for this early hour. You're a romantic at heart, Miss Temple."

"So is my niece, whether she realizes it or not. And I think she'd enjoy the adventure, though she would kick and scream every minute."

He grinned ruefully. "I know she won't come out while I'm here. Say good-bye for me, please? And take good care of her and yourself." He touched his hat in a farewell salute. "So long, dear friend. *Hasta la vista!*"

Garnet watched him leave through a slit in the canvas, stifling a sob in her throat. Had insomnia plagued him last night, as it had her? She had attributed her restlessness to fatigue and her throbbing breasts to strain. His lovemaking might have alleviated her pain, but the idea of sneaking through the dark and crawling into his bedroll was unthinkable. She had suffered all night, refusing even to reminisce about the blissful experience in the bunkhouse.

She picked at the plate of food Jenny brought her, but ignored her aunt's pleading about the magnificent sunrise. The pearly-pink translucence had faded from the eastern sky and the sun was in blazing ascent.

All the workers had gone from camp before Garnet left her tent. The acrid odor of scorched hair and hide assaulted her, the bawling of frenzied animals clamored against her, and dust burned her eyes and throat. She pulled her hat down low and tied the bandanna over her face, thinking she resembled an outlaw. She felt grimy, in desperate need of a bath.

Jenny didn't seem to mind any of it, not even the filthy flies buzzing after the blood and dung, or even the hovering buzzards. She was absorbed in conversation with Alma Duke, taking in information as if she expected to use it.

Recognizing Brant's sleek buff-colored horse some distance away, Garnet, on a sudden impulse, borrowed Mrs. Duke's binoculars and watched him in action. The accusation she had flung at him in rage last evening seemed absurd. He may have had seduction in mind, but hardly rape. After all, a few harsh words would not have stopped a man of his strength if he'd meant to use force.

No, it was herself she had really feared—her own vulnerability.

She returned the glasses. It was over. She had erected mountainous barriers between them, separated them forever. She sighed, feeling a sudden irretrievable loss. Forlornly, she asked if their hostess intended to accompany them back to the ranch.

"Why, sure, honey! I wouldn't let you two tenderfoots brave all that wild space alone. Seth should have made you take his pistol. It's dangerous for females to travel anywhere out here without a gun."

"I don't know how to shoot, ma'am."

"Better learn, gal, if you plan to live in Texas."

"I don't," Garnet said simply.

"Well...a wrangler will get our horses ready. Anybody like another cup of java before Fred dumps the grounds?"

The guests declined politely and Alma said, "Can't say as I blame you. That old potwalloper's been with us for twenty years and he *still* can't make decent coffee. His chow ain't nothing special, either, you may have noticed. I pity the poor fellas on the trail."

Jenny looked at Garnet. "Brant asked me to say good-bye for him."

"Isn't he coming to town again for supplies?"

Mrs. Duke answered. "Nope, we're sending Julio-Bear after them. The camp he's supervising is nearer Longhorn Junction. Brant's got to meet with the other trail bosses tomorrow, and him and Julio will be real busy from here to Missouri."

And so she was left with a secondhand good-bye, Garnet thought. Would he do that if he really loved her? Oh—what did it matter? Why should she care? Their trails were not likely to cross again, not ever.

Chapter 31

GARNET never wanted to see Brant Steele again. Throughout the longed-for journey home, the stagecoach to Corpus Christi, the ship to New Orleans, the steamboat to St. Louis, Jenny listened to Garnet's fervent declarations and smiled.

"Of course." Jenny would nod. "Now, I want to look at the new issue of *Godey's* I bought in New Orleans. Hoop skirts are definitely going out of style in Paris. Bustles are *à la mode* on the Continent now, though it'll probably be a while before the fashion catches on in America."

"Especially in the West," said Garnet.

"That's all behind you now," Jenny reminded.

"So's the bustle," Garnet punned with a mischievous grin. "All it'll do is make the *derrière* look larger, and most women don't need the emphasis."

"Including me?"

"Well, you did add a few pounds doing all that cooking for Uncle Seth! He's going to miss you."

"Yes, poor fellow, and I'll miss him. But *your* figure improved, Garnet, filling out nicely in the right places. You won't ever need puffs in your bodice, and your hourglass waistline enhances your hips."

Garnet sighed. What did fashion matter to her? She'd have to wear drab widow's weeds for another year at least, and then dress conservatively for the rest of her life...unless she married again. Her deportment would be monitored by her mother and the other Avalon matrons. She must not dance or appear to enjoy herself at any entertainment, especially a ball. She must be as proper and sedate at all times as if she were attending a church social. Her place at any gala would be on the sidelines, with the chaperones and the wallflowers. The tiniest departure from the norm would set tongues to wagging and bring sharp reproval.

Oh, Lord—what a future awaited her! She frowned and opened her book. Why had she chosen romance novels to occupy her during the long journey? Would this one have a happy ending? She was tempted to peek, but that would spoil this simple pleasure.

It was difficult to concentrate, however, and soon she was distracted by the scenery above New Orleans and the river plantations she could see from her deck chair. Suddenly, without wanting to, she remembered Great Oaks and the time they had spent there. Would the Northern colonel restore its grandeur? Oddly, she hoped he would. It must have been a paradise before the apocalypse.

How could anyone born to a magnificent manor on a vast stretch of lush countryside settle for a shack in the wilderness and a few livestock? To forget the beauty and the leisure of a gentleman's life for the hard work, privations, the crude existence of a struggling rancher! And why did Brant speak of the future as if there had been no past? She sighed. That required courage, sagacity, and resolve in measures she did not possess and probably never would.

"We're passing Great Oaks," she said to Jenny.

"How can you tell?"

"The landing has been rebuilt—and there's a new sign."

"So there is. And I suppose the new owner is pretending to be landed gentry. I hate to admit it, Garnet, but much of the Southerners' heritage was simply stolen from them under the hoary cliché about the spoils of war. There should have been some way for them to keep at least their ancestral homes."

"And their slaves?"

"Of course not! That evil had to go. But many landowners would have worked some of their land themselves, or with sharecroppers. There was no valid reason and no useful purpose served by razing so many towns and burning plantations and farms. There's just no excuse for it."

"I guess not," Garnet agreed, as the Great Oaks boundary receded from view. She had to resist an urge to go to the rail and stare at it.

"Stupid girl," she appraised the heroine of the novel.

"Who?"

"Maybelle in *Love's Lost Dream*. If she doesn't realize soon that the hero loves her, she's going to lose him to someone else. Isn't she silly?"

"Very," Jenny murmured. "But that won't really happen. It's only a romance—and they usually end happily. Maybelle will come to her senses."

"*The Lady of the Camellias* didn't end happily," Garnet reflected. "Marguerite died of consumption, you know."

"That was a drama, and the playwright was more realistic than most. Few French authors write the sort of frivolous literature you're reading."

"Or you," Garnet criticized, tapping the fashion magazine. "That will hardly enrich your mind."

"Touché!" Jenny grinned. "There's the first call to luncheon, and I'm hungry for some more New Orleans cooking. I bought a recipe book in the French Quarter to acquaint your parents with Creole food. The aroma of *bouillabaisse* makes my mouth water now."

"Your longhorn stews weren't so bad, either. In fact, I was getting accustomed to Texas cooking."

Jenny laughed, taking her niece's arm as they strolled toward the dining salon. "Well, it did put some much-needed meat on your spare little ribs! I'll make a few pots when we get home, and some chili con carne, too, if I can find the spices I need for that dish of Mexican heartburn."

Garnet quickened her steps across the deck, peeved at herself. Enough reminiscence! she decided abruptly. "I'm looking forward to a good old-fashioned boiled New England dinner! I trust Clara hasn't forgotten how to cook one."

"Your mother would never let her do that, Garnet. My sister and I were raised on boiled food, and on our trips abroad, Eleanor always preferred British cookery. Continental cuisine never appealed to her—and Texas food would appall her."

"Not only the food, Auntie," Garnet said wryly.

The entire country around Avalon was preparing for the unveiling of the Civil War Monument. It stood covered with a huge tarpaulin and draped in red, white, and blue bunting. The Stars and Stripes fluttered on every flagstaff, waving before buildings and homes. Street lamps and store windows were decorated in red, white, and blue.

Hammers tapped mesmerically and saws hummed plaintively as workmen constructed a platform for the honored speakers and guests. Veterans throughout Connecticut had been invited to the ceremony. Families who had lost relatives in the fighting could inter their own mementos in the base vault, which would be sealed during the ceremony.

Garnet had not yet decided which of her husband's few precious relics she would entomb.

The effusive welcome she received from her parents and friends convinced her that some of them had not really expected her to return alive. She was kissed, hugged, presented with flowers and gifts. Among the many callers at the Ashley residence were several other young war widows, some former schoolmates of Garnet's. One had already married again, and was clinging possessively to her new husband's arm.

"Maurine certainly has recovered from Oscar's death," Garnet remarked later to Jenny. "Remember how devastated she was when the telegram arrived after Gettysburg? Now she's proud of her new mate and unmistakably pregnant. Why, she almost seems to flaunt her condition!"

"Why not? It's certainly nothing to be ashamed of, Garnet. They seem very much in love. Besides, Jack Halston was a good catch—considering that he has all of his limbs, his eyesight, and his mental faculties. Not every Avalon veteran was so lucky, you know. Some of our men are pitifully incapacitated, and there's more than one village idiot now," Jenny said, horror creeping into her voice.

Garnet nodded sadly, wondering if some of the poor victims would not have preferred death to their living torture. Maybe Denny was infinitely better off.

After an examination, Dr. Forbes pronounced Garnet fully recuperated. He began immediately to prepare a medical paper on the curative properties of the Texas climate. Family rejoicing did not allay Jenny's private fears, however, for though her niece was physically sound, her emotional state was precarious. Jenny warned Eleanor that her daughter could regress to her former malaise in the atmosphere of continual mourning.

"Nonsense, Jennifer!" her sister scoffed. "She's well again, and happy to be home. Things may seem a bit strange to her, not quite as she remembered her life here, but that's only natural. After all, she has been away almost a year."

"And a lot can happen in a year, Eleanor. A little longer and she might have matured completely. In some respects Garnet is still a little girl masquerading in widow's weeds. Remember how she used to dress up in our old clothes? Playing lady, she called it. Well, a part of her is still playing lady, Eleanor."

They were in the sitting room adjoining the master suite. A hooked rug in many colors centered the polished floor. Blue ruffled chintz curtains framed the windows. Not a speck of dust was visible on the exquisite mahogany and rosewood furniture. Not a leaf had fallen from the floral arrangements or the crisp, green potted plants on their marble-topped stands.

Jenny thought the air must be sterile. Almost as if she had not moved during the last year, Eleanor sat in her favorite Boston rocker, working a petitpoint sampler. Without raising her eyes, she smiled at the image of her small daughter parading in hats and shoes too large for her, a tasseled reticule dragging the floor. But Eleanor refused to believe her sister.

"She's mature enough for her age, Jennifer. Garnet will never be sophisticated—it's not in her nature. But she's sensible and intelligent, and perhaps wiser than you think. Living through tragedy during one's early years is bound to leave scars. We must help her to build a new life."

"Here, Eleanor? In Avalon?"

"Why, of course. Where else?"

"Avalon went stale years ago, sister, when the shipping industry moved out. Except for the textile mills, it might vanish from the map. Many young people are moving to larger towns in search of opportunities. Those who remain will shrink and grow inward with Avalon. Why, Helene Bowles has married her second cousin from Hartford! Was there no one else available after her fiancé's death? Are there no eligible young men *left* in the country?"

Eleanor sighed. "Not many sturdy ones, I'm afraid."

"Well, there are some in Texas. It's expanding and it's lively, and your daughter knew a man there who wanted to love Garnet and help her grow. A real man, Eleanor. He could have made a real woman of Garnet."

Eleanor frowned, poking her needle through the black fabric. Texas had served its purpose and Eleanor was grateful to Seth—but she thought it would be best if they all forgot about it now. Evidently her sister wasn't going to allow that.

"Blatant virility has always been your idea of manhood," she chided. "I assume this Texan was male and muscular—long on brawn and short on brains."

"On the contrary, sister, and that's an unfair notion about Westerners. This one was a Louisiana planter before the war—the man I wrote you about after the steamboat accident. He saved our lives. Brant Steele is far better educated and more polished than he likes to admit, a gentleman in every sense. He could receive in the finest drawing room and lead a cotillion in the most elegant ballroom. But he's no Milquetoast, not by any means. How Garnet could have spurned him is beyond me."

"Perhaps her preference in men is different from yours," Eleanor suggested. "And perhaps she can't forgive what happened to Dennis. I know she'll never forget. Why, she sits on the parlor window seat all the time, watching the activity on the green."

"Out of boredom, most likely. What else is there

to do in Avalon? Let's give her a homecoming party, Eleanor. Please?"

"Before the dedication ceremony? Good heavens, no! We're hardly celebrating *that!* An afternoon tea, later on, will be just the thing."

Recalling the rollicking barbecue and hoedown at the Duke Ranch, Lacey Lee's fantastic escape, the roundup, Jenny shook her head at the thought of a tea party. "Well, my mind's made up, Eleanor. *I'm* going back to Texas. Seth needs me. It's nice to feel needed. I've always felt useless here, like a parasite on you and Henry."

"But that's not true!" Eleanor gasped, thrusting the cloth aside. "You're a blessing to us, Jennifer, and to our daughter. We love having you! You must never doubt that! Why, it would hurt Henry deeply to think you had ever felt otherwise. And poor little Garnet—"

Jenny interrupted. "Eleanor, please! You must stop regarding her as 'poor little Garnet.' She doesn't need pity any more. Or a chaperone. She may not be aware of it yet, but Garnet is perfectly capable of taking care of herself now. And I could never return to sedentary spinsterhood, not after all the activity of the past year. The idleness and the futility of my life would drive me mad. Then you'd have to stash me in the attic!"

"That's gibberish!"

"No." Jenny shook her head. "I never realized before how stifling leisure can be, Eleanor. It's an inane existence, and now I have a horror of my old ways."

"It's your choice, of course," said Eleanor hesitantly, retreating, as always, in the presence of a stronger personality. "But I think it's merely a temporary rebellion, fostered in the land of rebels. I hope you'll think this over very carefully."

Jenny excused herself a little later to find Garnet. She found her still positioned in the parlor oriel, her attention focused on the common.

"You're going to take root there!" she scolded. "The view can't be that fascinating. You've seen it all your life. Let's go strolling, Garnet."

"Did you invite Mother?"

"She's absorbed in her needlepoint, and I was getting cross-eyed watching her. What do genteel ladies *do* with all the embroidered linens, the miles of crochet, and the endless samplers of every axiom ever recorded in history!" Jenny frowned, bewildered. "To think I used to take my leisure the same way—that my whole world was bounded by an embroidery hoop! I'd rather darn socks and patch dungarees. Not so genteel, perhaps, but useful, at least. This idleness makes me restless and irritable."

"Me too," Garnet admitted, sorely missing her work in the Mercantile Mart. "A walk would be nice, Aunt Jenny."

The black parasol she took from the hall stand was not truly necessary, for majestic trees shaded the streets and parks all over Avalon. How different from the mesquites and scrub oaks of Longhorn Junction, the crooked trails worn through the buffalo grass in the square! Few ornamental plants were cultivated in the yards of Longhorn Junction, but even the smallest Avalon cottage had its rose garden, ivied chimney, and clematis-vined arbor and fence. Lilacs, forsythia, peonies, cherry and apple trees— oh, there was no place like Connecticut!

"And he thought that old blooming prairie was something," Garnet murmured.

"What, dear?"

"Nothing, Auntie. The green won't be the same after tomorrow, will it? It'll be difficult seeing the— the new monument first thing every morning."

"Draw your shades," Jenny advised.

"You can't shut out memories with blinds."

"Ah, that's wise! So you'll have to find another way, Garnet."

"You could help me, Aunt Jen."

"How can I help you?"

"By staying in Avalon."

"No, Garnet. I won't become your permanent crutch. I love you too much for that."

"What do you mean?"

"Dear, you can't lean on me forever. Unless you function on your own power now, you'll become a hopeless invalid. You must learn to sustain yourself. Travel your own path—to whatever destination."

"What if I take the wrong direction and get lost? I thought everything would be so clear in my mind once I came home, but somehow I'm only more confused than I was in Texas. Avalon has changed."

"Not Avalon, Garnet. You've changed. Texas affected you, like it or not."

Garnet twirled the parasol on her shoulder and it whirred like an agitated windmill. "If you mean Mr. Steele—"

"Why, I didn't mention his name."

"But he's on your mind," Garnet accused. "Too bad he wasn't old enough for you!"

"Too bad," Jenny agreed smoothly, then changed the subject. "Have you decided yet what to seal in the vault?"

"Not yet."

"You don't have much time."

"There's nothing I want to part with."

"But you can't be the only bereaved who doesn't contribute anything, Garnet. People here conform, you know, and expect it of others." She paused. "Actually, that's all custom is: conformity. Thank God, there's precious little of it out West."

"You should join the frontier promoters, Aunt Jennifer. You've been touting Texas ever since we came home. I'm surprised you haven't organized a settlers' train and offered to lead it."

"I would, if that were the only way back—and if I thought enough pioneers would join me."

Garnet shook her head. "Shall we go to the beach? I used to dream of Long Island Sound."

Jenny confessed that she had too, during the long, hot, dry summer when the prairie shimmered with heat mirages, and sudden Texas diabolos danced. "Why don't we drive the buggy to the shore and then on to Woods Road? Everything is so bright and beautiful!"

"And so *green*," Garnet cried.

Jenny nodded, smiling.

"And he thought that old prairie was something," Garnet repeated.

"*Now* who's thinking of him?" Jenny teased.

"Just comparing East and West, Auntie."

"And North and South? Yankee and Rebel?"

"How can I help it, when I think about the new memorial?" Garnet demanded hotly.

But Jenny said nothing.

Chapter 32

GARNET lay awake much of the night wondering what to place in the memory cache. She could not get comfortable. After so long on a flat cotton-linter pad, her feather mattress seemed too deep, too soft. If firmness was good for the backbone, then that featherbed should make her as limp as a rag doll.

How pampered and spoiled she had been before Texas! Doting parents, the best food, the most stylish clothing, servants. Warm winters by the fire, cool summers by the sea. Her own private room and bath facilities. If nothing else, Texas had taught her tolerance and endurance. Frontier hardships had strengthened her. A hot sun might still burn her tender skin, but it would not melt her. Wild winds might whip her hair and skirts, but they would not wilt her spirit.

She sat up and gazed through the windows at

the shadowy common. The canvas-camouflaged bulk
resembled a ghost ship run aground in fog. She had
to reach a decision before dawn. She sighed.

Moments later, she struck a match and set flame
to her bedside candle. How she had longed for this
familiar bayberry fragrance when the tallow stubs
of Texas sputtered in their rancid oils!

Unlocking the nightstand drawer, she removed
a packet of letters she had left behind when she
went to Texas. She untied the blue ribbon and
reluctantly began to read. Had they once seemed
romantic? They were a schoolboy's letters, hastily
scrawled on lined stationery like an assigned theme,
the youthful hand crossing the t's too heavily and
forgetting to dot the i's. Brief sketches were inadequate to convey the terrors of war, the privations
of a soldier's life, the fears of death and defeat. No
poetry, no passion, no hopes, no dreams, not even
a subtle promise of the future. The sentiment was
all the nostalgia of a homesick youth for home and
family. Some words were spattered and blurred,
probably with teardrops. Like Denny's tintype, the
ink was fading from black to brown. The spaces
between the lines were just bits of yellowed paper.

Garnet inserted the letters into their foolscap en-
velopes and slipped them back into the drawer. But
she did not lock it. These were not love letters, meant
for her eyes alone. They had obviously been meant
for sharing with others, and she realized suddenly
that she ought to have shown them to families and
friends.

In the foyer, Grandfather Ashley's clock struck
twice, its Westminster chimes resonating through
the silent house. Garnet yawned, snuffed the candle,
and composed herself for sleep, praying for divine
guidance.

She woke to a brilliant day, sunlit and sea-
scented, clouded only by memory and the imminent
event.

Eleanor knocked and immediately came in. "Hurry and get dressed, darling! Breakfast is waiting, and Clara fixed something special for you."

"I'm not hungry, Mother."

"Don't hurt Clara's feelings."

What about *my* feelings? Garnet wondered. Her head ached. Food would probably nauseate her. "I don't feel very well, Mother."

"Now, Garnet, it's just nerves. You'll be fine after the ceremony."

"May I come to the table in my robe?"

Eleanor's eyes widened in surprise. "Of course not, dear. You know we never dine together that way! But I'll send a tray up, if you prefer to stay in bed a bit longer."

"Never mind, Mother. I'll dress and come down."

"Good. Your black silk gown has been pressed, and you may wear my jet brooch."

"I thought perhaps your cameo?"

"Not today, dear. For this occasion, only black."

"Yes, Mother."

"And you mustn't be late," Eleanor reminded as she turned to leave. "Although the program doesn't start for a few hours, people are already gathering on the green."

"I hope it won't turn into a carnival, with vendors hawking souvenirs and refreshments," Garnet said. "That would be disgusting, Mother."

"People here would never allow it, dear. Don't worry."

A military band had volunteered to play. The mayor and aldermen occupied the patriotically decorated dais. Families of the dead heroes sat on benches and chairs provided by Avalon businessmen. Many veterans were there, all in uniform. Some of them were missing arms or legs, some were blind, many were scarred. They were hailed and cheered, and everyone determined not to notice the deformities, or to be put off by the grim-visaged stoicism with which Avalon's veterans observed the ceremony.

Mayor Grisby's bombastic address echoed scores of others everyone had heard. Reverend Hodge's eulogies recalled those of Army chaplains. The band played a brassy dirge. And then the tarpaulin was removed, and a bronze Union soldier was aiming his rifle at the musketed Minute Man across the green—an irony the designers had overlooked.

The audience applauded, praised, and admired the new sculpture, and all declared that the men whose sacrifice it commemorated would never be forgotten. The veterans, already largely forgotten, wore cynical expressions.

Finally, relatives of the dead were requested to come forward and deposit their mementos in the vault. Sealing it would end the occasion.

Garnet waited until she was the very last. She stood clutching the yellow oilskin pouch, inside which was the faded tintype. She walked to the monument alone—a diminutive figure, yet dignified in her sedate garb and posture, her expression solemn and serene. She gazed poignantly up at the statue, trying to visualize the person it represented to her. She hesitated slightly before placing her tribute. Then she moved back and joined the others as workmen troweled mortar onto the granite slab of the crypt and fitted it into place. Numerous wreaths and bouquets of flowers were placed around the base, and finally the minister's blessing and the sound of taps concluded the rites.

The spectators drifted quietly away. Garnet's parents and aunt walked home with her in silence. No one asked what she had interred. They were sure they knew. Not until she removed her black gloves and revealed her bare ring finger did they realize the extent of her contribution.

Three weeks later, as Jenny was preparing for her return to Texas, Garnet offered to help pack. She picked up a new petticoat, folded it, and placed it neatly in a valise.

"You're really leaving, Auntie."

"Did you ever doubt it?"

"Not really, but I kept hoping you'd reconsider. I'll miss you terribly."

"I'll miss you too, dear."

"Will you write to me?"

"Of course—and to your parents, too. But you know how uncertain the mails are. The pony-express routes haven't been restored fully yet."

"I wonder whom you'll meet on the riverboat this time?" Garnet mused softly.

Jenny shrugged. "No matter—they couldn't possibly be as interesting as our first traveling companions. Quite an adventure, all in all, wasn't it?"

Garnet nodded wistfully. "Except for the frightful explosion of the *Crescent Queen*. So many lives lost. We were lucky."

"Our luck has a name, Garnet, and he's somewhere on the Central Plains right now. But this journey may also hold some surprises for me. Going west, one never knows. I reckon that's what makes it so exciting."

"Reckon," Garnet teased. "You never used that expression before Texas."

"I never used an outdoor privy or bathed in a barrel, or did a lot of other primitive things before Texas," said Jenny. "Oh, I'm not exactly welcoming the hardships, but neither am I dreading them. Maybe that's the essential difference between us, Garnet. Texas left its brand on both of us. But I don't want to erase mine. I'm quite proud to wear it."

Garnet pondered the formal silk gown Jenny had mistakenly worn to the Duke Ranch barbecue. They had both been fashionably attractive but overdressed. "You were right, Aunt Jen. Avalon hasn't changed—I have. Everything's the same here, yet it doesn't seem the same to *me*. Something is missing, and, though I don't know what it is, I feel incomplete. I've been crying into my pillow at night. I'm really miserable! What's wrong with me, Auntie? What's lacking?"

"Garnet, I think you know the answer to that, but you want to hear it spoken. Well, I can't oblige. If they are to mean anything, the words have to be yours."

"I know, Aunt Jennifer. And I suppose what I actually came to say is that I—I want to go back to Texas with you. I don't believe I could be truly happy here again, not even content. In church, my thoughts wander sinfully. I don't care for visiting, and I was desperately bored at yesterday's tea party. Nothing but idle, prattling women sounding like a flock of magpies."

Jenny smiled, agreeing. "Not one profound or even interesting utterance the entire afternoon, and it'll be a repeat performance at a different location next week. But are you strong enough to return with me, Garnet?"

"I feel fine."

"I don't mean your health, dear."

"I know what you mean, Aunt Jenny."

"Have you told your parents?"

"It's my decision," Garnet replied, staunchly. "My life, my future. But I don't imagine they'll be much surprised. They know my wedding ring went into the tomb. So did Denny's photograph. I saved his watch and kerchief for his mother and sister."

"They appreciated it, I know. Mrs. Lane has aged terribly since her son's death, and I don't suppose her daughter will ever marry."

"Eileen is still mourning her brother and the beau she lost at Shiloh. But my giving them Denny's belongings was more than just a gesture, Aunt Jennifer. They should have them, and they should also share his letters, even though it is a little late." She paused for a moment. "And you know something? The ring was getting too small for my finger. I must have grown in the past year."

"A great deal, Garnet, and in more ways than one."

Garnet looked away, then back at her aunt. "Once I asked Uncle Seth why so many people went west, and he tried to explain. Only a few of the reasons made sense to me then."

"And now?" Jenny prompted.

"Well, I understand Brant Steele's reasons better, at least." Her eyes strayed to a westerly window, where brilliant rays of afternoon sun beckoned from the distant horizon. "He wants to settle in Texas, boss his own spread, help make something of the cattle industry. I could be a rancher's wife, if he hasn't given up on me by now. Do you suppose he has?" she asked after a long pause. "I'm afraid I didn't leave him much hope."

"Enough, I do believe. And, anyway, he's a stubborn hombre." As Garnet stared, Jenny produced a telegram from her reticule, grinning as she watched Garnet's expression. "This was sent from Missouri." She took a deep breath, and began to read. "'Dear Miss Temple. A wire from Seth informs that you are returning to Longhorn Junction. Please do not leave before I get to Avalon. Business here completed. Taking next train to Connecticut. Love and best wishes to you both. Brant Steele.'"

Joy filled Garnet's eyes to overflowing. "He really sent that?"

"Read it yourself."

"But when did you get it?" asked Garnet, hands shaking as she reached for the paper.

"Look at the date, dear. The housekeeper signed for it while we were out."

"Almost a week ago!" Garnet cried. "That means—"

"Yes—he's here. At the Avalon Inn. He arrived yesterday. I saw him briefly this morning. That's why I didn't take you shopping with me."

Garnet stared at her aunt, somewhere between laughter and tears. "Why, you...schemer! You and Uncle Seth plotted this, didn't you?"

"Guilty." Jenny smiled. "But Brant intended to come for you, Garnet—with a lasso, if necessary. He intends to have you, one way or another."

"Why did you keep this from me?" Garnet demanded. "You caused me so much worry!"

"And calendar-watching?"

Garnet gasped. "He told you about *that?*"

"Of course not! I sensed it when you came off that long excursion to the prairie. And a few weeks later I was certain. What else could make a single young lady so anxious for the monthly curse? This middle-aged lady understood...remembering a few experiences of her own. Spinsterhood doesn't necessarily mean celibacy, you know. Shocked?" she asked gently.

"Not really." Garnet gave it a moment's thought. "Does Mother know?"

"I doubt it, although I suspect your father realized there was more than culture involved in my trips to Boston and New York and Europe. I have never regretted a single escapade, never," her aunt vowed firmly.

Garnet laughed, delighted. "You're a wicked woman, Auntie!"

"Shh!" Jenny cautioned. "We must keep our secrets, niece."

"How much have you told Mother and Daddy about Brant?" Garnet asked hesitantly.

"Everything necessary, Garnet. After all, some of his family's finest *belles-lettres* are now in their library, and your father might like to express his appreciation. Your possession of Denny's personal belongings required an explanation, too. But they hold no grudge against Brant. Denny would have done his duty if their situations had been reversed."

"I understand that now, too."

"Brant is hoping to meet your parents, Garnet. But he's too well-bred to come to the house without an invitation."

"I'd like to see him alone first," Garnet said abruptly, then hesitated. "Do you think it would be too indiscreet if I went to the inn?"

"Not if I accompany you—and then manage to disappear."

"Order the carriage, Auntie! I want to get dressed."

"No weeds, please. You have some attractive clothes, and fashion hasn't changed much in this hamlet. Just wear a narrow crinoline—and your most frivolous bonnet."

"The gossips will call me a merry widow!"

"No, Garnet, not after all this time."

A mischievous grin played about Garnet's mouth, dimpling the corners, and her eyes twinkled. "At least I won't be Camille in Connecticut anymore! And, anyway, it doesn't matter. We won't be living here."

"Then you're going to marry him?" Jenny gazed at her steadily.

"Well, naturally. We can't cohabit in sin. I may not be so lucky the next time," she grinned shyly.

Smiling, Jenny hugged her. "This news will make him the happiest man in the country!"

Because he had listed Longhorn Junction, Texas, on the hotel registry as his home address, Brant Steele's presence in town sparked curiosity. Everyone knew the Ashleys' ailing daughter had been cured in Texas, and since Jennifer Temple had made a call on Mr. Steele that very morning, some revelation must be in the offing.

The desk clerk was not surprised when Miss Temple and Mrs. Lane arrived and sent a message to Mr. Steele's room, and he watched the ensuing

scene, when Steele appeared in the lobby—a sight
to behold in his Western apparel, obviously all new.
Saddlestitching trimmed the yoke, lapels, and pock-
ets of his fine gray wool suit, and a black string
tie set off the immaculate white cambric shirt.

Male loungers gawked and females were admiring
as he swept off his tall gray felt Stetson hat and
bowed.

Brant had never seemed more virile or more handsome, and Garnet relished the other ladies' whispers.
A demonstrative welcome in public was not seemly,
however, and she was forced to content herself with
a warm smile and gentle handshake.

"How nice to see you again, Mrs. Lane. You're
looking exceptionally well," Brant murmured in that
deep voice she loved so well.

And she was indeed radiantly lovely and entirely
feminine in a violet-blue silk gown with a heart-
shaped neckline and short puffed sleeves. The
flounced skirt flirted around her dainty matching
slippers. A circle of ruffled net and silk flowers
crowned her golden hair like an angel's wreath. She
was enchanting.

The sight of her slender waist caused relief to flood
Brant's face, and they shared a brief intimate, knowing look. Garnet had never been quite so flustered.
She was breathless and might even have been babbling nonsense, for all she knew.

Jenny excused herself and retired to the tearoom,
declining with thanks Brant's offer to escort her.
Then he and Garnet sat down—just in time, for Garnet's knees were trembling.

"How beautiful you are, Garnet!" he whispered
joyfully. "The costume, the color...perfect for you.
I was afraid you would still—"

"Be in mourning?" she finished, understanding
more than he knew she did.

"Yes. You're not angry about my wire?"

"Oh, Brant! I only learned about it today, *after* I

had decided to return to Texas with Aunt Jenny. It's true, Brant. I intended to go back to you before I knew you had telegraphed."

She sensed his tension and watched his hands flexing.

"Thank you for that, darling. If only I could take you in my arms now!" he said. "You know why I'm here, Garnet. God, how I love you. I want you for my wife! This is another proposal, and I'm sorry I can't make it more traditionally." After a long moment, during which they gazed into each other's eyes, he continued. "Jenny doesn't anticipate any objections from your parents. Do you?"

"No. They understand."

"They must be very fine people."

"I think so."

"How soon can we have the ceremony?"

"In a few days. I want it to be private, Brant."

"Thank you again, my love." He glanced at her gloved hands, his eyes lingering on the left hand. He couldn't tell whether the wedding band was there or not.

"It's gone," she said with unmistakable finality. "Sealed in the vault of the new Civil War Monument on the village green. Have you noticed it yet?"

A grave, remorseful nod. "Hundreds more will be erected all over the country."

"Don't feel bad, Brant." She longed to hold him. "I can talk about it all now—although there's no longer much point. And we have so much else to discuss."

"And arrangements to make," he agreed, crossing his long, muscular legs in the tight trousers and polished black boots. "In St. Louis, I bribed a tailor to make this suit quickly. I hope you think it's all right for the wedding. Or would you prefer something formal?"

"It's fine, Brant! What else should a cowboy wear, especially a cowboy who does his job so well? That long trail drive certainly didn't do you any harm! Tanned and slimmed you a little more, perhaps." She beamed at him, basking in his admiring return gaze. "Oh, Brant, I'm so happy!"

Brant decided to save the wedding bands for later, to surprise her. He'd bought a heavy gold ring for himself and, looking all over St. Louis to find just what he had in mind, a delicate gold band shaped like orange blossoms. The jeweler had assured him that orange-blossom designs were very popular just then, but Brant hadn't bought the ring for that reason. Orange blossoms seemed so right for Garnet. He smiled as he recalled the purchase of the ring, and his certainty that he knew Garnet's ring size. It would fit. He had no doubt of that.

Again he restrained his eager arms. "If I can't hold you soon, I may stampede."

"We have the rest of our lives, Brant...but I'm sure Aunt Jenny will give us a chance to be alone on the way home."

"Bless that wonderful lady!" Then, unable to resist any longer, he caught her hands impulsively and pressed them in his. "We'll have our own ranch, Garnet!" He rushed on. "We managed to get almost the entire herd safely to Sedalia, losing fewer than a dozen. They sold for a high price. The Dukes have promised me a big bonus, and they'll sell me some of their land. We'll build a cozy little house until we can afford a great hacienda."

He leaned forward on the edge of his chair. "Honey, the cattle business is booming, and Texas will be the center of it all. We'll stake hundreds, maybe thousands of acres of range, hire hands, develop our own breeds, and make our brand famous! When the railroads come to Texas—and they will—cattle can be shipped, which will be easier on them."

Garnet smiled, nodding vigorously, infected with his enthusiasm and certain that he could make all his dreams come true. He would take fate by the horns and master his own destiny, or she didn't know Brant Steele.

"I believe you, Brant. With all my heart, I believe it will all happen just as you say. I love you, Brant."

"I love you. We love each other, Garnet. Together we'll see our dreams come alive."

The others in the lobby were smiling at the animated conversation between the handsome, uniquely dressed stranger and the charming young Avalon lady, and all were openly curious. But Garnet didn't care. Let them stare! She was proud of Brant, and of their love.

"Yes," she whispered, yearning filling her voice. "And time is precious, darling. Let's get Aunt Jenny—and get our future together started!"

This was what Brant had wanted, waited for, and longed to hear. He rose and assisted Garnet to her feet, and with beaming smiles and lovingly clasped hands, the two strolled from the lobby in search of Jenny.

THE NEW NOVEL BY
KATHLEEN E. WOODIWISS

A ROSE IN WINTER

Erienne Fleming's debt-ridden father had given
her hand to the richest suitor. She was now
Lady Saxton, mistress of a great manor all but
ruined by fire, wife to a man whose mysteri-
ously shrouded form aroused fear and pity. Yet
even as she became devoted to her adoring
husband, Erienne despaired of freeing her
heart from the dashingly handsome Yankee,
Christopher Seton. The beautiful Erienne,
once filled with young dreams of romance,
was now a wife and woman...torn between the
two men she loved.

Avon Trade Paperback   81679-2/$6.95

Available wherever paperbacks are sold, or directly from the
publisher. Include 50¢ per copy for postage and handling; allow
6-8 weeks for delivery. Avon Books, Mail Order Dept., 224 West
57th St., N.Y., N.Y. 10019.

Rose 12 82

Bestselling Historical Romance
from Patricia Gallagher

ALL FOR LOVE   77818-1 ... **$2.95**

As Civil War sweeps across the nation, beautiful Jacintha Howard marries a war profiteer to save her family's Hudson River mansion, but surrenders her love to the guardian she has adored since childhood.

CASTLES IN THE AIR   75143-7 ... **$2.50**

In the aftermath of the Civil War, beautiful and spirited Devon Marshall flees Virginia. She becomes one of America's first women journalists—from glittering New York to Washington's elite circles of power—and falls in love with millionaire Keith Curtis . . . but a cruel fate will twist their passionate affair into a fierce battle of wills!

NO GREATER LOVE   44743-6 ... **$2.50**

Devon Marshall strives to forget Keith Curtis by marrying a wealthy Texan and moving to the rugged west. But her husband's election to Congress brings them back to the nation's capital. There Devon is caught up in a vortex of soaring power, corruption and social scandal that brings her face to face with Keith—the man she has never ceased to love!

MYSTIC ROSE   79467-5 ... **$2.95**

Star Lamont is a high-spirited Charleston belle . . . Captain Troy Stewart is a dashing rogue. . . . From their first shipboard encounter, Star and Troy clash in a battle of pride and passion, fury and desire, set against the fiery backdrop of the War of 1812.

Available wherever paperbacks are sold, or directly from the publisher. Include 50¢ per copy for postage and handling: allow 6-8 weeks for delivery. Avon Books, Mail Order Dept., 224 West 57th St., N.Y., N.Y. 10019.

Gallagher 2-83